*Totally Bound Publishing books by Roxanne Blackhall*

**Bristol Park**
Abbeydon Attraction

I0607631

Bristol Park

# ABBEYDON ATTRACTION

ROXANNE BLACKHALL

Abbeydon Attraction
ISBN # 978-1-80250-514-6
©Copyright Roxanne Blackhall 2023
Cover Art by Erin Dameron-Hill ©Copyright February 2023
Interior text design by Claire Siemaszkiewicz
Totally Bound Publishing

# ABBEYDON ATTRACTION

# Dedication

To my very own romance hero
and amazing husband.

# Author's Note

There are elements in this story that revolve around real estate development and while I have made every effort to research all the legalities involved, there is no getting around the fact that it's a murky subject that varies from state to state. I have based the events here on applicable laws and precedents but have also taken artistic license in their interpretation.

As we all know, not every business operates strictly within the bounds of the law, and the developer in Abbeydon Attraction is certainly in the questionable category. Which enabled even more artistic license.

In short, I hope you will enjoy the story and forgive any errors as they are entirely mine—whether conscious or not—and not the fault of the amazing people who helped guide my research.

# Chapter One

Dust rained down as Cat tugged on the rope handle to the attic steps. She coughed in spite of the handkerchief she'd wrapped around her face. Blinking to clear the grit from her eyes, she tugged again. Nothing. She let go of the rope and stared up at the thing, trying to figure out if she'd missed a latch or something — but no, it looked like any other drop-down attic access. A door with a rope and a handle hanging down, annoyingly just out of her reach unless she rose up on her very tiptoes. Maybe she hadn't pulled hard enough.

She propped a hand on the wall to steady herself and reached, her fingers just closing around the handle. Another stretch and she got a better grip. She braced herself and gave the rope a good tug. Something shifted, just a little. Cat tightened her grip, wrapping both hands around the handle and leaning back to give a hard yank. The rope snapped and she tumbled backwards, arms pinwheeling, dimly aware of a rhythmic pounding sound. She slammed into something hard. Large hands closed over her shoulders and pushed her upright.

"Whoa there. You okay?" The voice was deep and gravelly, tinged with a slight Southern accent that sounded like the voice on the phone when she'd talked with the local handyman the other day.

Cat whirled. A pair of concerned-looking amber eyes stared back at her from a handsome—and young—face. She'd been expecting some retiree. This man was maybe a few years older than she was. Wariness surged through her, and she tugged the handkerchief down and glared at him.

"Who are you and how did you get in?"

A hurt look crossed his features for a moment before he broke into a laugh. "I'm Nate Stewart. You left the door unlocked, and it's two. Little after, actually. I was knocking on the door for five minutes. And you're welcome." He nodded at the stairs. "That would have been a nasty fall."

*Yep, same voice. That drawl is unmistakable.* He was wearing a heavy jacket, and a knit cap was pushed back on his head as if it had been knocked askew. The pounding noise must have been him coming up the steps after she didn't respond to his knock.

"Uhhh… Thank you. We haven't properly met." She stuck her hand out. "I'm Caitlin, but everyone calls me Cat."

His hand engulfed hers. Warm and rough with calluses. "Good to meet you, Cat." His eyes crinkled at the corners and the ghost of a smile crossed his lips. "We've all been calling you Ms. Bristol, but I don't guess that's your last name."

"It's what's on my birth certificate. Mother never changed her name. I suppose my grandmother didn't either." Everyone she'd met here swore she was the spitting image of her grandmother. It wouldn't matter what she called herself — in this town she would always be Susan Bristol's granddaughter. The family name also came with fewer potential landmines than being the widow of Jimmy Corozzo. "The attic door is stuck."

Nate straightened his hat, then shrugged out of his jacket and hung it on the newel. His broad shoulders filled the space as he maneuvered past her on the narrow landing. At first glance, he looked like a typical burly, muscle-bound gym rat. Once the jacket came off, revealing a tight flannel and low-slung jeans, she had to rethink that assessment. He was big, but there was nothing of the hulking meathead to him.

He reached up and caught the attic release. Fresh dust rained down, pulling Cat's attention away from his denim-covered backside. And now the starry-eyed expression every woman in town sported at the mere mention of Nate made sense. Cat shook her head to clear those unwelcome thoughts. He was hot, and that was trouble she didn't need.

"I think I've got it." Nate gave another tug on the door then jumped back as the ladder came tumbling down, scattering bits of wood across the floor. "Huh. Dry rot. Look here. There's why it wouldn't open." The hook for the rope had pulled away and wedged into the hinge.

"Guess I'll need a ladder to get up in there and check things out." She peered through the swirling dust into the inky depths of the attic. Who knew how many years of what lay tucked away up there. "Thank you again, but I think we should head to the kitchen. I asked you here to talk about a job."

She headed down the stairs, shaking her head at her brusque approach, but she needed to establish some boundaries, and fast. Nate came with stellar references, and the only hint of anything inappropriate was a snide comment one of the old-timers at the general store had made about all the ladies calling on Nate. That and the gaggle of adoring fangirls. Not that she could blame them. He was definitely fine, but she didn't need a man in her life, especially one who had his pick of all the ladies in town.

She poured two glasses of water and set one in front of him. "I want to live here while going through Susa — My grandmother's estate." The word grandmother still felt strange to her — until recently, Cat had believed her grandmother had died before she was born. She perched on the edge of a kitchen stool and pulled out her rough project list. Time to see what the man was made of. "I can't be dealing with the repairs and going through all of this."

Bristol Park, once a bustling family resort, had long ago fallen into disuse and disrepair. And now it was hers. She'd taken a quick look around and it was overwhelming. Several rooms were filled to bursting with storage boxes and furniture covered in ancient sheets. Every closet was stuffed full. And down a long, creaky hallway she'd found the laundry, plus a small commercial kitchen and a formal dining room that looked like they hadn't been touched in over a decade.

"What's your plan?" Nate's voice cut into her thoughts.

"My first priority is safety — make sure there's a functioning kitchen and bath here in the main house, and a roof that doesn't leak. No major renovations. Just repairs. Like that attic access — I can't deal with the stuff up there without a decent ladder." She ignored his eye roll and continued. "After that, I'll decide what comes next."

His brow furrowed as he leaned forward, running his finger down the list in front of her. "This first part makes sense if you're staying here. The rest..." He raised his eyes to hers and shook his head. "My question is, why?"

Cat drew back from his narrowed gaze. His look said suspicion. He tapped the page, flashing ink on his wrist, the heavy black lines visible against his golden tan skin. Cat swallowed hard and pulled the notebook back.

"Because there's history here." She breathed the words through gritted teeth. History was something she'd never had growing up. One of the few things she'd loved about the Corozzo family. And now here was an opportunity to have it without the whole mess that came with *them*. To see something of her own history — one she'd been denied as a child. She snatched up the list and glared at him. This man wasn't her business partner. She didn't need to explain herself to him.

"Because it's what I want to do. I need a general handyman. Someone who can help me get the house in order. If that's not of interest to you, Mr. Stewart, then I'm sure I can find someone else."

He leaned back and crossed his arms over his chest. His mouth pressed down into a thin line, then crooked into a half-smile. "You're not likely to find too many folks willing to come all the way out here, and those you do won't be near as good. Plus, they'll cost twice as much."

He was right on that point. She'd already looked into available labor. If he didn't agree to help, this was going to be even more costly.

"I'm aware of that. It doesn't change the fact that either you are willing to work with me or you are not. So, which is it?"

He rested his elbows on the table and his eyes caught hers, held her gaze. "Conditionally." He held up his hand and ticked off items on his fingers. "I want to know what your ultimate goal is here. Are you planning to reopen or sell? It's a safe bet you've either gotten an offer on the place or will soon. Holding out, fixing it up, all of that could be a ploy to raise the stakes a bit, demand a higher price."

"I don't know yet. But if you think that I'm doing this for the sole purpose of personal profit, you can leave right now." Cat had no patience for that attitude, though she understood where it was coming from.

"I'll give you a month." He continued as if she hadn't said anything. "Get through as much of that list as we can, then we check in. You may think differently by then. I might think differently. And we reevaluate every month after that."

She nodded. "Seems fair enough. Anything else?" She didn't bother to try keeping the sarcasm from her voice, but he either didn't notice or didn't care.

"I want to see the entire list of interior projects. There may be some things you can double up on — if you need to rent equipment, or hire a contractor, there's no sense doing it twice."

"You think I haven't considered that?" She arched an eyebrow at him and gave him the look that'd had Jimmy's men quaking in their shoes. She hadn't taken over the operations of Corozzo Shipping for nothing — project and resource management came easily to her. Nate spread his hands wide and fixed her with a devastating smile.

"Let's just say two heads are better than one, and you haven't had much time to be thinking about this."

She tossed her notebook onto the table in front of him. "Here ya go, champ. Have fun. I'm going to see if there's a ladder around here that isn't rotting out. Find me when you're done playing administrative assistant."

\* \* \* \*

The kitchen door swing shut on Cat's retreating form, and Nate shook his head. When she hadn't answered the door, he'd let himself in just in time to see a tiny redhead perched at the top of the stairs, yanking on the attic pull. She'd almost knocked him off the top step when she fell into him. The contact was brief, but long enough to stir thoughts he didn't care to entertain. Like how small and fragile she felt. He shook his head again, turned back to the list she'd practically thrown at him and smiled.

It was a rough draft, but already a project manager's wet dream. Neatly organized into columns with weekly goals. Just like she'd implied, she'd already overlapped several projects. It looked like she at least knew what she was doing. Still, she was probably in way over her head.

"The only ladder I can find is not something I'd trust to hold me, much less you." She plopped down into the seat opposite him and smiled. "You find anything missing, or things you could improve?"

"Not yet." He didn't see a point in lying to her. "It could be workable."

She smiled again and tapped a manicured nail on the counter. "You got a ladder on that truck out there?"

It was his turn to smile. If she'd taken five seconds to ask, she'd have known. "Yep. Coulda saved you the looking."

"Maybe." She pushed back from the island and stood, beckoning him to follow. "Let's go see what's in the attic."

He tried to insist that she let him go first, citing the possibility of squirrels or even rats. She wasn't having any of it. He blew out an exasperated breath.

"Look, you're not dressed for crawling around in...well, whatever may be up there." He waved a hand at her skinny jeans and sweater. "I'm not sure how far that dry rot goes. The floor may not hold." She glared at him, grabbed his flashlight, and stepped onto the first rung. Which was how he found himself holding the ladder steady, looking up at her perfect, round ass as she levered herself into the attic space. A shuffling step or two, a sneeze, a muffled curse and some fumbling, then a click and light poured down from the doorway. Her head popped into view.

"Light works. That's something," she called down to him. "You coming up? Or are you worried about bats now? I promise, nothing up here to ruin your jeans."

*Damn pushy woman.* He climbed the ladder into the dusty attic and stood, surprised there was enough room for him. No sign of rodents or bats, though there were a few spiderwebs and lots of boxes and things draped with sheets. He tapped his foot along the boards, listening for the tell-tale sounds that would indicate the wood was rotted.

"Looks like there was a leak in the roof at some point." She pointed the flashlight beam at the ceiling.

Dark stains spread out from what was obviously a patch. Right over the access ladder. Well that explained the dry rot—wood got wet. Closed up, the ladder never dried out. Hello fungus. Still, he tested the floorboards before putting his weight on them. He had no desire to go crashing through the floor into a room below.

"Why are we starting in the attic?" Nate's mind flashed back to her list. So many projects and she chose to start here, but okay, she was paying the bills.

Cat chuckled as she yanked a sheet off a large mirror in the corner. "Who said 'we'? A lot of the furniture downstairs is in bad shape. I wanted to see what was up here. Some of it might be usable, or I can sell it. And I wanted to look for signs of roof leaks. I'd rather not have to do the roof in the middle of winter, y'know?"

She shifted a pile of boxes and brushed the dust off the side, turning it to the light. "Wanna bet these holiday lights are not LEDs?"

Nate shook his head and chuckled. Nice to see she had a sense of humor. She was going to need it for what she had planned. "No bet."

"Besides, old house, barely maintained and with a single occupant for the past ten plus years?" She poked a toe into a sheet-covered shape, sending a cascade of dust into the air. "Who knows what sort of furry or feathered critters might have taken up residence here."

He leaned back against a post and laughed. She had a point. A damn good one at that. He'd been trying to discourage her with exactly those worries. She stopped her explorations and glared at him, then her face cracked into a smile as well.

"Okay, Boss Lady," he said. "Let me rephrase things. Clock's ticking here. What do you want to accomplish today? Do you need me to help you sort through all this stuff?"

"No," she replied. At least she was straightforward. "How about you figure out what you need to do to repair or replace the attic stairs? I can't leave your work ladder here forever. I'm sure you can order one from somewhere, but what do I do until that arrives?"

He knelt at the access door, poking his fingers into the wood frame. "The whole thing's in bad shape. I'll run into town—Juan's got some lumber left from working on his garage. He won't mind me picking it up for this. Temporary stairs won't fold up, but they'll be better than a ladder until the replacement can get done. This whole frame's gonna need rebuilt."

He made it halfway down the main stairs before remembering his jacket hanging on the newel post at the top of the flight and nearly bumped into Cat as she came down, his jacket in her hand. "Thanks." He tried to ignore the jolt of excitement when his fingers brushed hers as he took the coat from her. "You done up there already?"

She shook her head. "I'm starting by cleaning up the dust." She handed him back his flashlight as well. Not like him to be that forgetful. "You aren't going to make it to town, pick up wood, and get back here before it gets late," she continued. "Let's just call it a day and start all this tomorrow."

He ignored the unexpected, and unwelcome, stab of disappointment at not seeing her again tonight and nodded. "Good call. I like to start early, but I'm guessing you don't want to hear saws and hammers at first light. Eight okay?"

Her eyes widened, then she smiled. "Wow, a whole forty minutes past sunup. Burning daylight there, aren't you?"

He nodded. "Good point. I'll see you at seven thirty then." He didn't quite catch the words she hurled at him as he left, but he was certain they weren't fit for polite company. Not what he expected from a prissy city girl at all.

# Chapter Two

Cat's gaze swept the attic, now cleared of years of dust and cobwebs and at least semi-organized into sections — things to throw out, things to sell or donate, things to keep, and a monster pile of things she'd have to go through before she could figure out what to do with them. She'd nearly missed a ladder rung coming down, she was so tired. All she wanted to do was shower off the grime and crawl into bed. Ten minutes later, with nothing more than cold water coming from the faucet, she stumbled down the basement steps to find a spreading puddle coming from the old water heater in the corner.

"Oh, you've got to be kidding me."

She made her way over to the thing and shut off the gas line, then the tap, stopping the flow of fresh water. "Just great." She pulled her phone out. Almost midnight. Too late to call someone to help. *Not like I can get a new water heater in the middle of the night.* She trudged back upstairs and found a couple of battered stockpots, half-filled them with cold water and put them on the stove. No way was she going to bed without cleaning up a little bit and jumping into an ice bath was even less appealing. Then she grabbed a stack of towels and a mop to get started on the sopping mess in the basement.

By the time the water had warmed up enough to be tolerable, she was wet and gritty and looked like she'd crawled through a mud puddle. She got the worst of it off, doing a final rinse in frigid water straight from the tap, then fell into bed shivering and exhausted.

Sharp pounding sounds pulled her awake. Dim light filtered through the sheer curtains, and she blinked, rubbing sleep from her face. She stumbled into the bathroom and swore when the tap only produced cold water. *Aw man, I forgot about that.* She opened her bedroom door and bounced off a broad back. Nate.

"Good morning, sleepyhead." A wide smile lit up his face, and she scowled back at him.

"I thought you were kidding about the seven thirty bit." She stifled a yawn behind her hand, and he chuckled.

"It's after nine."

Whatever. She waved a dismissive hand at him and padded down the stairs to the kitchen. He had the attic steps to build. She shouldn't have to babysit, and he shouldn't expect wide-eyed appreciation of him just doing his job. And now she'd have to add a new water heater to the growing to-do list. Ugh. No way was she facing today without... The smell of fresh-brewed coffee hit her as she pushed through the kitchen door.

She stuttered to a stop and cast a dazed look around the room. Last night, she'd left a pile of wet and dirty clothes on the floor, dirty towels in the sink, and several pans on the stove. Now, the kitchen gleamed, spotless in the pale morning light.

"I put a fan down in the basement to get some air moving down there. Your clothes and stuff are in the dryer. And I took the liberty of making coffee." Nate leaned against the kitchen door, his arms crossed loosely over his chest. "Didn't think you needed to be hearing me tearing apart the attic stairs at the crack of dawn, so I got busy down here instead. Figured I'd wait for you to get up, then run out for a new water heater. Nobody local's got one. Closest place is the home improvement store about thirty miles north."

Cat cupped her coffee in her hands and sank onto a stool, regarding him through the rising steam. She wasn't sure what to make of this guy. One minute he was a pushy jerk, and the next he was being nice as pie. And too fine-looking for her comfort.

"I should go with you." She concentrated on her coffee cup to keep her eyes from lingering on the way his tight Henley pulled across his shoulders. "To pay for things, I mean."

He shrugged and pushed himself away from the doorframe. "If you'd like. Otherwise I'll pick up everything and bill you. No problem. I'll be at a good stopping point in about an hour, then finish up this afternoon. Your call."

"If you're okay getting everything, I'll reimburse you. I've got a lot of work to do around here still. Starting with finding consignment shops for a bunch of this furniture." She cleared her throat and looked down. "Umm...thank you."

A big hand landed on the counter in front of her. "Hey, up here." The voice was just inches from her face, she tipped her head back to find him leaning down, elbows on the island and a gentle smile on his face. "You hired me to do a job." His voice was quiet, low and deep, and it made her breath catch. "And I'm not a total asshole."

He straightened and shook his head. "It won't take long to install the new heater. You'll have a hot shower tonight."

Cat breathed a little easier as he moved away. Nate was trouble she did not need. A pretty boy with a side of just-cocky-enough? That was one big fat nope. She'd been suckered by that type once, and that was more than enough. Nate might be on top of things, handy and amazing to look at, plus kind and nice as well, but it was a pretty safe bet that he played that game with every woman he worked for.

\* \* \* \*

Cat pushed through the doors of the general store and grimaced as half a dozen pairs of eyes settled on her and the rumble of chatter came to a sudden stop. The eyes belonged to a group of older men playing card games around the wood stove. She'd seen most of them in her earlier trips to town. As always, they eyed her with expressions that combined curiosity and suspicion.

A throat cleared to her left, and she turned to find Juan standing there with a broad smile. His deep brown eyes soft and kind.

"Ms. Bristol, welcome back." Juan's smile was infectious, and she was grateful for any sign of friendliness in this place. It didn't hurt that he was a good-looking man with his wiry build and a shock of salt and pepper hair standing out against olive skin.

"Thank you, but it's just Cat, please." She'd said the same thing to him each time. She figured she could say it until she was blue in the face, unless these folks decided she belonged here, she'd be Ms. Bristol. That, or Susan's granddaughter.

She wandered the small grocery section, picking up a few things she had somehow missed in her whirlwind trips to town. The store was eerily quiet as she came up to the register.

She leaned over the counter and whispered to Juan. "Is there something wrong? Everyone is so..." She glanced over at the group of men and all of them quickly looked away, as if trying to pretend they hadn't been staring.

Juan chuckled and leaned forward. "Don't mind that crew." He nodded at the older men who had resumed their card games. "They take a while to warm up. Anything else for you today?"

Cat snagged her groceries, about to say no, but something nagged at her. If she was going to live here while clearing out her grandmother's house, she might as well get to know the place. And the people.

"Yeah," she replied. "How's the coffee next door?"

Every eye followed her as she entered the coffee shop attached to the general store. She stifled a yawn and ignored the curious stares from the women gathered around a central table.

"Word of advice." The voice came from near her left elbow. The attractive blonde who'd been in the center of the group of ladies now stood next to her. "Stick with straight coffee. I don't think the other drinks would be up to your city standards."

Cat adopted the calm smile she'd cultivated when she'd been working the casino. Before she met Jimmy. Before a lot of things. That smile had eased her into Jimmy's large family and smoothed out many business meetings. It was the smile she'd put on when confronted with evidence of yet another of Jimmy's indiscretions, or when she found herself face-to-face in public with one of his many mistresses. Cat screwed that smile firmly into place and stuck out her hand.

"I'm Cat," she said. "Thanks for the advice. I never developed a taste for those fancy drinks. Always been a straight coffee person, myself."

The other woman blinked a time or two and shook Cat's hand as if on autopilot. "I'm Gina Tellis," she replied. "I teach at Abbeydon Academy. What's got you in town today?"

Well, the woman certainly cut straight to it. Cat ordered and paid for her coffee before responding. "I wanted to check with the local antiques and consignment shops. There's a bunch of furniture at the house that I don't need. And frankly, I needed to get out. I asked Nate to fix the attic access, and the sound of the power tools was driving me nuts."

She grabbed her coffee and glanced over at the table of women, half of whom she'd seen around getting doe-eyed and breathy at the mention of Nate's name. They were all trying to appear like they weren't watching her. Gina caught her by the elbow and steered them toward the table.

"Nate's a good man." Gina's words came out on a sigh. An angular Black woman who looked like she could be related to Grace Jones nodded her agreement while she scooted her chair over to make room for Cat and introduced herself as Rachel. The other ladies gave their names, and all wore expressions that reminded Cat of lovesick teenagers. *Dear Lord, I've landed in the Nate Stewart Fan Club.*

"How bad is the place?"

"I've never seen inside."

"Are you going to sell?"

"What are you planning?"

The table erupted in questions and comments so fast it made Cat's head spin. She had no illusions. She was the outsider here. A curiosity, her value yet to be determined. Just like the older men she'd seen gathered around the wood stove at the general store, whatever she said to these ladies would be all over town by the time folks sat down to dinner.

"I haven't decided yet," Cat said. The entire table fell to a hush as all six women stared at her. "I lost my husband a year ago, and then found out about my grandmother. I'm just taking things one day at a time for now."

All around the table, eyes went wide, and then narrowed. Cat had gambled with that one. A young widow was either mourning her late husband, or out hunting for a new man and a potential threat. She sighed and looked down.

"I didn't feel like I had any direction after Jimmy passed. Like I was just...adrift." She let those words hang for a moment. It was true. She had felt directionless and uncertain. She'd also known if she hung around, Mama C would be trying to marry her off to some second son or cousin, like Marc whatever his name was that she'd tried to hook Cat up with on New Year's Eve. All Cat had wanted was out, and then her attorney Dominico Santieri had given her the letter about her grandmother and the will.

She drew in a long breath and brought her head back up. Gina still looked skeptical, but Rachel and the others all bore expressions of sympathy. Cat hated herself just a little for playing that card, but dammit, if she was going to live in this town, even temporarily, the last thing she needed was to run afoul of the Nate Stewart Admiration Society.

"Wait, so you lost your husband and your grandmother so close together?" Rachel's eyes were wide with borderline horror at the idea.

"Yeah," Cat replied. "Though, to be fair, I never knew my grandmother." A few gasps echoed around the table, and even Gina was leaning in. "It was always just me and my mom. Then she passed a few years ago."

Gina's eyebrows went up. "What about your husband's family?"

There was the sticky part. Cat didn't want to bring up the Corozzo clan. The family owned a list of casinos in Vegas and Atlantic City, several hotels and the largest shipping company on the East Coast. And she didn't want to be tied to them in any way.

"My in-laws are…well, they're complicated," Cat replied, and it was true. "They'd smother me." Also true. "I just needed…something simpler. Easier."

Gina's laugh echoed in the cafe. "Well, it's sure as hell gonna be simpler here!"

And with that laugh, Cat edged into new friend territory. She may still represent potential competition, but she'd given these women enough of herself that they could see her as one of their own.

Chatter erupted, and Cat breathed a sigh of relief to have the attention focused on something other than her personal life. Content to sit and listen for a bit, her ears perked up when Rachel mentioned a large corporate developer had just bought a property up the road from Bristol Park. She made a mental note to ask Dominico to look into it, then cringed as the talk turned to children.

"I'm sorry." Cat pushed back from the table. "I've got a few more errands to run and…"

The ladies all nodded, offering murmurs of understanding.

Cat thanked them and headed to her car. She'd barely pulled onto the road when her phone quacked, the strident ringtone she'd programmed for Dominico. She tapped the button to answer.

"Don't tell me," she greeted without preamble. "We got an offer on the property?"

A rich chuckle reverberated through the phone, and she could picture him sitting back in his big leather chair, hands laced over a belly that strained at his expensive suit. "More like due diligence. And I'm not sure I want to know how you already knew about this."

Cat laughed. "The gossip chain is strong around here, and I think I just fell in with its central link. Talk to me."

"That's my line," he shot back. Dominico never said hello when answering the phone. It was always "talk to me." Unless it was his mother. Then it was, "Si, Mamma." The sound of papers rustling carried through, followed by the creak of his chair, then Dominico cleared his throat.

"TravelCorp just purchased a nearby parcel. Small — only an acre. They've made inquiries into a finger of land that's owned by a large agricultural firm — there is a five-acre field that abuts their recent purchase. And they've got a lot of surveying going on, along with preliminary impact studies. It looks like they're gearing up to purchase a large chunk in the area. But I don't know what their plans are yet."

He paused a moment, and Cat's brain whirled over the new information. "I want to know what they've got going on. This could be an amazing opportunity, or the money pit of a lifetime. Either way, I don't want to be in the dark." Cat chewed on her lower lip. "While you're at it," she continued, "can you do a little background on someone? Nothing too deep. I just want to know what I can about this guy." She rattled off Nate's information.

"Are you worried about him? Sounds like a local handyman to me."

Cat hauled in a breath as she turned down the drive into Bristol Park. "Not worried, no. He's well liked. Respected. Big guy. First glance, you'd think jock or meathead, but that doesn't ring true. He's…"

Cat struggled to put her finger on whatever it was that had her asking Dominico to go digging. She told herself it was just smart business. After all, he would be working around the place—with no one else around. "There's just something about him. More than meets the eye, y'know? And he's practically got a fan club of women here."

The chuckle that vibrated the phone this time had lost all its warmth. *"Donnaiolo?"* The syllables came from Dominico as if he spat them out, like he didn't want them touching his tongue any longer than necessary.

"Something like that." Cat cleared her throat, her teeth sinking into her bottom lip as she tried to avoid a direct answer. "Yeah, okay, a lot like that."

Dominico's sigh was heavy and slow. "Not every man is Jimmy. But yes, I'll see what I can find."

"I know that," she snapped back at him, and immediately regretted it. Dominico had been the one person who had tried to hold Jimmy accountable. The only one who had not advised her to do what every Corozzo wife had done for generations—look the other way. Find a hobby. Take a lover of her own, just do it discreetly. No. Dominico had dragged Jimmy's womanizing ass to church for confession, believing if

Jimmy had to tell the priest he'd known since his confirmation that he was sticking it to multiple women other than his wife, he might change his behavior.

No such luck.

"I've hired the guy to work on the house," Cat said. "I don't care who he's sleeping with. But I don't want to accidentally step in the middle of some lover's quarrel or find myself dealing with a string of pissed off women because their favorite Lothario is otherwise occupied in legitimate handyman work."

*And speak of the Devil.* The man in question strode down the porch carrying power tools back to his truck. There was no getting around it, Nate was walking sex appeal. Everything about him screamed 'look at me and want me'. His shoulders strained the seams of the faded button-up he wore and the way his jeans highlighted his ass and other assets ought to be flat-out illegal.

Cat blew out a breath. "Just send me an email with everything. And thanks!"

She hung up with Dominico and tried to look at Nate with a more dispassionate eye. No one could be that perfect looking. She studied him, looking for some flaws. From the shiny black curls that peeked out from under his knit cap and light stubble on his jaw to the large hands placing power tools back in their cases as gently as if they were fine porcelain. She shook her head to clear those thoughts. That was the kind of thinking that had gotten her married to Jimmy, and while her life had taken a turn for the better in many ways, being married to a devastatingly handsome man who cheated on you at every opportunity was no picnic.

Nope. The ladies of the Nate Stewart Appreciation Club could keep him. Caitlin Bristol-Corozzo was done with pretty boys. She had no interest in the man beyond his ability to help her get this place in order. And that was that.

* * * *

Nate slid the toolbox back into his truck and sketched a short wave at Cat. She sat in her car, glaring at him as if he were some distasteful thing she'd stepped in. Not the reaction he was used to from women. Not that he wanted her attention like that. Hell, he didn't want any woman's attention like that. He'd given them up. Besides, he'd lay odds she was a lights-out and missionary type.

Every now and then, he had caught the hint of a crack in her perfectly polished exterior, but otherwise, she was all ice princess. Strictly work and business. He slammed the tailgate shut then leaned back against it as she climbed out of her car.

"Any luck at the shops in town?" Nate had warned her trying to offload the antiques here would likely end in failure. The local stores just didn't have enough business to support bringing in an entire house full of new stuff. Her expression tightened further, telling him everything he needed to know. He bit his tongue to keep from rubbing it in.

"No." The word slid out so softly Nate barely caught it. "You were right. They're all chock full of stuff that isn't selling."

*Wait. Did she just say I'm right?* That was unexpected. Here he was thinking he had her pegged.

"Got the temporary ladder in." He needed to stay focused on the job at hand. She likely would tire of the place before too long. Abbeydon was off the beaten path, quiet and mellow. Not the kind of place you'd find the lifestyle she was obviously used to. She reminded him far too much of the women he'd grown up around, and he was sure she was equally afraid to muss her hair or break a nail on her hundred-dollar manicure. "I also got the water heater installed."

The smile that broke across her face looked genuine and lit up her eyes until they sparkled. He needed to shut those thoughts down right now.

"Really?" She jogged up the steps, then turned and waved a hand at him. "You coming in? It's cold out here. I can make coffee."

Nope. Nate didn't do hanging out and being social. He was here to do a job. That was a lesson he'd learned early on after moving into town. Those coffee invites led to places he didn't want to go, from mild flirtation to outright come-ons. He'd never taken any of those offers. Sure, it was tempting, but Nate didn't do casual, and besides, he'd come here to enjoy a quiet life, free of drama. More importantly, free of romantic entanglements.

"Sure." His mouth answered before his brain engaged, and the rest of his body went right along, pushing up from the truck then climbing the porch steps. "I'll brew the coffee while you check things out, make sure they're up to your standards."

A flicker of something passed over her face — a tiny thing like a grimace of pain that tightened her mouth and made her eyes look dead before being replaced with the bland, pleasant smile reminiscent of a retail clerk or cocktail waitress. She held open the door and gestured him in.

"I'll take you up on making the coffee." She was out of her coat in seconds and sprinting up the stairs. Still not fast enough to keep him from noticing the way her black pants clung to her curves. Dammit. That train of thought needed to come to a halt. He pushed into the kitchen and headed for the coffee maker.

She popped into the room just as the machine beeped, the eager, open smile back on her face. "That looks great. Thanks!" She brushed past him, pulling cups from the shelf, leaving a scent of soap and roses in her wake. "Cream or sugar?"

Nate shook his head. Her perfectly manicured nails gleamed against the chipped mug as she handed him a coffee. She poured a second cup and took a sip. Black. That was unexpected. She hooked a stool out and sat, looking up at him expectantly. He should finish his coffee and go. Before she got to whatever it was she was about to say. Instead, he slid onto the stool across from her.

"You knew I wouldn't have much luck in town." It was a statement, and it didn't sound like she was blaming or accusing. Just stating the facts.

Nate nodded. "Most of those places are barely holding on." He lifted his coffee for a sip and looked up to find her eyes glued to him, as if waiting for him to continue. "Not enough traffic through here anymore."

She leaned her elbows on the table, lids half-closed over those dazzling eyes. "You did tell me." Her eyes closed for a moment, and she shook her head. "Still, had to try. I was expecting a makeshift ladder up there. You built a staircase."

The rapid change of subject had his head spinning. "Ladder stairs. No telling how long it'll take to find a replacement for the drop-down ladder, and I figured you needed something sturdy if you're gonna haul all that furniture down." He dared a broad grin and a wink. "Especially since it's likely gonna be me doing the hauling."

That got a chuckle from her. "Yeah, speaking of that..." She thumbed her phone awake and tapped the browser.

"I'll save you the trouble," Nate spoke up. She gazed at him over her phone and his breath caught. Then it hit him. Her moves had a practiced air about them. Even the bland plastic smile earlier. It felt like something she had honed, perfected, to elicit the desired response. He sure was suckered right into it. Ah well, he'd gone and opened his big mouth already. Couldn't back out now.

"There's a couple towns on the main road that attract larger crowds," he said. "Locals and tourists. Lots of antique places, but I'd start with the Schuberts. They run a bed and breakfast and have a couple antique and consignment shops." Beatrice and Alvin would treat her fairly, that much he knew. They were good people.

"I'd like to get this stuff done as soon as possible. You don't think it's too soon after the holidays, do you? Those places always seem to get clogged with donations after New Year's."

Nate pulled out his phone. "Only one way to find out." He pulled up the number for Catskills Consignments and slid his phone over to Cat. "Give them a call."

He waited for her to copy the number then pocketed his phone and rose to drop his mug in the sink. "What's on the agenda for tomorrow, Boss Lady?"

She scrunched her nose up, and the transformation took his breath away. Gone was the practiced plastic perfection, instead, she looked adorable. Though he supposed even that could be a calculated move on her part. Somehow, he doubted it. This felt more real.

"Don't call me that," she whispered. "It's...weird."

The desire to apologize, to reach out and place his hand over hers while uttering words of assurance that he would never do that again was so strong he shoved his hands into his pockets to keep from doing just that. "Well." He cleared his throat. "You are the boss..." He let that hang in the air. He was opening himself up for some potential grief, pulling something flirtatious like that, but it was better than him feeling like an anxious puppy craving her affection.

"And I have a name." The Ice Princess was back, and Nate heaved a sigh of relief. That, he could deal with. "I think the downstairs bath. The toilet leaks so bad I had to shut it off, and the door into the second guest bedroom is stuck, and..."

Her voice faded from his consciousness as Nate flashed back to her list. The one where she'd outlined every project for rehabbing the place. He'd lay odds that list was now a color-coded spreadsheet. Hell, he'd bet she'd done a Gantt Chart. But why? She didn't need to do all of that just to stay here while cleaning out her grandmother's things.

"See you tomorrow morning, then." He sketched a salute and headed for the door. "Seven thirty, right?" He shot the last over his shoulder and was gone before she could reply.

# Chapter Three

"You gave up Corozzo Shipping for this?" Tom Corozzo unfolded his long frame from the sleek black sports car and shielded his eyes against the sun. "I don't get it."

Cat eyed her brother-in-law. Former brother-in-law. She wasn't sure what to call her late husband's younger brother. "You didn't have to come all the way out here," Cat replied. She'd told him and his wife as much on the phone. But Lucia Corozzo was impossible to argue with. A darling woman who could also be a holy terror. And if she wasn't bedridden with morning sickness, she'd have been standing in the drive right along with her husband. They did practically everything together, still acting like newlyweds after eight years of marriage and two kids, plus one on the way.

All things Cat never had with Jimmy. Six months after their marriage, he had dumped his struggling shipping business into Cat's lap and made it clear he wanted as little to do with it as possible. Ten years later, he was gone.

"Well, don't just stand there." Cat opened the screen door wide and waved him in.

Tom paused at the door, running a finger along the worn and dirty brass sign. *Bristol Park.* Her grandmother's home. The grandmother she'd never met. Cat had no ties here. No childhood memories. She could close the door and walk away. Tom was right, she'd given up a successful business for this crumbling old family resort.

But it was a chance for independence, for a life that was hers. And she was going to grab it and run with it. She still didn't know what she was going to do with the place. The property was huge—two hundred and fifty acres of woods, riverfront, cabins, mess hall and the house. For now, it was like discovering secrets from an unknown past. And it had possibilities. So many possibilities.

Tom whistled as he stepped into the entry. "This place is a museum."

Cat had to agree. Even after cleaning, the dark-paneled wood and heavy drapes sucked up what little winter light filtered through the windows. A nervous laugh threatened to bubble up and Cat tamped it down fast. The whole thing felt surreal. One minute, she'd been trying to figure out what to do with her life a year after Jimmy passed away, and how to get away from the overbearing Corozzo family—Tom and Lucia were the only ones she could stand. The next, she found she was the sole owner of a dilapidated property in Abbeydon, New York, at the edge of the Catskills. When she'd first laid eyes on the place, all she could think of was Dirty Dancing and Hollywood images of family vacations in days gone by.

"I can clean up the second guest room if you wanna stay the night," Cat said as they climbed the stairs to the second floor.

The look of horror on Tom's face almost made her laugh. He was a city boy, through and through. "You don't have to do this. You don't have to live here. You have options."

Cat surveyed the small guest room with its worn furniture and dark draperies. It wasn't the condo she had shared with Jimmy, but it was hers. No domineering mother-in-law. Former mother-in-law. Whatever. No Mama C trying to get her married off to keep Cat, and the business, in the family. She'd taken care of the business by selling it to Tom.

"You're right," Cat replied. "But I want to."

She'd been here just under a week, and the place was feeling oddly like home. For the first time in her life, and in a place she'd never seen before, Cat felt a sense of belonging. Tom's expression was dubious, but as they came back down the stairs and into the dim light of the entry, Cat saw the place not as it was, but as it could be.

Sunlight filling the entry hall and making the herringbone-patterned wood floors glow. The tall ceilings giving the room a bright, airy feeling. Tom sneezed and the vision disappeared, leaving Cat staring at the faded and dusty drapes. Those were coming down. Soon.

Tom enveloped her in a bear hug. "If you need anything"—he whispered fiercely above her head— "you call me. No arguments. No stubbornness. You call. If you don't wanna talk to me, I get it. Call Dominico. One of us will take care of it—no Mama C." He held her out at arm's length. "That's a promise."

Her throat constricted and her eyes burned as she fought back unexpected tears. As much as she liked Tom, and loved Lucia, calling him wasn't going to happen. Despite his promises, he was a Corozzo. That, and seeing the happy couple with their adorable children was too painful a reminder of her own failures in that department.

\* \* \* \*

"Thanks for coming with me." Cat grabbed a stack of plastic storage tubs and nodded when Gina held up a label maker. Going through her grandmother's things was turning into a bigger task than she'd imagined. When Gina had asked if she could help, Cat's first instinct was to say no, but she nipped that in the bud and fast. She didn't know what she was going to do with the place yet, but whatever it was, having people on her side could only benefit.

"You got Mister Handyman working today, or is he taking the weekend off?" Gina consulted the list Cat had given her and tossed a couple more items into the cart. She'd mercifully not mentioned Nate until now.

"I have no idea," Cat replied. The truth was, after the first few days, she'd given him a list of projects and a set of keys, then let him do his thing. It was easier that way. She could ignore his comings and goings, and not be distracted by the tight jeans he seemed to favor. She glanced down at the list one last time. "I think that's everything."

"So, what is all this for?" Gina poked at the bins balanced precariously in the cart. "It looks like you're ready to tackle the world's largest organizational project."

Cat let out a laugh. Though a little blunt at times, Gina had proven to be good company, with a surprising sense of humor. "That's what it feels like." Cat grimaced, thinking about the mess she'd left at home. Boxes upon boxes of business records, family photo albums and important papers were easy. But the other stuff? Ugh.

"There's goodness knows how many years of stuff in the house." Cat wheeled them into a checkout line, mentally totaling up the costs. This wasn't a planned expense. "I thought it would be easy. Just go all KonMari on the place and divide things into keep, toss and donate piles, but..." She shook her head and thumbed open her phone, flipping to the pictures she'd taken after Tom had left the day before.

"There's just too much to go through, and it's going to get in the way of the work." Cat turned the phone to Gina and let her scroll through the images. The attic had been the easy part. It seemed like every room in the house had a stack of boxes and every storage space was crammed full.

"Was Susan a hoarder?" Gina whistled at one particular picture. She pointed at the screen — the room Cat thought of as the library, except it was wall-to-wall with boxes.

"I'm not sure," Cat replied. "I'm not seeing random stuff, or like she went crazy on the home shopping channel or anything like that. It looks like she just kept everything."

Gina scrolled again before handing the phone back. "Any chance of tossing it all? How much is worth keeping after being boxed up so long?"

Cat paid for her items, and they headed out to Gina's truck — part of the reason Cat had accepted Gina's offer of help. Her little two-seater wasn't the right choice for a trip to the home improvement store.

"It's mixed," Cat replied. "There were boxes of industrial napkins — the paper kind. Those are trash, which is a shame. But there are also boxes with old fliers and advertisements for Bristol Park. And boxes filled with vintage tableware. Trouble is, you've got to open every box and look inside to figure it out."

And that was why the piles of plastic tubs and the label maker. Trash, she could ditch right away. Everything else could go in the tubs to be dealt with later. Labeled bins would be far easier to manage than room upon room of mystery boxes, half of them falling apart with age.

* * * *

Back at Bristol Park, Nate was nowhere to be seen and his truck wasn't in the drive. Cat breathed a silent word of thanks. She wouldn't have to put up with Gina's coos of longing over the hot handyman. She didn't even want to imagine how awkward that would get. They unloaded the truck and Cat plastered on her best smile.

"You want to come in?" she asked. "You said you'd never seen inside."

Gina's eyes went wide, and a big smile crossed her lips. "Hell, yes! Thanks!" She bounded up the steps with Cat. "Your grandmother closed the place down just before my senior prom."

Cat nodded as she led a starry-eyed Gina through the lower floor. "It's been interesting, digging through all the boxes and seeing everything that went on here."

Gina pressed herself into the big dining room window and wowed over the view. "I was devastated when she closed. We all were. Everyone had their prom here. But we wouldn't." She pointed down the hall. "Where's that lead?"

Cat chuckled. "The library sort of connects the main house to another wing and the staircase to the guest rooms. It's still filthy, and a wreck. The sunroom is almost clear." She led Gina into the big, glass-enclosed space that commanded a stunning view down the hill.

"Everyone loved the place." Gina whispered the words. "Girls were in tears when they found out Bristol Park was closing. At the time, I didn't understand it. Now?" She sighed and turned away from the window. "I realize she kept it open as long as she could. For the community. But then, I was heartbroken I wouldn't have my prom here. Like my mother had. And my grandmother, I think."

"More than a few generations," Cat confirmed. "The pavilion is still there, but it's in kinda rough shape. It's amazing how much a part of the community this place was. And it's a little sad to see it come to this."

Looking through all the old fliers had given Cat a sense of missing out on something she couldn't quite put her finger on. There was history here, but it wasn't just that. There was community. A sense of belonging and a pride of place—things she had certainly never had growing up. Even after marrying Jimmy, she had never felt like she belonged. Not really.

"Hey." She shook herself from those thoughts. "I'll put on coffee. Thank you again, seriously. I appreciate the help."

Gina clapped her shoulder. "What are friends for?"

\* \* \* \*

Nate eyed the thin rungs of the fold-up ladder, certain Cat wouldn't like it. They had already looked at three stores, and countless attic access options, and she had vetoed everything. She wanted something sturdy and reliable, and he wasn't about to disagree with that.

"I know you're kidding." Cat's voice came over his shoulder and a jolt of electricity tingled his skin as she stepped close. Ten days of knowing her and he still couldn't control his body's traitorous response. "I thought the guy said this was their most robust model."

Nate swallowed his laughter, barely. There was nothing robust about the thing. It wobbled at the slightest touch. He might trust it with Cat's weight, but he wasn't about to climb it. He could leave the temporary stairs in until the work was done and do this part last, but they were in the way on the landing. There was no getting around it. A solid fold-up ladder was the only option.

He skimmed the installation instruction sheet, looking for a weight limit, then laughed when he found it — two hundred and fifty pounds. Considering the last time he'd stepped on a scale he was two and a quarter, it was out of the question.

"Yeah," he replied. "I don't think you're going to find what you're looking for in an actual store. These are more…uh…quick-and-easy solutions."

Cat scowled as she reached past him, a whiff of soapy rose scent tickled his senses, and he shook his head. She grasped the ladder in both hands, her slim fingers easily closing and overlapping on the beams. He didn't need to be thinking how nice those small hands would look on a different kind of wood. They wouldn't wrap around it quite so easily. *Nope. I don't need that image. Not at all, thanks.* She gave the ladder a good shake, mercifully ending any sexy thoughts he might be entertaining.

"This is a no," she muttered. "Where would I find the old-fashioned kind of thing?" She turned back to him, hands on hips, as if expecting him to produce an answer. Immediately. *Yep. Ice Princess.*

"Umm...old-fashioned kind of thing meaning...?"

She blew out a breath, ruffling the curls that tumbled over her forehead. "You know...the kind of ladder that slides down. Like was there before."

Well, that made a whole lot more sense. "You know those are going to be bulkier, right?"

Cat raised her eyebrows at him, adopting a perfectly innocent look that he didn't believe for one second. "If you need to bring in extra help..." She trailed off and shrugged.

He chuffed a laugh and stuck the installation sheet back on the shelf. "C'mon." He grabbed Cat's sleeve and tugged, urging her out of the aisle with him. "Let's head back. I'm betting you can find what you want online."

Back at his truck, her fingers tapped a rapid rhythm on her leg and a frown creased her forehead. Something was clearly bugging her, she vibrated with energy and impatience. She turned in the seat to face him.

"What about Juan?" The words blurted out. "I mean, sure I could just order online, but everyone ordering online is one of the things killing small businesses. And I like Juan. And Abbeydon General Store."

Nate stared at her, completely at a loss for words. That was the last thing he'd expected to come out of her mouth. He hadn't figured she'd care what happened to the businesses on Main Street.

"Uhhh..." He blinked and swallowed hard, his thoughts getting tangled up as she stared at him with those impossibly blue eyes. "Yeah." He stabbed the key into the ignition, just for something to do and cleared his throat. "Yeah. Good idea."

Cat fished her phone from her purse. "I'll give him a call. If he's got time now, we can swing by on the way back to Bristol Park."

Nate grunted a response, too confused by whatever had just happened to do much more than that. He stayed that way all the way back to Abbeydon, barely responding when she hung up with Juan and told him to go to the store. The more time he spent around Cat, the more she confused and aroused him.

Inside the shop, Juan waved them back to the office, leaving his daughter Charlie in charge of the register. "After you called, I checked a couple of my usual suppliers and I think I may have found what you're looking for."

Juan was all smiles, like his usual friendliness had been cranked up to eleven. Come to think of it, Cat had that effect on almost everyone. Even the normally testy Gina seemed to like her. Juan spun his laptop around and pointed at the screen.

"What d'ya think?" He sat back, his grin taking over his face. "Perfect, right?"

Cat whistled long and low, flashed Juan the brightest grin Nate had ever seen and then leaned into the screen. That megawatt smile wasn't even directed at him, and he was still knocked flat by it. Then she was all focus. He'd seen that look. On a hawk about to nab a ground squirrel.

She was staring intently at the ladder on the screen, and Nate had to admit, Juan had nailed it. Sturdy treads that looked like narrow stairs, a handrail, even brass fittings. It was so pretty it would be a shame to tuck it up into the attic. It would be a helluva job to install, but it *was* perfect.

"And the price isn't that bad." Juan pointed again. "That's my price, but I won't take…"

Cat stopped him with a look. "You'll take your normal markup, please." Her voice was soft, but there was no missing the demand. "It says it'll be here in a few days. Really? That's amazing."

Nate pushed up from the chair, dimly registering Juan's response that the company was only a hundred miles away. There was no sense in him hanging around while they dealt with business, Cat would tell him when the thing would arrive. Back in the store, he grabbed a coffee and leaned against the counter to listen to whatever the latest gossip was. Anything to keep his mind off Cat charming the pants off Juan. Or the fact that he couldn't seem to keep his mind out of the gutter.

# Chapter Four

"You ready?" Nate looked across the bulky box at Juan. The attic ladder assembly had arrived by lunch on Monday, as promised, and it wasn't small. When the Ice Princess had ordered this one, he'd looked at the box size and scoured the company's site to check out the videos to see if he'd need help on the installation.

He'd teased her a bit about choosing the biggest, heaviest ladder available, when she could have opted for a lightweight and super-strong aluminum model. She'd given him an icy glare for that, and though he'd never admit it, he agreed with her. Metal wouldn't be right in the old Victorian home.

"Let's do this." Juan let out a groan and gripped his side of the box. With a quick count, they hoisted it into Nate's truck. "Didn't expect this thing to be so big, did you?"

Nate nodded absently as he tied the load in place. After the hassle they'd had searching for the right ladder, the last thing he wanted was something breaking because the box shifted during the drive.

"That's why I grabbed the scaffolding," Nate said. "No way I'd be getting this in place otherwise."

Juan slammed the tailgate shut. "You gonna be okay doing it yourself? I know you're good, man, but this sucker's big."

Nate checked the ties one last time. "I downloaded the instructions and already got everything ready, and the whole thing installs in pieces. Pretty smart design. I even pre-framed the opening. Just don't tell Cat." He winked. Juan shook his head and laughed.

"Hey, Papa!" Charlie came out of the shop waving her phone in the air. She squeaked and drew up short when she caught sight of Nate and her cheeks flushed vivid pink. Nate tied off one last hitch and leaned against the truck. Charlie was slowly growing out of her schoolgirl crush on him. Thanks in no small part to the young man she'd started seeing. Juan gave his daughter a pointed hurry-up look.

"Did you check the weather this morning?" Charlie bounced on her toes, worry creasing her forehead. "Because there's a storm coming."

She held the phone up, and Juan's eyes went as big as saucers when he saw the radar. Nate didn't get it. It was coming into late January. Sometimes storms happened.

"Ah crap," Juan muttered. "Have you called Cat? Or Beatrice and Alvin?"

Charlie nodded, but any words she said were lost as Nate finally caught up. He pulled up the radar on his own phone. A big snowstorm was barreling down on them. Shit. Shit. Shit. Cat had taken Juan's panel truck with a load of antiques up to Catskills Consignment. Hopefully she'd have the sense to check the weather, or she'd be stuck driving home in this mess. An elbow in his ribs pulled him from his thoughts.

"According to Alvin, Cat left maybe fifteen or twenty minutes ago," Charlie said. "But she hasn't answered her phone."

Twenty minutes into a little over an hour drive. Not too far to turn back. Especially if she'd dawdled around town a bit before leaving.

"You guys keep trying to reach her," Nate said. "I'll get out to Bristol Park and get the generator set up in case power goes out."

He was in his truck and pulling out when an idea hit and he leaned out the window to yell at Charlie, still talking to her dad on the front steps. "Hey, maybe try texting. If she's driving, she won't answer the phone or check voicemail. Maybe she'll see a text alert."

Charlie gave him a thumbs-up and Nate headed for his place. He'd have to fill up the large gas cans. Maybe he should stop and get food just in case. If this storm was as bad as it looked, it could be days before the roads were cleared. He'd get up there, drop everything off, leave a note for Cat, then get back home.

Hopefully before the snow started. The last thing he wanted to do was get stuck all the way out there in the middle of a damn snowstorm.

No, scratch that. The last thing he wanted to do was get stuck anywhere with the Ice Princess. She was lovely to look at, but the way his brain turned to very non-family friendly thoughts around her — down that road lay trouble. Besides, she blew hot and cold with him, and he wasn't sure if she wanted to slap him or sleep with him to scratch some country-fling itch.

\* \* \* \*

The highway stretched gray and mottled with salt and sand, and the wind had Cat gripping the wheel until her knuckles blanched white with the strain. She swore under her breath and slowed to a crawl as she crossed a bridge, the empty truck acting like a sail in the wind. At least it wasn't snowing. Yet.

The weather had looked clear—or at least reasonably clear—when she'd left the fussy little bed and breakfast. Beatrice had invited her to stay, but she'd declined. Perhaps foolishly, but the idea of staying in one of the cutesy rooms was too much. Cat had never been one for theme rooms—maybe because she'd grown up in Vegas around so much overdone tackiness. While the Schubert's B&B was nice, each room was decorated in a particular era—Victorian, Roaring 20s, Vintage Hollywood. Cat just wanted to get back to Bristol Park.

Her phone had been ringing off the hook for the last ten minutes, but she couldn't take her hands off the wheel to answer, and she was terrified if she took even a few minutes to pull over and check her messages, the weather would get worse.

At the end of the bridge, the truck slid on a patch of black ice and Cat turned the wheels into the slide. Brittle fingers of fear spiked through her spine and her stomach roiled. The taste of cinnamon filled her mouth as the tea Beatrice had served threatened to come up. The guard rail loomed, and Cat braced for impact, then the wheel jerked in her grip as the tires bit. Maneuvering carefully, she guided the truck out of the slide and pulled to the shoulder.

She ran shaking hands through her hair and blew out a sharp breath, then fumbled the phone from her bag. Multiple missed calls and voicemails, and a mountain of texts. Dammit. The phone buzzed again, and she jumped. Nate. She thumbed the text icon.

"Storm front moving in fast. If you haven't left the area yet, go back to Beatrice and Alvin's."

Other texts from Charlie said the same thing, and Charlie's voice in her messages sounded close to panic. A message from Beatrice told her if she hadn't gone too far, there was room for her at their place.

Cat groaned, muttering curses under her breath as she pulled up the radar to see a fast-moving storm coming up behind her. There was nothing for it, she'd come too far to turn around. She'd have to try to beat this thing home. She tapped out quick responses to Nate, Charlie and Beatrice, then tossed the phone into the passenger seat before pulling onto the road, and driving as fast as conditions allowed, hoping to stay ahead of the weather.

No such luck. Fifteen minutes later, the windshield wipers flicked away the first flakes of slush and snow, and Cat's fingers ached. There was nothing between her and Bristol Park but narrow, rural roads, and at the rate she was going, the time was going to at least double.

She had to pull over three times when the snow got so heavy she couldn't see the road. Each time, she checked the weather, calculating how long she'd have to wait before a break or thin spot in the storm. And each time she sent texts to Charlie, Beatrice and Nate.

By the time she pulled into the drive, the falling snow was the least of her problems. It was the wind that was the real hell. She struggled out of the truck against wind that blew so hard it stung her exposed skin and she stumbled going up the steps. The storm door flew from her hand and banged against the wall.

Cat fumbled with her keys, but the front door swung open, and Nate's big hand closed over her jacket and yanked her inside before slamming everything shut behind her.

"What are you doing here?" The words sputtered from her mouth without thought. She tossed her bag down and struggled from her coat. The truck's feeble heater was enough to prevent freezing, but it had still been a chilly ride. Her eyes burned and her fingers ached from clenching on the wheel during the long drive. All she wanted was a cup of soup and a hot shower. Instead, she was faced with Nate.

"I came here to make sure the generator was gassed and ready to go, then the weather shifted. I shoulda left then, but I wanted to make sure you got back in one piece."

He nodded out the window. His truck sat in the drive, buried in snow. Well, that sucked. He couldn't leave in this.

"You didn't have to do that." She hung her coat and headed to the kitchen. Screw him. He decided to stay, that was on his head. Didn't change her plans. He could sleep on the couch.

"No, I didn't," he replied, following right on her heels. "But it was the right thing to do. It's called being neighborly. In case you hadn't noticed, we tend to take care of each other around here."

*What in the world has got him so prickly?* It wasn't her fault he'd stranded himself. Cat pushed through the kitchen door and stopped so quickly he ran into her back.

A pot bubbled and steamed on the stove, filling the kitchen with an amazing smell. The rest of the room gleamed as if it had just been polished and a pile of receipts and a battered laptop took up one end of the big island. Cat sniffed. Onions and garlic and something spicy.

"I figured you could use something to eat when you got back." He brushed past her and crossed to the stove. "Me too, truth be told. Last thing I ate was breakfast at Dolly's. I wasn't sure what you had here, so I stopped for groceries as well."

Cat darted a glance at his face, half-expecting to see a grumpy look. And she deserved it. He was being nice, and she was acting like an ass. Instead, his look was more one of amusement. And very disconcerting. She cleared her throat and found her voice.

"Thank you. The last hour all I could think about was getting home and getting some hot soup." Her own grouchiness faded a bit. "I'm sorry you got stuck out here because of me."

He lifted a shoulder then turned to the bubbling pot. "It's ready, if you want to grab a bowl. Nothing fancy. Spicy chicken soup."

Cat laughed as she pulled bowls from the cupboard. "I don't suppose you got sour cream or tortillas to go with this?"

He dropped a wink that had her thinking of things much hotter than soup and nodded at the counter where several small bowls sat filled with sour cream, grated cheese, sliced green onions, and what looked like toasted tortillas.

"I seem to recall someone saying she wanted things around here done right. No cutting corners." He poured coffee into a mug and slid it across the counter to her. "And certainly, no forgetting all the trimmings when making soup. Though the store didn't have any cilantro."

Cat's jeans clung just right as she stood. "You cooked," she said as she grabbed the dishes. "I'll get these."

Nate looked away with a nod. He didn't need to be thinking about the curves of her ass right now. Or ever. Desperate for something to do, he powered up his laptop. "If you don't mind multitasking, I can go over what's been done this week, and what you wanna do about your bedroom."

She half-turned to him and nodded. He sorted through the receipts, even though they were already in perfect order. Anything to keep his eyes off her ass. It wasn't like he'd never seen a nice ass before.

"Basement's got a new sump pump. Replaced the cracked dining room window and got all the storm windows up."

Her sweater rode up as she reached over the stove, exposing a swath of creamy skin. He picked up another receipt, stabbing at the numbers on his keypad.

"Got the master bedroom all cleaned out. Will you want to move into that room right away, or do you wanna wait for a new bed or something? I guess we could move the guest bed in there for the time being."

"What happened to the bed that was...?" She swung around, a horrified look on her face. "Oh! Yeah. Ugh." That was the bed her grandmother had died in. She closed her eyes and gave a little shudder. "I'll stay in the guest room tonight. That'll do until I can get a new bed. What else?"

She plopped onto the stool next to him and looked over his shoulder. His pulse went up at least a few points.

"The attic ladder is installed." He entered the numbers from the receipt. His insistence on computerized bookkeeping had caused a few grumpy expressions when he'd first come to town—a place where business was still done on a handshake—but people had soon got used to it and learned to appreciate the transparency it provided. They could see where every penny went.

"What? Really? Today?" She pushed back and nearly ran out of the kitchen. The sound of her footsteps on the stairs was followed shortly by a soft thump as the new ladder landed in place. Then came a high-pitched squeal of glee—a sound he never imagined coming from the woman he thought of as the Ice Princess. He planned to keep on thinking of her that way—it was far more comfortable than the other thoughts he'd been having about her. Like how his hands would fit oh so nicely at her waist. Or how good her ass would look up in the air in front of him. Her feet thudded down the stairs and the kitchen door burst open.

"Thank you! That's amazing. That just came in today. How did you get it done so fast? With everything else you did."

Nate smiled and pointed out the window. "I kinda got snowed in. Wasn't gonna sit around reading a book or knitting. And you took forever getting home."

"So, uh…" She fussed around the sink, folding and refolding the towel, then finally tossing it on the counter and grabbing the silverware from the drainer. "Did you get the other guest bedroom cleaned up as well? I mean…unless you'd rather sleep on the couch?"

He fought the urge to laugh, actually bit his tongue to keep from making some smart-ass remark, or worse, a crude joke. She hadn't planned on him staying here, that was for sure, and the two upstairs guest bedrooms were joined by a shared bathroom. Nothing like a little forced proximity to make friends out of people. Or turn them into enemies. Still, he didn't relish a night on the couch. He'd already checked out that possibility and as unappealing as it sounded, it looked even less comfortable.

"Yep. The second bedroom is all made up."

Silverware slipped from her hands, clattering to the counter.

"Look, I can sleep downstairs if you'd rather. Me bunking here wasn't part of the bargain." He crossed his fingers hoping she wouldn't take that offer. The only couch big enough for him was lumpy and hard.

"No." The word came out as a whisper. "No." That time it was louder, firmer. "I'll admit I considered that when I first saw you here. You didn't need to stay. But you're right, it was a nice thing to do. And you've been working the whole time. And you cooked dinner. And…" She pulled the cuffs of her sweater down over her hands, a gesture that made her look like a little kid. "I can't imagine any of the furniture down here would fit you. Or be comfortable. And it's silly when there's a bed upstairs. I mean, we're all grown-ups here, right? And there's a bathroom between the rooms. And…"

"Or we could move the bed from your room into the master tonight."

Cat gaped at him. She'd been babbling. She knew it, but somehow hadn't been able to stop herself. The idea of being that close to him all night was unnerving. Or possibly bumping into him in the bathroom. She swallowed. Hard. She'd been a virgin when she met

Jimmy. He was the only man she'd ever seen naked in person or touched. While he'd been a total player and their sex life had dwindled over the years, he hadn't entirely neglected her. Now that the grief was fading, her body was reminding her that she was a healthy woman with certain appetites that were no longer being satisfied. And she needed to get those thoughts right out of her head. An affair with Nate was not on her agenda. Now or ever.

"How long will that take? I'm exhausted." She stifled a yawn. With food in her, the stress of the long drive in the snow was taking its toll. She was ready for bed. "And why didn't you say that to begin with? The part about moving the bed tonight."

He gave a crooked smile. "I did. I told you the master was cleaned up and asked if you wanted to move in right away or wait or what."

*Oh yeah, he did. And if I was fully awake, I'd have caught that.* She wasn't sure whether he was just having some teasing fun, if he was being a jerk, or if he was trying to seduce her. Though she imagined it was normally the other way around — women seducing him. Not that she cared either way.

"Y'know what. Never mind. I don't want to take the time to do that tonight. I'm going to bed. Do you need towels or anything?"

"Nope." He shot her another smile. "Found all that earlier. G'nite."

She waved at him and climbed the stairs, barely remembering to save taking off her clothes until she was safely behind her closed bedroom door. She'd just settled between the sheets when the sound of footsteps echoed down the hall. His bedroom door clicked shut, and moments later, light shone under the bathroom door. Cat turned her eyes away from that narrow band of light.

Would he be in pajamas? He hadn't planned to stay, so he wouldn't have anything. Maybe he'd sleep in his shorts. *Or naked.*

She hissed in a breath at the idea of Nate stripped down to his underwear. He was a big man — tall and broad shouldered, forearms corded with muscle. Did he have more ink? A hairy chest? A line that traced down his belly…

A soft click sounded in the quiet room. No light shone under the bathroom door. He'd closed the door leading into his room. She fought the urge to get up and slip into the bathroom, to see if his bedroom light was on.

*Oh, knock it off! You're not sixteen!*

She rolled, putting her back to that side of the room and trying not to think about Nate in bed just a dozen steps away.

# Chapter Five

Nate flipped the pillow. Again. Punched it into shape. Kicked the covers off. Pulled them back up. Every time he moved the bed squeaked as if in protest. He sat up and glared at his phone. Five in the morning, and he'd done nothing but toss and turn—just like every night this whole damn week.

Seven nights of even less sleep than his normal. He could blame it on being snowed in, or on the bed—too small, too soft, too noisy. Or the temperature—too hot and stifling thanks to an over-active radiator. All of those would be true, but none of those reasons would explain the throbbing hard-on he got every time he thought about Cat.

He shoved the covers off and surged to his feet, pacing the small room. Women were trouble he didn't need. Especially a woman like the Ice Princess in there. Too many complications and risks involved.

He grabbed his bag and started throwing on clothes, thankful he always kept a tote with a few changes in his truck in case a job got dirty. Still, he was having to do laundry every other day. He eased out of the bedroom and crept down the stairs, avoiding the squeaky tread three from the top.

A little early for his daily hike, but it wasn't like he was getting any sleep. Not with her in the next room. Not when every night, he climbed into bed with the smell of rose soap coming from the bathroom after Cat showered. He didn't know why she hadn't switched to using the master bathroom. Especially after a couple of near embarrassing moments—the first morning, she'd walked into the bathroom while he stood at the sink, brushing his teeth, fortunately, already dressed. Then he'd walked in on her as she got out of the shower—he had been quick to turn around, and she was equally fast at grabbing a towel, but the flash of skin had had him raging hard for nearly an hour.

Outside, he rummaged in his truck until he found his headlamp. Two hours till sunup and the moon already set made for a very dark hike, even with the reflective snow all around. The early morning air bit through the heavy mask he wore, but he welcomed the cold. Anything to get his mind off Cat.

He looked to the skies—clear as a bell. Stars created pinpoints of light so sharp they seemed like diamonds in the sky. The heavy storm had come, dumped tons of snow on the area and passed on. He flicked the headlamp on and trudged down the drive. Might as well see how much damage there was. If he was lucky, he'd be able to plow the drive and get home today.

A downed tree over the main drive dashed those hopes. Shit. He'd be all day cutting that up. There'd be no hope of help until the roads were cleared. He circled the first set of cabins and the dining hall—everything seemed fine there, but they'd have to check the rest once the sun was up.

The sky was brightening in the east by the time he made his way around the base of the little hill, and there his breath caught in his throat.

Heavy snow covered everything, turning the world into a winter wonderland. The broad field lay pristine and white, stretching from the pavilion to the cabins. Snow-covered trees served as a backdrop and the pre-dawn light made it all look otherworldly. Beautiful, and so very quiet. His fingers itched to pull out his phone, text Cat and tell her to come look. Come look at this place she owned.

His phone pinged with an incoming text. Cat.

*Hey, are you down by the cabins? There's a light bobbing around down there. I tried knocking on your door, but no answer, so I hope it's you.*

Nate chuckled as he pulled his gloves off to type out a reply.

*Yep. Me.*

He debated telling her about the driveway but figured that was best saved for in person. Who the hell did she think would be traipsing around the property at the ass crack of dawn after an epic snowstorm. No one else could have gotten here. The closest neighbor was over a mile away. Not something the average person was gonna hike.

That damn tree. Even if he could go home today, he shouldn't. Leaving her out here by herself with more storms coming did not sit well with him. No matter how uncomfortable she made him. No matter how much he had to battle every urge to touch her, he couldn't leave her to fend for herself.

Shit.

The question was, how did he get that through to her and not have her think he was coming on to her. He was pretty sure she figured him for a playboy. While there was a point when he'd wondered if she was looking for a brief country fling, he'd quickly had to revise that thinking. Now he was certain she was repulsed by the idea of a man like him — or at least, a man like she pictured him to be.

He was just fine with that.

Up the hill, the kitchen light came on, casting a warm glow on the snow outside. Cat stood at the sink — he'd guess filling the coffee pot since he hadn't made any yet this morning. He watched her move through the kitchen — her curls piled on top of her head in a riotous mass that begged to have fingers tangled up in it. More unwelcome thoughts.

He tucked his head against the wind and resumed the climb up the last bit of hill.

Cat tapped her fingers on the counter, willing the coffee to brew faster. Outside, the world was white and silent. The howling winds had ceased, leaving a tangle of broken branches and bits of what looked like one of the cabin roofs strewn across the yard. At least she hoped it was a cabin roof and not part of the main house.

She squinted out the window. A large, bundled up figure trudged through the snow, headed straight for her porch. Nate was up every morning just after dawn — before she was willing to even consider getting out of bed — but what in the world had he been doing traipsing around before sunup? The possibilities sat like a hard knot in her stomach. Heavy footsteps sounded on the porch. Cat went to the door and flung it open, then stopped in her tracks.

Nate had dropped his scarf and peeled off his jacket and long-sleeve shirt. His T-shirt, wet with sweat, clung to his body and steam rose from his skin into the cold air.

"What…? Why…?" Cat struggled with finding words, any words. She cleared her throat and tried again. "What in the world are you doing?"

He looked up from unlacing his heavy boots.

"I run or hike every morning."

He swept his hat off and went back to his boots, as if that statement answered everything. She supposed maybe it did. A little snow had to be nothing to this mountain of a man. Still, he didn't need to be stripping outside. And how naked did he plan to get?

She felt heat rush to her cheeks at that last thought. Though it was no worse than the things that had been running through her head every night since they'd gotten snowed in a week ago.

"I've noticed," she replied. "But do you have to strip on the porch?"

"If I wait to take all this off when I come in, I'll overheat."

Had he been reading her thoughts? She'd undressed him enough times in her mind. He dropped his boots under the bench on the porch and gathered up his jacket and shirt. Cat stepped back and held the door for him. The hat had matted his curls down to his head and a fine sheen of sweat turned his skin to satin. She pressed herself against the door as he passed, the sheer size of him filling the frame. This close, he smelled of spice and smoky wood.

"Did I see your light out on the drive?"

Nate hung his coat and turned to her. "Downed tree." That hard knot twisted. "I don't think it's too bad, but gimme a bit to get a shower and something to eat, then we can check it out. I've got the tools to take care of the tree, I think. I've got my plow blade, I can do the drive, too, but it's gonna be a while before the road is cleared."

Cat opened her mouth, determined to say something, anything, semi-intelligent, when all she could think about was how much she'd like to get the rest of his clothes off him and drag him into a hot shower to warm up.

The sound of her cell phone mercifully interrupted those thoughts before she could do something as stupid as say it out loud. She nodded at him and grabbed her phone.

*Dominico.*

She left Nate in the hall and retreated to the dining room where she'd set up a makeshift office. Dominico calling could not be good news.

"Let's hear it."

"And good morning to you as well." He laughed as he spoke. It was a running joke between them. His brusque manner of answering the phone had put her off at first, then she'd adopted it. She'd never been one for small talk. Just get to business. While Dominico teased her about it, she knew he also respected her for it.

"Good morning." She chuckled. "Now talk to me. You calling first thing in the morning means something serious."

Dominico rattled off something about zoning ordinances and variances. "It's all preliminary," he continued, "but it looks like they're setting up for something big. I'm looking into it, trying to see what they've got planned, but so far, coming up blank. Which means either they're keeping things close to the vest, or there are other players on the board here. Either way, their plans could mean good things for you, or bad. If they're looking for a variance, this needs to be public. Are you planning to sell? Or keep the place?"

Cat looked out the window, across the broad expanse of snowy field to the river, visible below the hill. Did she really want this? She had enough saved. She could go wherever she wanted. Buy a house almost anywhere. She had a good education and experience. She could get a job anywhere. Somewhere the Corozzo family name meant nothing. Or maybe she'd go back to her maiden name. That'd be easier.

Tom had said it. She didn't have to do this. Except something in her needed this. That sense of home, of belonging, had grown.

"Caitlin? Are you still there?"

Dominico using her full first name shook her. "Sorry…" She took a deep breath and blew it out slowly. "I'm not selling."

# Chapter Six

Nate tossed the last branch onto the pile. The winds had taken down a couple of trees, but spared the rest, and there was thankfully no damage to the main house. The older outbuildings hadn't been so lucky. A couple of cabins had collapsed under the weight of the heavy snow, and the big pavilion had some serious issues — they'd be lucky if the roof stood up to another storm. Just more work to be done.

He shook his head. He'd overheard the Ice Princess' side of a phone call he assumed was with her attorney and could fill in a few blanks, including that she wasn't interested in selling. The only reason he could imagine for that was her thinking of renovating and reopening the family resort. Which was either the most ridiculous thing he'd ever heard, or the most amazing.

There was no doubt the town needed fresh life, and he knew from town gossip that her grandmother had had offers on the place, but she'd never wanted to sell. Susan had insisted a corporate developer would ruin the charm of the town. An opinion Nate shared. Maybe, so did Cat. Which was the ridiculous part. With her porcelain skin, delicate build, and designer duds, she looked like she belonged in New York or DC, wrapped in silk and talking art or politics. Not up to her ass in snow.

He glanced up to where Cat was putting salt and sand along the freshly shoveled front walk. He'd lay money that she wasn't used to the amount of physical labor she'd done today, but she'd gone the whole day without a complaint. Even when she slipped on an icy patch and landed on her oh-so perfect ass. Instead of fuming and storming back inside, as he'd expected, she'd laughed, picked herself up, and gotten right back to work.

"Hey, Nate. What brought you to this town?" She dropped the bags onto the porch and stomped slush from her shoes.

"Why? What difference does that make?"

Her eyes went wide, and she took a step back.

*Jesus, man, don't be a dick.* He cleared his throat and tried again. "I like the quiet." He didn't want her asking questions, getting personal.

"What do you know about the developers buying up local properties?"

Well, that was unexpected. "Think it's time we call it a day? Sun's headed down and the temp will drop along with it. Let's get inside."

She nodded and kicked off her boots before hauling open the front door. The entry was uncomfortably warm after hours outside, and Nate quickly stripped off layers. A muffled curse sounded behind him. She'd pulled her sweater over her head, but a button had caught in her hair. Her tee rode up, exposing silky smooth pale skin and abs that said she was no stranger to working out.

"Hang on." He grabbed her flailing hands and found the offending button. He tried not to think about the soft skin just inches away, or the soapy scent that came from her, even after a day working outside, bundled up against the cold. He finally got her hair loose and stepped back as she whisked the sweater over her head.

"Thank you."

Was it his imagination, or was her voice a little breathless?

"But you didn't answer my question."

She led the way into the kitchen and headed straight to the coffee pot. Nate sat down at the island, watching her. She was small, but curvy, and moved with an easy grace that spoke of confidence. *And toughness.* That didn't jive with the image he had of her — an uptight and driven Manhattanite. The Ice Princess.

"Ah. Well." He shoved his hands through his hair, trying to find the words. All he knew was gossip. Some big corporation wanted to put in an outlet mall. Or a big summer water park with river access. Some of the stories made sense and others were pure fantasy.

"I'm guessing you know more than I do," he said. "I can't imagine you haven't done some research."

She offered a small smile. "Nothing came up in preliminary searches. The sale of the Miller place caught me off guard. TravelCorp has purchased an adjacent property and initiated environmental impact surveys. But no hint of their plans." She slid a cup of coffee over the counter to him, then sat down, her own cup cradled between her hands.

"I don't know the truth of it," he replied, "just rumors. There was talk a big company offered your grandmother a decent price for the place a while back. She didn't take it, obviously. According to gossip, she was a bit pissy about it all, in fact. That was just about the time I came here. Since then, there've been rumblings here and there."

"So, you haven't been here all that long." She chuckled and looked down at her cup. "Funny, I took you for part of the landscape. All except the slight Southern accent."

"Small towns will do that to you." It hadn't taken him long to feel at home in the town. Getting everyone else to agree with that sentiment had taken nearly a year—still quick by local standards. "I do not have an accent."

She rolled her eyes at him, and he had to chuckle. "I worked very hard to get rid of it, but yeah, I guess it comes out every now and then. You don't sound like you're from New York."

It was her turn to look a little uncomfortable. "That's because I didn't grow up there. You don't like talking about yourself, do you?"

*Ha! She's one to talk.* He cleared his throat, desperate to get them onto safer territory than the inevitable follow-up questions about where he was from. "Facts are hard to come by when it comes to developers, but it's not too hard to put two and two together. Outlet mall, entertainment complex, water park. Maybe a casino. Who knows?"

"Not exactly the kind of development that will help this town, now is it?"

Nate shrugged. "Guess that depends on who you ask."

The half-smile and quirked eyebrow she shot at him spoke volumes. She had asked him, and he was being evasive.

"Look, I've got my opinions same as anyone else around here. And I don't harbor any illusions that you're asking me for advice. So, you wanna know what I think?"

He rose and refilled his coffee before answering. She sat, quietly tapping her fingers on the handle of her coffee mug. He didn't even think she was aware she was doing it. A little gesture of impatience that belied the calm look on her face. Juan was right—she had a hard streak. Where did this lady come from? And who the hell was she?

"This used to be a good town—family vacation destination, camping, outdoorsy life, all that stuff. It's got potential to be something like that again, but big corporate developers aren't the ones to make that happen. They come in and all the quiet charm goes away, replaced with sprawling buildings, and dead-end minimum wage jobs. The folks who make places like this come alive? They're bought out or shut out. Either way, they're out."

She nodded, pushing herself back from the island. "About what I figured. Drive's cleared, but according to Duane at the Sheriff's, the roads won't be done till tomorrow at the earliest. Guess you're stuck here another day."

The sudden change of topic struck him as odd. Had he said something wrong?

"About that..." He pulled up the weather app on his phone. "We're due for more storms. You might lose power out here. There's a generator, and I already cleaned and gassed it up, made sure it still works.

But...uh... I don't relish the long drive, in nasty weather. And I don't think you should be stuck out here alone if you get snowed in."

The pan in her hand clattered on the stove. She turned back to him, one hand on her hip. Her eyes traveled over him — cold, assessing.

"Fine. Stay here. But we're moving me into the master bedroom tonight."

\* \* \* \*

Silvery moonlight painted the room in a thin glow. Cat glared out the window. After midnight, and she wasn't any nearer to sleep than she'd been hours ago when she and Nate had finished changing the beds around. She'd found herself standing on the opposite side of the bed from him, laughing over something he'd said. And then she'd looked up and caught that tawny-eyed gaze on her.

No amount of logic, or reason, or anything else could stop the rising tide of desire that ran through her in that instant. And that just made no sense at all. Sure, Nate was good looking. Sinfully, deliciously so. But she'd been down that path and it was full of nothing but heartache and humiliation.

Even thinking of Jimmy and his endless string of affairs did nothing to quench the thirst, but no way would she act on that. She'd primly thanked Nate for his help and, claiming exhaustion, shoved him from the room.

Cat tossed the covers off and rose. She might as well put all that energy to use somewhere. Twenty minutes later, earbuds in and music cranking, she was mopping the floor in the room she'd dubbed the library — what else did you call a room with three walls of bookshelves and one wall of floor-to-ceiling windows.

Cat twirled the mop and worked in time to the rhythms of her favorite workout playlist, swabbing years of dust and grime from the beautiful wood floors. This place must have been a showstopper in its day. And it would be again. All her life, Cat had felt out of place—a burden to her single mother who hadn't wanted a baby, and herself a barren wife who couldn't keep her husband happy enough to stay faithful.

Something in the house spoke to her. Even in its current state, in the dead of winter, there was beauty here. She would bring that all back to life. Make it part of the community, the way it was to all the people in the general store who had fond memories of Bristol Park back in the day. It could be that again, for a new generation.

Cat plunged the mop into the bucket—ugh! Time to get fresh water. She propped the mop in the corner and grabbed the bucket.

"That is a lot of floor." Nate's voice echoed in the empty room, penetrating even the blaring horns of *You Can Leave Your Hat On*. Cat dropped the bucket and whipped her earbuds out, whirling to face the door.

Nate leaned against the jamb, thumbs hooked in the pockets of impossibly low-slung jeans, a flannel open over a gray undershirt.

"How long...?" Cat gulped air, swallowed hard. "How long have you been standing there?"

A slow smile crossed his full lips, drawing them up into a sensual smirk. "Long enough to know you've got some moves. Couldn't sleep." He crossed to her and bent to retrieve the bucket. "I'll refill this. You might wanna mop up the spill."

Cat tried not to watch his retreating back. And she definitely didn't notice how good his ass looked in the jeans. Or how the undershirt was low enough and thin enough to show traces of extensive tattoos on his chest.

She ran the mop over the spill, then went down the hall to the laundry room to rinse it in the deep sink. Big mistake. Nate stood by the basin, his broad shoulders almost filling the narrow space. Cat shoved the mop into the sink as quickly as she could and stepped back. Something about him overwhelmed her senses and turned her brain to mush.

*You're just horny. It's been a while. Get a grip. This is the last kind of thing you need. Jesus. Buy a vibrator.*

"What has you up?" Nate's voice was a soft, low rumble. Not helping things at all.

Cat focused on wiping her hands on a paper towel, anything to keep from looking at him in the confined space. "We took down the curtains in the master bedroom and the moon is too bright."

Yeah, that made a whole lot of sense. She had insisted on taking the curtains down. They were dusty and smelled like stale perfume. Chanel No. 5. No mistaking it. Her mother wore the same thing — well, the cheap knock-off version. She'd claim she wore it because it was classy, but that scent would always be mixed with stale booze and pot in Cat's mind.

It didn't help that the curtains looked like they were straight out of the seventies — big yellow and orange flowers on a green background. Cat couldn't imagine what had possessed her grandmother to buy those things, everything else in the house was tastefully done. Except the master bedroom. Which was a design horror show that included a shag area rug and a fuzzy toilet lid cover that matched the shower curtain, and the throw rugs. All now gone.

"So, you decided to do some late-night housework?" Nate nodded toward the library down the hall and gave a low whistle. "Most people would brew a cup of tea and maybe read a book. You decide to tackle mopping the largest room in the main house."

He hefted the freshly filled bucket and grabbed the mop, trudging down the hall with both and leaving her to follow along behind.

"You're gonna be sore later on." He set the bucket down, then to Cat's horror and delight, stripped the flannel off and began mopping the floor.

Complicated patterns of ink traced up both arms from wrist to shoulder, then joined with designs that crossed his chest and disappeared beneath the edge of the undershirt. His arms flexed and bulged as he swiped the mop over the floor. She forced a swallow past her dry throat.

"Why are you up? And you don't have to do that." She waved at the mop in his hands. He made the big industrial-size mop look like a child's toy. *Just how tall is this guy?*

"Told you," he replied. "Couldn't sleep."

Cat's brow furrowed at that. He was being evasive. Maybe this was part of some elaborate seduction scheme. She hadn't fallen for his charms the way all the other women in town seemed to have, so he was upping the effort. She bit her lip as he bent to wring out the mop and cords of muscle popped on his forearms. She'd never imagined that a man mopping a floor could make her think sex, but that was exactly where her brain went every time his hips swiveled as he changed directions with the mop. Okay, maybe it wasn't her brain going there.

Yeah, she needed to buy a vibrator.

He finished the last swipe of floor, propped the mop in the bucket and turned to her with a sigh. "I don't sleep much anyway. Few hours a night at most." He leaned back against the wall, the move highlighting his long legs and broad shoulders. "Heard noises and came down to check it out. This room is huge, and it looks like you've already gone over everything at least once. You really are gonna be sore."

She hated to admit it, but he was probably right. She went to the gym regularly, but nothing that would have prepared her for the amount of physical labor she'd been doing since she'd arrived here.

"Yeah," she replied, "but it's gotta get done, might as well do it." Besides, she wasn't ready for bed yet. She wasn't ready to face the cold sheets and too big mattress that conjured up inappropriate thoughts of a certain hot handyman.

The windows rattled and the lights flickered, making both of them jump a little. The house groaned in the wind as icy pellets of sleet drove against the glass.

"Well, that's gonna make clearing the roads a bit more difficult." Nate had abandoned the mop and bucket and stood staring out the big windows into the darkness beyond. "There'll be a layer of ice on top of everything else. Hopefully..." his voice trailed off and he shook his head. "Nah, not even gonna think it."

The lights went out, plunging them into darkness.

Cat's gasp echoed in the dark room as Nate felt his way around to the wall switch. His hand brushed the wall, but found soft, feminine fingers instead of a switch.

"Already thought of that." Cat's voice, close to his face. He stepped back, dropping his hand as the click of the switch going up, then down punctuated the constant pelting of sleet on the windows. The lights stayed off.

"And to think it was moonlight that was keeping me up." Cat chuckled. "Why is it so dark in here now?"

Nate slid his hand around the doorjamb, feeling his way into the hall. There was a flashlight in his toolkit on the porch. "Storm brought in clouds," he replied. "It's black as black out there now. I'll get the generator going. Do you have a flashlight close?"

A hand brushed his along the wall, making him jump. Cat, moving behind him. The echo of her breathing accompanied by that clean soapy scent. Her hand flattened against his back, and he sucked in a breath as her fingers trailed around his side and over his arm.

She was just going past him. This wasn't some seduction. Though, dear God, in that moment, he wished it was. Her hand grazed his chest and his stomach lurched, tightening into a knot as a white-hot bolt of desire shot through him, making him think the wall seemed like a good place for some middle of the night fun.

Then her hand was gone. She'd found the wall and was moving down the hall toward the kitchen. A moment later, a triumphant "aha" rang in the dark and a flashlight beam flashed against the tiled floor.

Nate crossed to her and stepped into the light. "Will you be okay for a minute in the dark while I borrow this to grab the light in my toolbox?"

Wordless, she handed him the light, her fingers cool against his. Another jolt went straight to his groin and his dick twitched. *Down boy.* This was not the time or the place. Fucking a client was never on his list of things to do. Especially one that wore designer yoga pants to mop the floors in the middle of the night. Though her dance moves did not make him think socialite. No, she moved like she was on a club floor and angling for attention. She sure as shit had his.

He grabbed his flashlight then made his way back to the kitchen. Cat moved around the room, carefully unplugging the coffee pot and toaster. "I don't know about this place, but..." She swallowed as if choking back some memory. "Maybe a blown fuse, and..." She gave a nervous-sounding laugh, looking less like the prissy city girl and a lot like she was struggling not to cry. Which made no sense.

"More likely the storm knocked down a power line or took out a transformer," Nate replied, trying to offer a calm and rational note. He didn't think he could handle her crying. "If the sleet keeps up, there'll be a lot of that. Still a good idea to turn off anything you don't need on. Generator can power most of this place, and I got extra cans of gas, but if the weather doesn't clear..."

Her eyes went wide, then that about-to-cry look settled into something far easier to deal with. Determination. "Got it. Conserve where we can. Looks like work's done for the night then."

Nate nodded. "Yeah. Let's get the generator up and running, and make sure everything's set. The boiler and water heater don't need electricity, so there's plenty of heat."

They could turn the blower off and just use the radiators. That would keep the place warm enough, and without the fans going, the generator would have less to power. If the storm blew through quickly, they might get out of here in a day or two. If it knocked down more lines, or closed a lot of roads, it could be another week before the main road got cleared.

# Chapter Seven

Cat picked her way down the icy slope to the pavilion overlooking the river. The storm had raged for an entire day, leaving everything covered in sparkling ice. It was beautiful, in a strange, bleak way. She'd been on the phone with the sheriff first thing in the morning and learned she wasn't the only one without power. All of Abbeydon was down.

Downed power lines and blown transformers had left most of the region with power outages. The utilities company was already hard at work but had to wait for roads to be cleared. The conservative estimate was two to three days before they'd get to the road in front of Bristol Park.

Cat swore as her feet slid, and she went down on her ass, skidding down the slope until she was able to dig her heels in and stop herself. Two to three more days stuck here with Nate Stewart.

At least he was nice to look at. Too nice, honestly.

*Speak of the Devil.* Nate waved at her from the edge of the pavilion. Apparently, a little record-breaking snow and sleet storm were not enough to stop this guy from doing his morning torture hike. She'd heard the door open and close and had rolled back over in bed, tucking the blanket more firmly in place. If he wanted to freeze his oh-so-fine ass off, let him.

Then he'd texted. And sent a picture.

Cat slid down the last few feet to Nate and looked in the direction of his pointing hand. The roof of the pavilion sagged under the weight of snow and ice and about half a tree lying across it.

"Ah, man." Cat stepped onto the wooden boards and her feet skidded like she was on an ice rink.

"Careful there." Nate's hand caught her elbow as he guided her to the rail. "Hold on and make your way around if you want to get a better look. It must've come down pretty early on, and the wind blew the sleet everywhere."

Cat inched her way along until she was close enough to see the full damage. One entire corner of roof gone and a big portion now sagging. Cat pulled off her gloves and grabbed her phone, snapping pictures from every angle she could get. She turned back to Nate to see him shoveling sand and salt onto the floorboards.

"You think the pavilion can be salvaged? Not the roof, obviously, but the rest?"

He leaned back against a side railing and crossed his arms over his chest, surveying the space.

"Floor's solid enough. So're the support beams. Don't see why not. Roof's beyond my abilities alone, but it'll have to wait till the snow melts. Nobody's gonna do much of anything if there's still threats of storms."

Cat groaned—she hadn't thought of that. That meant leaving the leaking, falling down mess for a while. And another last-minute project for her list.

"Still," he continued. "Could at least clean up the mess. Maybe remove the damaged parts so it doesn't pull everything else down."

He strode across the floor as if it were dry as a bone, not slipping even a tiny bit. In two breaths, he was beside her, looking up at the damaged roof. His breath plumed in the air.

"We'd have to get the snow off before we could do any of that." She kicked her toe at the pile of broken branches, ice, and snow under the caved in roof.

"Easy enough if the good weather holds," he replied. "I can get up there and just shovel it all over the side."

The idea of him, of anyone, climbing around on that roof was enough to make her shudder. She could see the holes from the underside, and God only knew how solid the rest would be. Still, she couldn't wait for the snow to melt before starting clean-up. Might as well just tear the whole thing down if she was going to do that.

"Did you know this pavilion is over one hundred years old?" Dominico had done some digging and the list of details he'd sent was mind-boggling. Both about the property, and the family she'd never known.

"The May Pole may be even older," she continued. "Or at least, the tradition of it here. There were spring celebrations at Bristol Park every year. The pavilion was built in 1905 for when they hosted their first cotillion out here. Can you imagine? Girls in long dresses and corsets making their way across that mass of lawn."

The property had been bigger then and included a logging camp in what was now protected forestry land, deeded to the state in the 1950s.

Nate tugged off his gloves, sketched a low bow and offered his hand. She hesitated only a moment before slipping her fingers into his calloused palm, then gasped as his other hand grasped her waist. Two steps and a turn and they were twirling around the floor, Nate leading with gentle pressure of his hand. He moved with easy grace and confidence, steering them away from the icy patches until they'd crossed the entire floor. When he stopped, they stepped apart, both looking away as if embarrassed.

Cat's breath caught in her throat. She loved to dance. She missed dancing. Though Jimmy was never as smooth and graceful as Nate.

"You're full of surprises." She'd finally found her voice, but apparently not her tact.

Nate lifted a shoulder in a half-hearted shrug. "Daddy insisted on schooling and martial arts. Momma insisted on dancing lessons."

That was more personal than anyone in town had ever gotten out of him. Somehow, with her, it had just slipped out. Like the idea of asking her to dance. Hell, he'd been to a few cotillions, at his mother's insistence. Even served as escort for a whole different set of Ice Princesses who didn't have brothers to walk with them at their debut.

*That was another lifetime.*

She'd felt good in his arms. Light on her feet, fluid, following his lead as if she knew his every move. He hadn't danced in years. Hadn't wanted to. That wasn't who he was anymore. Not that he was sure that had ever been him. He'd walked away from that life. Good riddance.

"I'll see what I can do about getting that tree shifted," he said. "At least keep it from tearing down the rest of the roof. My bet is that'll take up most of the day. That is one big piece of plant life."

He tossed the shovel into the wheelbarrow and grabbed the handles.

"How, exactly, are we getting up that hill?" Cat waved a hand at the snowy slope. The Ice Princess was back. "I slid most of the way down."

"Oh, ye of little faith. If you'd taken a look around, you might have seen the path I laid down earlier."

Cat unleashed a stream of less-than-polite language before falling into step behind him.

"I didn't schedule much for the next couple weeks because I knew the weather would be unpredictable," she said, huffing up the hill with him. "And Valentine's is just around the corner—nobody likes to work on Valentine's Day."

Nate grunted some non-committal response. He didn't do Valentine's Day. Hadn't in years.

"We'll have to rush a bit to get things done before Easter," she continued. "That's family time. I don't expect you, or anyone to work the holidays."

Nate wheeled into the storage shed. They unloaded the wheelbarrow and put away the tools, working in silence for a few minutes.

"That's almost two months from now," he said. "Besides, what about you? Won't you be visiting family for Easter?" He didn't know why he was opening that can of worms. But she'd started it.

"My family's all dead."

*Ouch. Touché.*

"Even the in-laws?"

She scowled at him. "That's not a place I belong anymore. No ties. What's your excuse?"

"Sometimes I think my family wishes I were dead." There it was again, more personal than he ever got. "Doesn't matter. I'll send cards to my parents and brother and chocolate bunnies to my nieces and nephew."

"Don't you get invited to have dinner with someone in town? Or go to church services?"

Nate threw back his head and laughed. "Yep, and nope."

She blinked at him, her mouth working as if in shock. "But...why...wait...then...?" She cleared her throat and stuck her hands on her hips. "So why don't you go?"

"I've no desire to spend my holiday listening to the preacher talk about the resurrection or hanging around a bunch of crotchety old folks. I do not wanna spend any day, ever, around women who are just looking to hook me up with their daughter, or niece, or hell, themselves."

A pink flush crept up her face, and she looked away. Well, that finally got her off the personal subjects. He didn't want to embarrass her, but he didn't want to be talking family ties either. Judging by her responses, neither did she. Maybe he should have googled her before he took the job. There was more to her than met the eye.

"So yeah, we can play a bit of catch up," he said. "If you're okay doing a lot of this work just the two of us. Like you said, not too many folks around here are gonna wanna work."

She swung the shed door closed and latched it, then headed straight for the house. "I haven't exactly been sitting on my ass." Her words carried back over her shoulder.

Nate shook his head and followed. No. She hadn't been. In fact, just the opposite. She'd been hustling around the place, doing things she probably shouldn't have been doing. His opinion of the prissy town girl was in need of a fast revamp. The trouble with that was it opened him up to thoughts he didn't need to be entertaining. *Like dancing with her and thinking how good she feels. Or admiring her ass. Little things like that. Fuck.*

# Chapter Eight

Nate hung the towel up and glanced at Cat. She stood by the big windows, a pensive look on her face and tension etched in the lines of her body. She could swing from lighthearted to serious in the blink of an eye. Just as he'd begun to think the Ice Princess was thawing out, she'd turned cold and distant again.

"Roads are clear." He leaned against the sink. The weather had turned nasty again over the weekend, then the sun finally peeked out on Monday. He'd spent the last two days dealing with that damn tree on the pavilion and hadn't paid any attention to the roads. The sheriff had called yesterday afternoon to update them, and Nate had gotten the text this morning that they'd finished the main road out to Bristol Park late last night. "If you wanted to go anywhere."

She lifted a shoulder and shook her head. "Everything's still closed — power just got restored yesterday. Folks are still scrambling. And it's not like I've got anywhere to go. Aside from returning Juan's truck, and he already said that could wait. He needs to plow the snow from the parking space, or something like that." She cleared her throat and looked down into her coffee cup. "You go on, though. I'll be fine here. The generator works in case the power goes out again."

The set of her shoulders, pulled in like she was protecting something, and the tight expression on her face told a different story. She didn't want to be alone, but she didn't want to admit it, either. What did he care, anyway? The hell of it was, he did.

"Nah," he replied. "We should go over our progress. See where we are. It's been a month."

She glanced back up at him and nodded. "I'm planning on keeping the place," she announced. "So, we'll be looking at everything on that list, and adding new items. You said we could reevaluate every thirty days. Thoughts?" She tapped the master list that now hung in the kitchen. "Changed your mind yet?"

She probably didn't want to know his thoughts. Hell, he didn't want to admit them even to himself. "I kinda figured you'd gone past the clear out grandma's stuff stage." He stole a glance at her, relieved to see a small smile curving her lips. "I'm up for it. But uh...figured if it was okay with you, I might start working on one of the small cabins. Maybe just stay there till the work here is done."

She glanced back at him, one eyebrow up, but she said nothing.

"It's a long drive to my place," he continued. "Easier to stay here on a good day. With the weather and all..."

"Do whatever you want," she interrupted. "If that makes sense to you. Fine. But there are plenty of rooms here in the house. Why bother with a cabin?"

Nate sucked in a breath. Every night, knowing she was just a few doors away, sleep was even more difficult to come by than usual. He didn't think she needed to know that.

"People talk, Cat," he whispered the words, knowing the threat of gossip would hit her hard. "Me staying out here makes sense, but as we get more and more work done, people would start to talk about why I'm staying in the house."

Thirty days. Barely a month of knowing her. That was it, and he was getting all tangled up in her. Despite knowing she was the last thing he needed. Thirty days, and he was torn between the desire to do unspeakable things with her and the need to protect her from even the slightest hint of gossip.

"Yeah, I suppose the town ladies thinking you were in my bed might ruin your chances of getting a little play." She smiled as she said it. As if it were a joke. What the hell?

It wasn't the first time someone assumed he was enjoying the company of a woman or three. He usually ignored it, knowing the truth would sink in. He'd never taken any of the women up on their offers, and scrupulously avoided even the appearance of doing so. Cat didn't know him yet, and damn her for thinking that of him. He cursed himself for even caring what she thought.

"That's not the reason," he muttered. "Not even close. That's not my style. Or haven't you figured that out by now?"

She whirled to face him. "What's that supposed to mean?" Her hands fisted on her hips and her face lost the soft smile, replaced instead with a look of demand. The Ice Princess was back, and she was not happy.

He crossed to her in a heartbeat, getting close enough to tower over her tiny frame. She didn't back down. Only stood there, glaring up at him.

"Don't you think if that was my game, I'd have been working on seducing you?" He spoke softly and inched closer. So close he felt the sharp exhale of her breath.

"Who knows how you work?" She hurled the words at him. "You can't deny you've got a whole host of admirers. Most of them women."

Something in her face changed. A flash of pain. Of shame. Her arms moved to cross over her chest—protective, shielding. Lightbulbs went off in Nate's head. He'd bet anything she'd been cheated on. He'd read her all wrong. Well, maybe not all wrong. That hot then cold thing. Her interest, her desire for him, he was pretty sure that was real. As was her distaste. She clearly wasn't looking for a boy toy. In fact, she was probably just as torn up about her interest in him as he was about his desire for her.

*Well, shit.*

He sighed and rested his butt against the kitchen island, giving them both some space. "Can we start this conversation over? I think there's been some misunderstandings."

Cat nodded, but kept her arms crossed. Nate tipped his head at the island beside him, inviting her to join him. She shook her head and shot him a glare. Yeah, she'd been hurt. Bad.

"I wasn't worried about what any of the women in town think about me." He looked directly at her, maintaining eye contact even though it felt like her stare was boring straight into his soul. Hell, maybe it was. "You're trying to build a business. It's not gonna benefit you if people start gossiping about you and I playing house up here. That's all I was thinking."

Her lips curled into a one-sided smirk as she chuckled, but her arms uncrossed and her posture relaxed.

"Okay, maybe not all I was thinking." He laughed and looked away from her. Was he really going to admit this? "It's damn distracting sleeping down the hall from you. Or trying to sleep."

Yep, he was going to admit that. Nate pressed his hands against the counter until the edge dug into his palms and dared to glance back at her. Cat's eyes had gone wide, and her mouth hung open for a split second before closing with a snap.

He pushed himself off the counter. Back into her space. Close enough to smell the clean, soapy scent of her. Close enough to touch if he wanted to — and damn he wanted — but he held back. Her breath hitched, and her breasts rose and fell sharply. Aw, hell. She wasn't wearing a bra. The outline of her nipples printed firmly into the soft fabric. His fingers itched to touch, to reach up and palm those lush curves. Instead, he bent his head and placed his mouth near her ear. Goosebumps rose on her skin as his breath washed over her.

"I don't think I'm the only one distracted," he whispered.

Her gasping intake of air was all the confirmation he needed. Nate straightened and took a step back. A look of raw need filled her face briefly, so briefly that if he hadn't been looking right at her, he'd have missed it. It was gone with a shake of her head, replaced by a confused look that made him want to laugh. She'd had no idea he'd been struggling to keep his mind and his hands off her. She'd thought him bent on just another conquest. This was one time he was happy to disappoint.

"All the more reason for me to move to a cabin," he said. "We're grown-ups, Cat. Not kids ruled by our hormones. I think we can handle a little mutual attraction without losing our heads."

Cat laughed out loud at that one. "You think so, huh?" Her voice was husky, damn sexy. Whatever thoughts were going through her head had to be good ones. Her parted lips and shallow breaths exuded desire. The warm flush creeping up her neck, and the smoldering look in her eyes only added to the temptation.

The urge to cup her cheek in his hand and kiss her until she confessed everything she wanted was so strong, Nate had to turn away from her to keep from doing just that. He strode to the kitchen door, tugging it open and casting a glance back at her.

"Sure," he replied. "Unless of course we want to."

He let the door swing closed, cutting off the colorful words she flung at his back.

# Chapter Nine

Cat pushed the cabin door open, prepared to jump back if any furry creatures had taken up residence and thought to complain about the intrusion. Dust turned a beam of sunlight into a swirling kaleidoscope. Cat turned her head and sneezed.

"Doesn't look too bad." Nate pressed close behind her, gazing into the small cabin. His warmth radiated into her, even through the layers of clothing they both wore. The goosebumps on her neck had nothing to do with the cold and everything to do with thoughts of what he'd said just a few days ago.

Cat stepped out of the doorway and gestured for him to go ahead. When she'd realized Nate was serious about moving to a cabin, they'd quickly decided on the first set of four—they were closer, and frankly, in the best shape.

"Ten years," Cat whispered as she stepped through the door. At some point, someone had removed anything upholstered—something Cat was eternally grateful for. A dining table and chairs sat pushed against one wall, and in the bedroom, a pair of nightstands still framed where a bed would have been.

"It's not as bad as I feared," she said, poking around the kitchenette. A stray pot lurked in a cupboard, and one drawer yielded an odd assortment of utensils.

Nate picked a two-burner hotplate up off the counter and nodded at the microwave and mini-fridge in the corner. "I'm thinking these are trash."

The lopsided grin he shot her sent pleasant shivers down her spine until she squashed that response. He was dangerous, that's all there was to it. Nate's very existence screamed sex, as if some airborne lust potion came off him in waves. From those eyes, that looked like tiger's eye stones were somehow on fire, to the silky curls, broad shoulders and even the way he stood—easy and comfortable, every move speaking of quiet confidence. And he backed that up with competence. Nate had excelled at everything she'd seen him do. He never took shortcuts and always put in the extra effort to ensure a job was not only done, but truly finished.

She could only imagine how he might be in bed. There would be no quickies or less than satisfying sex in Nate's world.

"Yeah," Cat replied, shaking herself before those treacherous thoughts bloomed into actions she might later regret. "The wood pieces might be salvageable." She gave a chair a shake and it seemed sturdy. "A little bit of elbow grease and these could still work. Doesn't look like this place has any leaks. Small miracle, really."

She tried to ignore the view as Nate bent to inspect under the small bar sink. The kitchenette wasn't made for serious cooking. Back when this place had been functional, most guests took their meals in the dining hall. The kitchens in the cabins were more for coffee and snacks or heating up pizza.

"You think you'll keep the kitchens?" Nate stood, looking insanely huge in the small space. "I mean, down the road, if you plan to rent these places out again."

Cat leaned against the wall, opposite him. The idea of crossing the room, of being that close to him, was unnerving. "I don't know," she replied. "The guest rooms in the house had coffee pots and microwaves—like a hotel room. I think that's smart. The cabins were meant for longer stays. It makes sense to keep a functional kitchen. Maybe not a hot plate."

She eyed the battered old electric thing, too reminiscent of the weekly rentals her mother had often shuttled them through. Peeling wallpaper, ratty bedspreads, wheezing air conditioners and dirty kitchenettes crammed into a corner of a one-room efficiency—those were the images of her childhood.

She'd used a friend's address when she applied for her first job working as a server in a casino restaurant—her mother had insisted no one from a reputable place would hire her if they knew where she lived. Cat had folded a towel over the end of the bed to press her interview outfit and refused her mother's help with her hair and makeup. She wanted to look professional, not an area where her mother had excelled.

She'd landed the job, no problem. Unlike her mother, she'd kept her job—squirreling away tips and bonuses so Sophia Bristol wouldn't spend them on booze. Or worse. A year later, barely seventeen, Cat had met Jimmy—the casino owner's son. He was twenty-one, handsome, and already so charming it was hard to believe he'd noticed someone like her. But he had.

"Hey…" Nate's voice cut into her thoughts. "You looked like you were a thousand miles away."

Cat scowled at the little kitchenette. "Over two thousand." She shook herself. He didn't need to know that. She swallowed, forcing history into the past where it belonged. "Yeah, these places need a kitchenette. But it's got to be nice." No aging hotplates or microwaves that smelled of stale bar food or the leftovers Cat had often brought home from work.

"So, aside from getting rid of the dust bunnies, and putting in some furniture, what do we need to do so you can move in down here?" Cat wanted, no needed, to talk about something other than the stupid kitchen. That little unexpected trip down memory lane was not something she cared to share. Ever.

Nate pushed up from the counter he'd been leaning on and strolled into the bedroom as if he expected her to follow. Even memories from childhood didn't put a damper on the flutters of anticipation in her stomach when she stepped through the bedroom door and into the small space with Nate seeming to fill the entire room.

"The bathroom's in decent shape," he commented. "But the blinds in here are shot." He poked a finger at the grimy looking mini blinds. No amount of cleaning would make them serviceable. "Other than that…" He turned in a circle, nodding here and there. "A good cleaning. New paint. A bed. I don't need anything else. I can bring a coffee pot from home."

That thought brought her up short. "What? Wait. But you take coffee at the house…" The words tumbled from her lips before she could think.

Nate winked and his lips broke into a broad smile. "You've gotten used to me making your coffee in the mornings."

Cat sputtered, unable to come up with a quick response. He was right. She had gotten used to waking up to the smell of fresh coffee. Yeah, okay, and coming into the kitchen just as Nate returned from his morning workout was a visual treat. The idea of stumbling downstairs to find a cold coffee pot was not appealing. Even less appealing was the idea of missing the sight of him flushed and sweaty while he stripped off the layers after his morning hike. It was a good way to start the day. And she needed to turn this conversation, and her thoughts, around. Right now.

"If you're going to fix this place up, we might as well go ahead and finish it like a rental," she said. "Paint, fully furnished. Get the kitchenette done. No half measures." She flung open the closet door, gratified to see it was empty. "Put in some nice wooden hangers."

She moved back into the living room—anything to get some space between them. His proximity made it hard to think straight. "Seating in here." She gestured around the room. "Maybe a television. Maybe not. I'll have to think about that."

Nate cocked his head and crossed his arms over his chest. "That's a lot of work just for me to have a place to crash."

Cat gave him her sweetest smile. "Any job worth doing…"

She marched out of the cabin, desperate for fresh air. The conflict of emotions swirling through her was dizzying. Whatever he was playing at, he was good. She'd lost at that game once and had no intention of losing again. Ever.

\* \* \* \*

"More paint." Juan's chuckle echoed in the early morning quiet. Nate had come in before the store opened to avoid the local gossip mongers. He wasn't sure he could keep a straight face if anyone asked how Cat was doing. Every time he thought of her, he got goofy. Not a great idea, especially since she seemed determined to keep him at a distance. Her expressions around him still ranged from dislike to obvious interest and desire. He was never sure which he was going to see from one minute to the next.

After inspecting the cabin yesterday, she'd been distant, reserved. By dinner, she was back to her normal self. Then this morning, she was up before her usual and had joined him for a cup of coffee. They'd sat at the kitchen island like an old couple, reading news headlines to each other and talking over their plans for the day. Nate hauled in a slow breath and pushed thoughts of Cat aside.

"Yeah," he replied. "Just one thing after another. Thanks for ordering this stuff. Saves me a trip to the big box shop."

Juan rang up the gallons of paint. "Always a pleasure. You know that." He leaned his elbows on the counter. "How are things going out there? Ms. Bristol always seems nice when she comes into town."

Nate forced himself to not smile. *Oh yeah, Ms. Bristol is definitely nice. Even better to look at.* Anyone could fall victim to the gossip monster, and the last thing Nate needed to do was feed that beast.

"You know how it is — things you figured would be tough are quick and easy, and things you figured would be easy turn into nightmares." He nodded down at the paint and other supplies Juan had ordered at his request. "Fixing up one of the cabins. I'll be staying at Bristol Park until the job is finished. It's just too long a haul, and the idea of her being alone…" He let that thought hang in the air.

"Oh, hell no," Juan replied, predictably horrified at the idea of Cat being alone—like her grandmother had been. "It's good of you to do that. That property is too big for just one person, and too far out for anyone to be alone. Especially after…well…you know."

Susan had been well loved, and while Cat was a stranger, she was Susan's granddaughter. Cat had also gone out of her way to cultivate a pleasant relationship with just about every shop owner on Main Street. And most of the gossip crew. It was impossible to find someone in town who didn't think highly of her.

Now if he could only get past the feeling that she'd acted to carefully inspire that perception. Still, in the barely two weeks before they'd gotten snowed in, Cat had done what it had taken him over a year to manage—gained the town's respect.

"You ready for your truck back yet?" Nate nodded his head at the still-snow-covered drive that led to Juan's house behind the store.

"Nope," Juan replied. "Not too worried about it anyway. If it isn't in the way out there, might as well leave it be. I won't need it till I start doing spring gardening runs."

He unlocked the front door, and Nate was practically bowled over by the usual crowd coming in for their morning gossip session. Grant Bishop, Lyle Redman and the rest of the crew of retirees converged around the wood stove and the volume in the place about tripled.

"Hey, Nate. Y'all get through that snowstorm okay?" Lyle sat down at one of the tables and pulled out his dominoes. "That was a record breaker."

The others agreed, a chorus of "ayuhs" and "yeps" rising in the room. Nate sat the paint cans down. So much for coming in before the place opened. He hadn't counted on these guys waiting for Juan to open the damn door.

"Yeah," he replied. "Came through it okay. Not too much damage, and most of it already cleaned up."

Grant Bishop came over and clapped Nate on the shoulder. "It's a good thing you were out there when that storm hit." He shook his head and something like a grim smile crossed his face. "Woulda hated to think of her cut off out there with no one around to help."

He gave Nate's shoulder another pat and joined Lyle setting up dominoes. That might have been the least grumpy thing he'd ever heard out of Grant Bishop. Juan flipped the sign to open and grabbed the paint cans then ushered Nate out the door before anyone else could start asking questions.

"Grant's one soft spot," Juan said once they got to Nate's truck. "He sorta had a thing for Susan."

Nate tucked the paint cans onto the passenger side floor and tossed the bag into the seat. "Huh." Nate wasn't sure what to say about that. Susan Bristol had been a lively woman, still beautiful in her seventies. She had been one of the first people to trust him with odd jobs. Even if it was just tidying up the drive and laying new gravel—and he'd barely seen her or spoken three words to her—that went a long way toward other people calling him for work.

He'd seen her cuss a blue streak a time or two, and she could get incredibly grumpy when people were idiots. She had been smart as a whip and generally sweet and pleasant most of the time... Much like her granddaughter, come to think of it. Still, he couldn't imagine her with the always grouchy Grant Bishop.

"Oh, he never said anything to her. He couldn't when they were younger." Juan sighed and shook his head. "He grew up around here. Grew up seeing the Bristols, spending summers up there — all the town kids were welcome at the river and the picnics, segregation be damned. Grant was maybe a couple years younger than Susan. I think he had a schoolboy crush on her that he never outgrew."

That explained a whole lot. Bishop had joined the military and married a woman he met overseas. She'd passed away only a few years later, and when Bishop eventually retired, he came back to Abbeydon.

"Susan's husband had passed before Grant got back," Juan said. "And rather than say anything, he held on to his fear and kept his feelings quiet."

That last comment stabbed at Nate. As he was struggling to keep control of his growing attraction to Cat and having the argument with himself over how much he should share with her. He'd already pushed the line. Any further and he'd have to quit working for her — he'd never slept with a client and had no intention of starting now. No matter how tempting Cat was, he sure as hell didn't need to be even thinking about sleeping with her. That was a road he didn't want to go down.

It didn't take a rocket scientist to figure out that Cat was sinking every penny into the property — eventually, that well would run dry. If Bristol Park wasn't up and running by then, and bringing in money, she'd be sunk. Then what? She'd have to sell. Or find investors.

There was another road he didn't want to go down. Too many painful memories along that route.

\* \* \* \*

The sun streamed through the bare windows as Cat stirred, glaring at the offending beam of light. Curtains for the bedroom needed to move up the priority list. She rolled and thumbed her phone on. Valentine's Day. One of the few days Jimmy had set aside for her and her alone. Last year, she'd still been in shock. Jimmy had died the weekend after Thanksgiving. They'd gone out with friends on the Friday night, celebrating some occasion or another—a deal that went well, a promotion, didn't matter. Then home, and sex.

In the morning, he'd gone out—supposedly to play tennis, or something, but she knew. He was seeing his mistress. At least he'd had the courtesy not to die in another woman's bed. No, not Jimmy Corozzo. He wouldn't do anything so tacky. Partying at clubs and sleeping with a string of women was one thing. Having a heart attack while doing it was something else entirely. It would have been indecent. He'd pulled into the garage at home but didn't come inside. Cat came running when she'd heard the horn blaring. His head had dropped forward and hit the steering wheel.

The next few months were a blur of family—Jimmy's family—telling her what to do, taking over her home and cooking meals she didn't eat. Noise and people everywhere when all she'd wanted was quiet. Peace and quiet and a place to think. To decide what in the world she was supposed to do. This wasn't anything she'd ever been prepared for. Marry smart. Marry rich. Marry someone who could take care of you for the rest of your life. That's what her mother had drilled into her from the time she could walk. Nothing about how to deal with being a widow before she'd even turned thirty.

Cat shook herself. That was over a year ago. All of that mess was a year ago. She'd left it behind. She'd done the year of mourning. Wearing black. Not seeing anyone but family for those first weeks. Living in the uncomfortable silences that stretched between the even more uncomfortable chatter created to cover the silence.

She stretched out on the bed, then rose and grabbed her robe. Coffee. And maybe pancakes. Or waffles. Something indulgent. Something just for her... The scent of coffee wafted up the stairs. Oh yeah. He was still here. Nate Stewart. The first man to turn her head since she'd met Jimmy.

*Jesus, Cat. Couldn't find some guy in the city where a crazy affair wouldn't even be a blip on anybody's radar. No. You have to go and have a case of the incurable hots for the small-town local handyman...* And if his comments about the holiday dinner invites were anything to go by, she wasn't the only one down with a case of the 'I wants'. She could attest to that from talking with Gina and the rest of the Nate Stewart Thirst Club. And yet, he clearly wasn't interested. Though that could be just a game. A show for her benefit.

She pushed through the kitchen door. Nate sat at the island, cradling a cup of coffee in one hand and his cell phone in the other. He looked up and nodded a greeting at her as she made her way to the coffee pot.

"Wondered if you'd ever wake up."

Cat sipped her coffee and glared at him over the rim. "It's barely sunrise."

"It's nearly eight. Happy Valentine's Day."

She took another look at him. His usual curls lay damp and combed back, shining blue-black in the morning light, and he was dressed, not in pajamas, or sweats, but in jeans and a tight Henley.

"I suppose you did your usual morning routine. What form did the torture take today? A ten-mile hike in the snow, uphill, both ways? Or was it jogging in snowshoes?"

The coffee cup didn't do much to hide his smirk, but his brows knitted together in a frown that looked at odds with the expression on his mouth.

"I think you need to drink your coffee. Save the comedy routine for later."

Cat ignored him and dug through the big cabinet where she'd stuffed all the old appliances and pots and pans she wasn't using, but wasn't quite ready to get rid of. She was sure she'd seen a waffle iron…yep. There it was. Now, to hope it still worked.

"That thing looks older than you."

He stood behind her, coffee cup in hand, eyeing the waffle iron, uncertainty written on his face.

"Look who's talking about comedy." She grabbed a cloth and wiped the machine down before opening it up to inspect the surfaces. "It's not too bad. At least it's not a cloth covered cord. My grandmother-in-law still had a toaster with a cloth cord. That thing was a fire hazard, but she insisted it made the best toast. Wouldn't use anything modern."

Satisfied everything looked in working order, she plugged the thing in. Might as well see if it worked before making batter. The little light came on and in minutes, the surfaces were too hot to hold her hand over.

"Well, Mister Skeptic. No sparks flying, so maybe this old thing will make some waffles." She poked his chest to move him out of her way. He was still disarmingly close. "Or are you not eating carbs? Maybe you're all about protein in the mornings."

He didn't reply, he just went back to sipping his coffee while reading the news on his phone. Cat pulled out eggs and milk and butter, then added a pack of breakfast sausage. Might as well have some protein. Ten minutes later, she was pouring batter for the first waffle and crossing her fingers this would work.

When she turned back to the island with a platter of waffles in one hand and sausages in the other, she was surprised to see he'd set their places and poured them both a glass of milk.

"Can't have waffles without milk." He winked and sat back down before pushing the syrup and butter across the table for her. "Ladies first."

The waffles were perfect. After they ate, he stood and cleared the dishes. For such a big man, he moved with ease. So fluid. Every move was graceful, economical, efficient. It didn't hurt that his ass looked amazing in the tight, low-slung jeans, and his shoulders seemed about a mile wide.

Yeah, it was time to stop that train of thought right there.

She poured herself another cup of coffee then crossed to the big window. The world around them was beautifully white. And quiet. So quiet. Out here, the snow brought a hush she'd never known in the city. Cat sighed, her breath fogging the glass.

She'd looked forward to this day. As soon as the reality of Jimmy's death had hit, she'd determined she would walk away from the Corozzo family and find her own life. She hadn't known about Bristol Park then. She hadn't even known about her grandmother. She'd been prepared to be all alone in the world, and here she was.

Hardly alone. Dominico was just a phone call away. She hadn't been able to walk away from him as her lawyer, or her friend. She could always call Tom and Lucia, not that she ever would. And now there was Nate. She'd known him a little over a month and yet he already seemed like a fixture in her life.

It had been over a year. Maybe it was time to think about other men. She was allowed to do that. Just not this one.

# Chapter Ten

A sleek black car pulled up in the drive. Cat shoved her fingers through her hair, twisting it on top of her head in a messy bun. Dominico stepped out, all dark suit and polished loafers. He barely glanced around him before mounting the steps. She threw open the door before he could knock, greeting him with a hug and kiss on the cheek.

"You said this was urgent but wouldn't talk on the phone. I could have come to you, y'know."

In the entry, Dominico shrugged out of his coat. "I wanted to see this place. Besides, why would I have you drive all the way into the city?"

Cat hung his coat in the hall and gestured for him to follow into the dining room, she couldn't imagine Dominico perched on one of the kitchen stools. "I'll steam some milk for coffee."

He waited until she'd poured two cappuccinos, then nodded out the window. "Nice view." The dining room commanded a view over the barren trees and standing pines to the frozen river below. Dominico heaved a sigh and opened his briefcase, spreading folders out over the table.

"TravelCorp is not taking this lightly." He pulled a pile of papers from a folder and slid them across to her. "You're refusing to sell, so they're pulling out all the stops. They've requested economic feasibility reports — which is ridiculous, considering Bristol Park would be an as-of-right development and what they're proposing would require a variance for zoning, at the least."

Cat glanced down at the paperwork, the words and numbers blurring and swimming into a confusing mess. "I thought we did our due diligence on this place. What is all this?"

Dominico held a hand up, quieting her.

"We did. But TravelCorp wasn't in the picture yet. Not that we could see anyway. They're just trying to make things complicated and more expensive for you. It's a common tactic to encourage owners to sell."

She looked at the papers again. Ordering those studies would cost an arm and a leg. Money she didn't have, not if she wanted the rest of this project to work.

"This is a resort property, already zoned and permitted — though those are expired, it shouldn't take this much to renew. This is all stuff that a company would have to do in order to develop the property, but we're not doing that. I'm not about to fund the research they would have to do if they bought this place. This is ridiculous. Bottom line it for me," she said. "Do we need to do any of this? Do we need to fight them? And how?"

Dominico waggled a hand back and forth. "We can stall. They can continue to push, which means it could end up in court."

Cat pressed her lips together to stop the string of profanities she wanted to scream. When she'd first learned of Bristol Park, her only interest was curiosity — about the grandmother she'd never known and the family history she'd been denied. Then she'd seen the opportunity. The chance to rebuild not just the resort, but herself as well.

"You know the family will help…"

"No."

Dominico sat back in his chair, his eyes wide. "What do you mean?"

"I mean, no." She shoved the papers back to him. "Stall as long as possible. If they're at this stage of development, they've got to be doing their own impact studies."

He sighed and shook his head. "You don't have to do this alone."

"Yes, I do." She smiled and patted his hand. "You know I do. If I accept help from them, I'm back in. Someone else controlling my life. Telling me what to do. Who I can see. This place will be run by committee — all Corozzo family members."

"You are a Corozzo."

Cat laughed. "Only by marriage. What life do you think I'd have in that family? Seriously?"

He looked away, the sad expression on his face saying it all.

"Exactly." She softened her tone — she didn't want to hurt Dominico. He was her friend. "I'd have Mama C trying to set me up with every second cousin or third son. Someone who isn't that important in the scheme of things, who doesn't have the burden of carrying on the family name, but who needs a good wife. And everything here would be theirs. Not mine."

She shook her head again and sniffed back the tears that threatened. "I couldn't give Jimmy a baby. I ran his business for years, kept his home, did everything he ever asked of me, except that one thing. Still, he fucked around on me. And everyone knew it. Nobody cared. Not even you."

"Don't go blaming yourself for that. Not for any of it. Jimmy was a slug." Dominico spat the words out, then wiped his mouth as if saying them left a bad taste. "Really, you should…"

Cat silenced him with a look. "I don't have to think about him, or families who care more about the lack of another son being born into the world than they do about cheating husbands."

Dominico patted her hand gently. "People care, Cat, they just stay silent. The men because they don't want to get called a pussy, or have the others say they're whipped. The women because they don't want to lose what they've got."

"That's so wrong."

"*Così fan tutte.*" He waved a hand dismissively, but his smile was kind. "Yeah, it is. But don't think it's because nobody cared." He leaned back and sighed. "Still, you're right about Mama C. She'd be nagging every day to get your ass married off, tied to some nice guy in the family. Only because she loves you and respects you."

Cat uttered a short laugh. "More like she knows I'm useful and wants to keep that in the family. She tried to set me up on New Year's Eve — Marc Grenotti, Jimmy's smarmy cousin. If I'm married off, it's harder to leave. And the money goes right back into the business."

He nodded. "That's how family businesses run."

"Yeah, well, screw that." She pointed out the window. "This is my family business. No Mama C or marrying somebody I don't love necessary."

"You loved Jimmy."

His words hit like ice water. She had loved Jimmy. Despite it all, she had loved him. Stupidly, foolishly. Naively. She wasn't that stupid anymore. "I was a lot younger then."

She gathered up the papers and skimmed through them again, then tossed them back at Dominico.

"Stall them. And find out why this is the first we're hearing of this. I've got a feeling the executor or someone knew this was coming, and if I'm right, I want that person's ass in a sling." She chuckled and patted Dominico's hand again. "Figuratively speaking, of course. Then let's clean this mess up, and I'll show you around."

\* \* \* \*

Nate double checked the list and marked off the last items as he left the store. That damn house was turning into a never-ending pile of projects as one thing kept leading to another. He'd just started painting the cabin when the washing machine had quit working. He'd managed to get that repaired and a new one was on the way. Then the lawyer had called, all in a tizzy about something, and insisting on hauling his ass out here to talk to Cat in person. The new mattresses had arrived just that morning—three of them, new pillows too. Trouble was, she'd only ordered bedding for two beds. Hers and his. So here Nate was getting new sheets for the third bed.

"Y'know, you're a hard man to find."

The soft, husky voice startled him from his thoughts, and he nearly dropped his keys. Despite not hearing that voice for years, he didn't need to turn around. Erin Blake. His ex-fiancée. *Shit.*

"What do you want?"

Her hand closed over his bicep, squeezed. He turned and her ice gray eyes were inches from his. There was a time when her very presence would have had him shaking with need. Now, he felt nothing. He pushed her hand away.

"Oh, come on, Nate." She leaned against his truck and smiled, giving him a look under her lashes. "You never used to be difficult."

"People change. Would you mind moving? I've got places to go."

She crossed her arms and didn't budge. "Nate…" Her voice was a seductive purr, her deep red lips curled in a pout that should have seemed cute. "It's been a long time, I know we had some problems, but…I don't know, I thought maybe we could talk. Over dinner." She reached out and traced her finger from his shoulder to his elbow, then tugged at his hand.

Nate caught her wrist and pulled her away from his truck. "Not interested." He was in his seat with the door shut and locked before she could recover. He didn't wait around to see her response. Knowing Erin, she could easily decide to block his way, forcing him to either run her over — and then blaming him for it — or get out and move her out of the way, again, blaming him for it.

His ex was good at blaming him for everything. He glanced in the rearview — she stood, one hand on her hip, waving, as if she knew he'd look. *Dammit.*

Erin was another problem he didn't need right now. She'd popped up once or twice in the first couple of years after she left, always with excuses for what had happened. Always with some new need she expected him to meet. He hadn't seen or heard from her since before he came to Abbeydon and he liked it that way.

Nate pulled into the drive, eyeing the big black car parked in front of the house. Not the ideal thing to drive out here in the middle of February, but hey, to each their own.

He let himself in, struck, as always, by the changes they'd accomplished in such a short time. The entry hall, once dark and depressing, was bright and welcoming after they'd cleaned the years of grime from the front windows and removed the heavy velvet draperies. Gone was the old, sagging furniture, replaced with comfortable modern pieces interspersed with a few well-chosen antiques. Gone too was the unused smell and any traces of dirt or dust. There was still work to be done, especially in the back part of the house they hadn't yet reopened, but the main rooms at least were livable.

Laughter carried in from the dining room. He hung his coat, dropped the bags on the hall table and kicked his boots under the bench. Cat would have a fit if he tracked road grime onto the area rugs she'd unearthed from the attic and cleaned herself. He opened the dining room door to find Cat sitting at the table, a cup of coffee cradled in her hand, and a heavyset, dark-haired man who had to be Dominico Santieri—Cat's attorney. According to her, a serious hard-ass with a marshmallow center.

"You must be Nate." Santieri rose and offered his hand.

Nate shook. At least the guy didn't play the let's see who can crush whose hand first game. "And you'd be Mr. Santieri."

The man laughed, a good-natured sound that matched the friendly look on his face. "Please, it's Dominico. Cat's told me about you. How much of a help you've been. She's been showing me around, telling me her plans for the place." He nodded, the smile tightening a bit as his eyes focused on Nate.

"There's still a lot to be done. Especially outside. But it's going well." He turned to Cat. "Everything's in the hall. You want me to take care of it so you can keep chatting?"

She shook her head. "No, I've got it. I need to start dinner anyway."

The moment she was out of earshot, Dominico pushed a chair toward him. "Sit." He waited until Nate complied, then smiled. "You had to expect she'd ask for a background check on anyone working in her home."

Nate nodded, unsure where the man was going.

"You're a long way from your Georgia roots. What I want to know is why a man who graduates with degrees in public and international affairs from Princeton and Harvard, of all places, disappears for a few years? Apparently doing volunteer work in some interesting places. And then you wind up in this little town, working as a handyman. You've lived a colorful life."

Nate winced. Those were years he didn't care to think about—when he'd been young and naive and focused entirely on the path his parents had put in front of him. Then Erin happened, and his eyes had been opened. He'd walked away from it all.

"No more colorful than your own, I'm sure."

Santieri chuckled at that. He leaned forward in his chair, elbows on the table. "I'm not here to be an asshole. Fact is, I don't really care why you took off because I don't believe you're a threat. There are some unusual things in your background, sure, but who doesn't have a few skeletons in their closet, right?"

Nate arched an eyebrow at the man. "So, what's the purpose of this discussion then?"

"How much have you told Cat?"

Nate sighed. "I don't recall," he replied. "I don't see the need to get personal with my employer."

Santieri nodded and sat back. That seemed to satisfy him in some way. Truth was, Nate didn't see the need to get personal with anyone.

"I would like to know how you go from being groomed for a career in politics to this."

"I like the quiet."

The older man gave a hearty laugh at that. "That is something you and Cat have in common." He rose from the table, surprisingly agile for his size. "Oh, one other thing." He laid a hand on Nate's shoulder and leaned close. "I don't believe for an instant she's nothing more than your employer. She doesn't see it, yet."

He straightened up and headed toward the kitchen, leaving Nate alone at the table. Shit. The man was right. He'd been denying it for days, hell, since the moment he'd laid eyes on her. Desires he'd long thought dead came raging back to the surface every time he was around her. Getting to know her had only made things worse. He could ignore physical desire, he'd gotten very good at that over the years, but hell, he actually liked her as well.

How had Santieri spotted that?

\* \* \* \*

Cat poured Dominico a brandy, slowly trickling the amber liquid into a balloon glass she'd found in the dining room's china hutch. A fire crackled in the hearth, transforming the nearly cavernous living room into something almost cozy. She poured a second drink for herself, then sat.

"When I first got here, the only rooms open down here were the kitchen and the dining room. Everything else was closed off. Doors latched, windows boarded up or covered in plastic." She sighed and leaned back, looking around the room again. "Look at this place. It's gone from practically abandoned to this. Sure, we've got a way to go yet, but we've come so far so fast."

Dominico cradled his glass, swirling the brandy as he glanced about the room. "I only saw the pictures you sent, and Tom's description was colorful. It's a remarkable transformation." He sat the glass on a table and leaned forward. "Cat, what are you planning to do here? With this place? It's too much for just you."

She'd known he would ask. It was his job as her attorney, and his duty as a friend. Still, it bristled. She fought back the urge to tell him it was none of his business. Instead, she took a deep breath and blew it out slowly before answering.

"Bristol Park used to be a successful family resort. That sort of thing is becoming popular again." When she'd first arrived, she wasn't sure what she'd do with the place either, but the ideas had started and, over the last couple of weeks, become more and more clear.

"This is an ideal location for a four-season event space. We're not that far from New York City, Philadelphia, New Jersey, plenty of places along the

Eastern Seaboard are in driving distance. That's why this area used to be so popular. Weddings, weekend events, summer camps, river tubing, cross-country skiing—"

"I'm not saying the place isn't suited to all that. And I sure as shit am not saying that you can't handle it—I know better. But...it's just you here." He spread his hands and waved around the big living room.

"Eventually, I'll hire staff. There's an entire wing of the house I haven't opened yet—guest rooms, staff rooms and another big room that looks like it was being used as a rec room of sorts. Plus, there are staff cabins. You know the history."

Dominico nodded, slowly sitting back in his chair, sipping his brandy. "What about Nate?"

"What about him?" The defensive tone in her voice surprised her. Nate had confused and infuriated her when she'd first met him, now she was ready to go to bat for him.

Dominico's chuckle was unexpected. "Do you think I'm blind? You rely on him far more than just a paid handyman. And he's living here."

Cat stared into the amber depths of her glass, trying not to think about Nate's warm amber eyes. "He's trusted in town. Has a solid reputation for doing good work—and that's hard to come by around here. And you ran his background, told me there were no problems." She huffed out a short breath. "Him staying here just made more sense. It lets us get more work done, especially when the weather's bad. And he's been an amazing help. I don't think...no, I know I wouldn't have gotten this far, this quickly, without him. So, what about Nate?"

She glared at Dominico, but he was expressing the same concerns she herself had at first. Today, she trusted Nate. And she didn't trust easily. That was a big change. Dominico was right to question. She would do the same.

"What has he told you about himself?"

Cat sat back, a little nonplussed. "He doesn't talk about his past much. I can put two and two together though." She rolled her eyes. "It doesn't take Sherlock Holmes to figure out he's had a good education, and probably comes from a well-off family but doesn't have a great relationship with them. Maybe he's the black sheep. Maybe he just didn't like the expectations of him. I don't care."

She sipped her brandy, thinking. What else did she know about Nate's life? "He's mentioned an ex, in passing. No details. I don't even know if he means ex-wife, fiancée, girlfriend, or hell, business partner. I don't think he has any kids—never mentioned them. Everything else is more recent. What he's done since he came to town."

Those details weren't hard to come by. Though Nate was reluctant to talk about himself, others in town weren't so reticent and would happily sing his praises if given the slightest provocation. If the town talk was to be believed, Nate was not only honest and hardworking, but an unbelievably nice guy who'd give the shirt off his back if he thought you needed it. The ladies still loved him, but he didn't seem to pay them any attention. In fact, just the opposite—as far as anyone could tell, he never dated and scrupulously avoided even the appearance of being interested in a woman.

"You told me he was fine. Nothing to worry about. Why are you asking about this now?" It was possible his staying here had caused some juicy gossip.

"Relax, Cat." He gave a soft smile. "I didn't find anything worth worrying about. I would have told you if I had, you know that. Though folks in town aren't going to gossip to some stranger from the city. Juan Neeman at the general store was a bit more forthcoming."

*Ah crap, what did Juan have to say?* Cat narrowed her eyes and glared at Dominico, silently urging him to skip the dramatic build up and get on with it. As short as he could be on the phone, he did love a good story.

"Don't worry, nothing salacious. Instead of thinking unsavory things, seems everyone believes Nate to be a saint for coming out and helping the way he has, and even staying on the property so you wouldn't be alone—like your grandmother was." He paused a moment, eyes closed. He'd be saying a silent prayer for the dead. Old school Catholic habits died hard.

"Older folks in town knew her well. They weren't too thrilled at her being all alone out here after she had to let the last of her staff go. They remember this place as something good for the town. All of that goodwill seems to be spilling over to you—have you seen pictures of your grandmother?"

Cat nodded. She had. Beyond the one photo the executor had shared, she'd found a photo album and boxes of old pictures when she'd cleaned the master bedroom. Seeing herself reflected in images of a woman she'd never known had been a bit unsettling. Her mother was a tall, leggy blonde with model-like good looks. Cat was small and curvy, with a riot of curly red hair and blue eyes. She looked nothing like her mother.

But she looked exactly like the woman in the pictures she'd seen. And her mother looked exactly like the man with his arms around the woman who looked so much like Cat as she cradled a newborn infant—Cat's mother.

"Yeah," Cat whispered. "It was a little creepy."

Dominico nodded. "It gave me a bit of a shock, yes. You bear a striking resemblance to Susan Bristol. It's no wonder Juan, and others who've been around for years, took to you so quickly. It had to be like seeing a ghost— or the dead come back to life." He crossed himself. That Catholic reflex again. Cat didn't think he was even aware of doing it.

"Okay, there's no naughty gossip going on. Nothing in Nate's background I should worry about. So, why are you pushing on this?"

Dominico rose, stifling a yawn. "It's late…"

He stopped when she glared at him.

"Fine. I'm not pushing. I just want to make sure you're looking at everything with a critical eye. You've got a lot at risk here." He cleared his throat. "And let's be honest, it's been over a year since Jimmy passed. You're a young woman, and Nate Stewart is a good-looking man who is very, very different from Jimmy. I can see that in an instant. I'm not blind, nor am I naive enough to believe you wouldn't at least be considering that. All I'm saying is—be careful. If you want to live here, do business here, think about long term."

"I'm not interested in a casual fling." Not that the thought hadn't crossed her mind. It certainly had. She wasn't blind either.

"No, you're not the type." He heaved a sigh. "That said, you could do worse. You've always been good about using your head. Don't let that change. Just remember, he's not Jimmy." He leaned down and kissed her forehead. "I'll be headed back to the city early tomorrow morning. This place…" He spread his hands wide and looked around as if in wonder. "It's a lot and I never would have imagined you here, but it's beautiful. And I understand."

Cat curled her feet under her, staring into the dying fire, listening to Dominico's footfalls as he climbed the stairs, then turned into the guest bedroom. Nate was already upstairs—he'd pointedly excused himself not too long after dinner, leaving her and Dominico alone. What did he know? Had Dominico said something to Nate? Or had Nate said something to Dominico?

She rose and carried the glasses into the kitchen. Sounds from upstairs told her Dominico had gone to bed. She should too, but her brain wouldn't quiet. What was Dominico getting at? Be careful, he'd said. She supposed he might worry the women in town would get jealous that Nate was staying here. That she was getting something they wanted.

Cat chuffed a laugh. Ridiculous. She wasn't getting anything. Well, except that dancing in the pavilion. No, it wasn't like Dominico to worry about that sort of thing. More likely he was worried about her falling head over heels and getting hurt, then having to live in this small town where Nate was practically part of the landscape.

Again, ridiculous. He was hot, but… But nothing. She wasn't head over heels, but Dominico was right, she'd begun to see him as far more than just a handyman. And it wasn't just her libido talking, though it wasn't exactly quiet, especially when Nate stripped down to a T-shirt and pants in the front hall after his morning workout.

She shook her head. Going to bed was out of the question right now, she was too wired. She slipped on shoes and grabbed a pair of light work gloves, then turned down the hall to the closed-off wing. Might as well do something if she couldn't sleep. She'd cleared out all the old furniture early on, but the cleaning seemed like a never-ending job.

# Chapter Eleven

Snow clung to Nate's boots as he trudged up the porch steps. Outside the cabin door, he slipped them off and changed into shoes less likely to tear at the drop cloths already down. Emergencies with the house kept getting in the way of painting, and today he finally had free time. He figured he could knock most of the small cabin out in a day, maybe two.

It was surprising how little work there was to do. Other than a good cleaning, a paint job and furniture, it really only needed new screens and appliances in the kitchenette. A perfect place for him to stay while he continued working here. He'd spent a few sleepless nights tossing and turning, mulling over the things Dominico had said. Wondering what the man had said to Cat. She'd certainly been eyeing him oddly ever since Dominico left, and they'd spent the weekend tiptoeing around on eggshells. Far from their usual banter. Though this morning had been different.

He scanned the now empty kitchen space. Cat wanted it fully outfitted, so they'd already ordered a new mini fridge, microwave, water kettle and coffee pot. Not that he figured on making anything more than coffee. Though if he wanted to create some distance between him and Cat, taking his meals alone would help. The dining table and chairs had cleaned up nicely, and the new bed was due by the end of the week.

He stripped off his outer layers, stuck his earbuds in and got to work. Painting was sort of a zen experience for Nate. The repetitive motion let him zone out, giving him space to let his mind wander. The first thought, as he ran an edger along the bathroom window frame, was the way Cat had looked this morning when he'd come back in from his hike.

Her hair still tousled from sleep, a ridiculous pink fuzzy robe half-hanging off one shoulder, revealing some slinky tank top and matching shorts underneath. Fuzzy pink socks on her feet. Leaning back against the island, cradling a coffee cup. It was sexy and silly at the same time. There was something so unconsciously comfortable about the moment that it had hit him like a punch to the gut. He'd stood in the kitchen doorway, trying to pull air into lungs that refused to cooperate. Then she'd looked up at him and flashed a shy smile — completely devoid of any of the practiced perfection she usually displayed.

Nate's hand slipped, smearing paint along the windowsill.

"Shit." He wiped the paint off and shook his head. He could have said something that morning. Maybe should have. In light of the conversation with Dominico, he'd given her a bland good morning and retreated to the bathroom to shower. By the time he'd come downstairs again, her guards were back up and the smile she bestowed upon him was more like what he was used to seeing—pleasant enough, but it didn't light up her face the way a real smile did.

Yeah, moving to the cabin was a good plan.

The sound of grinding gears echoed down the hill. Cat had said something about a propane tank inspection. The main one for the house was in reasonable shape and probably due for filling, but the big tank that served the cabins and the mess hall was ancient.

Nate poked his head out the door at the sound of Cat's voice carrying down the hill as she chatted with the driver. The man got out of the truck and followed her down the path toward the mess hall. Nate turned back to his painting—Cat had things under control. She didn't need him sticking his nose in.

He'd just finished the living room when Cat came in with a pile of fabric in one hand and her tablet in the other. She slid into a seat at the little table and spread the fabric out.

"Propane guy went fast," Nate said, watching as she tapped away on the tablet, then arranged and rearranged the squares of fabric.

"Oh, yeah," she replied. "He was out to fill the main tank, and I asked him to take a look at the second one. You were right, it's in bad shape and would need replacing. But the plumbing around it is fine." She leaned back and surveyed the squares on the table. "Can I get your opinion?"

Nate crossed the room and stood behind her. She pointed at the tablet where there was a picture of a simple loveseat and matching chair.

"I like this look," she said. "It's clean and classic. It won't look dated in a few years and can easily be reupholstered. A good long-term investment. I want to furnish this cabin and one other in this group. They're the only ones in good enough shape. I figure this one we'd do with a big bed, set up for a couple. And the other with two smaller beds, like friends sharing."

Nate leaned down and took a closer look at the sofa. "It looks nice," he said. "I think you've got the right idea with the layouts. But why do you need my opinion?"

Cat waved her hand at the fabric squares. "I can't decide which of these I like."

He glanced at the table. A row of three different grays sat to the left—one solid, one checked and one with a subtle stripe. To the right were a pair of geometric prints that looked like every couch in every hotel he'd ever stayed in. In the middle was a gray bumpy-tweedy fabric flecked with tiny spots of bright color.

"It's your place, not mine. What I think shouldn't matter." Nate scanned the fabrics again. All good choices. The geometric prints were a bit generic for his taste—especially if she wanted to make Bristol Park really stand out. Any of them could work. A loud huffing exhalation brought his attention back to her.

"Yes, I know that. But I'm asking." She crossed her arms and glared at him. "You've stayed in hotels, I assume. I know you've traveled. I'm sure you have an opinion."

Nate could only nod. He had an opinion, sure. Maybe he should just say what he thought and move on. But that would never be enough for Cat. She'd want to talk about it, and talking about the future put his head in a strange space that he couldn't define even to himself. Much less put into words.

"Fine," Cat grumbled. "I'll start." She pushed the geometric prints off to the side. "I think these are safe, but boring. And don't fit with the atmosphere here."

Nate heaved a sigh. Fine, if she was going to keep going, he might as well play her game. "Agreed," he muttered. She looked at him in mock surprise—her eyes wide and her hand fluttering at her throat as if she was shocked, absolutely shocked. Nate tried to scowl at her but only managed to laugh. Somehow, that broke the weird awkwardness he'd been feeling.

He dropped into the other seat and pulled the geometric prints from the table. "You think they're boring, and I think they're generic. Those are a no."

He tapped the plain gray and the checkered gray. "Same thing here. The fabric is nicer, but these still look like a hotel room."

Cat swept them off the table. "That was how I felt. They screamed suit." She tapped the gray stripe. "This comes in all sorts of colors—the stripe can be black, or lighter gray, or just about any color." She pulled up another page on the tablet and turned it to him.

"Colors could be interesting," Nate replied. "The neutrals look even more like a suit, though. Honestly, I'm liking the bumpy one."

Cat smiled and something told him he'd just hit on her favorite. Maybe it was the fact that she'd placed it in the middle, but no...it just seemed like the best choice.

"I wasn't sure about it," she said. "I like it, but it's a bold choice."

He pulled all the other squares from the table and really looked at the tweedy one. Varying shades of gray made the nubby texture look even more interesting. The surprising part was the tiny flecks of bright blue and orange that somehow just worked. He picked the swatch up—sturdy, heavy and surprisingly soft.

"It's the most expensive choice," Cat mumbled. "Of course. But it's not outrageous. It has a good warranty and wear rating. And I like it. But I needed another opinion."

Nate tossed the swatch back to the table. The set up made sense now—she'd framed it as three choices, with a couple variations in an attempt to not sway him to her choice. She could have just as easily taken the fabrics to the coffee ladies. Why had she come to him? The possible reasons for that tugged at him, making him tongue tied for a moment.

"You don't think this is too much?" Her fingernail flicked at the little spots of color. Nate tried to imagine the swatch as an entire loveseat.

Suddenly he had a perfect image of the cottage completed—the gray nubby loveseat, a side chair in a bright color. Throw pillows. An area rug. Art on the walls—maybe something from a local artist. The crisp white walls and polished wood trim a perfect neutral backdrop. Cat looking like some beautiful fairy in bright yellow, flowers in her hair, laughing and smiling up at him in the warm sun.

He pushed back from the table and stood. The images too real, too vivid and too damn uncomfortable. He swallowed hard and waved his hand at the tablet. "I'd do the chair in something different. Maybe one of the accent colors."

Why the hell was he continuing the conversation? He needed to leave this shit to her and not get involved.

Cat was smiling at him as she flipped to another page on her tablet.

"You mean like this?" She turned the screen to him and there was the side chair reimagined in a blue and white stripe, labeled turquoise chevron. Exactly what he'd been picturing.

"Yeah," he replied. "Uh..." He shoved his hands in his pockets. Everything about this talk had gone weird and didn't help him deal with the tangle of feelings he had about Cat. "I uh...need to..." His gaze roamed the room as he struggled to find something, anything to say. She sucked in a sharp breath as if she'd had a big realization.

"Oh!" She jumped up and gathered all the swatches. "I'm sorry. I'm keeping you from finishing. I should have saved this for dinner. Or the morning. Or just..."

She paused at the cabin door, her eyes wide and looking as confused as he felt. "Thanks." She took off, hurrying down the steps and up the path back to the house. Leaving Nate even more confused and conflicted than before.

# Chapter Twelve

"The what?" Cat looked at the man, not sure what he meant by access risers. She'd called the same septic company her grandmother had used, but it had been several years since they'd been out, and he was apparently a new service tech.

"There should be a cap," the man replied. "Couple of them. Do you know where the pump tank is?"

Cat forced herself to maintain a pleasant smile. She'd told the company when she'd called that she didn't know anything about the system. She'd assumed they would send a tech who had been to the property before.

"I explained on the phone," Cat began, but the man waved a hand at her.

"We need to find the pump tank and the access risers," he said.

Cat ground her teeth together. That was all he seemed to be capable of saying, and she was running out of patience. Time to try another approach.

"What, exactly, are we looking for?"

If the man rolled his eyes any harder, they'd fall out of the back of his head. Cat started thinking the alphabet backward to avoid telling him to just leave and send someone else who could actually be helpful.

He rattled off a long list of 'could be' features that were so vague, and so varied, as to be useless. Then he said something about a 'leach field', and her ears perked up. That term she knew. Nate had said something about needing to make sure to keep the leach field free of debris. Then he'd pointed out a large area behind the staff cabins. She stomped down the mad urge to call Nate and have him deal with this mess, but when she'd outlined her plans for the day, he'd been clear he'd be tied up at the cabins all day.

"Would the uh…pump tank be near the leach field?" Cat eyed the man hopefully.

He launched into an explanation how it might, or it might not, but Cat didn't want to stand here listening to him give a lecture that didn't teach her anything. She gestured for him to follow and led the way to the leach field. And lo and behold, along one side were a pair of what looked like raised manholes capped with hinged lids. She made a silent note to map the damn property and all the utilities to avoid a repeat of this experience.

"See now," the guy said. "We coulda just started here and saved all the trouble."

Cat's lips curled into a smile that she knew was not pleasant, but she kept her tone sweet. "Well, I wasn't sure what you were looking for. Do you need anything else from me?"

He grunted out a "no", already at work lifting first one cap, then the other, before nodding again and leaning down to inspect something inside the hole.

Unsure whether she was supposed to stand there and admire him in action, or get lost so he could do his job, Cat retreated to the staff cabins — still within sight — and propped herself up on the porch railing to wait.

The occasional sounds of hammering floated over the air from the cabins on the other side of the mess hall. Nate had finished the interior painting yesterday and said he was going to put up screens and do some repairs on the porch today. Maybe she should go over and see how he was doing. Or just enjoy the view.

She shook her head. Bad idea. It was bad enough seeing him every morning in his clinging T-shirt. This morning, she'd been very grateful for the cup of coffee in her hands. It had been the only thing keeping her from sliding her hands under his shirt and dragging her fingertips over the ridges of muscle on his back.

"Ma'am." The septic dude waved a hand at her, and Cat pushed herself off the rail to go see what he wanted. "Looks like everything's in order. It just needs routine maintenance."

If everything were in order, the drains wouldn't be running slow. Nate had commented the tank probably needed to be pumped, so that was likely what the guy meant by routine maintenance. Right now, the ease of city plumbing and a sewer system she didn't have to think about sounded very appealing.

"Okay," Cat replied. "What does that entail? What do you need? And what is the cost?"

The guy glanced down at his clipboard, scribbled a few things then looked back up at her. "I'll need to get the truck down here. Looks like there's a road right behind those buildings." He pointed back at the staff cabins, and Cat nodded.

"It's pretty straightforward, since your access risers are above grade. I'm gonna suggest we do this in two shots—one today, to take care of the immediate problems you mentioned, and one after the threat of frost and snow are past."

"Why do that?" Cat asked.

"If the tank is empty, it'll take several days before water starts getting to the leach field again, and you don't want that to freeze over. It's kinda complicated."

Cat was pretty sure it wasn't complicated at all. That sounded like basic physics. If she understood the purpose of the leach field correctly, it made sense. He handed her an estimate sheet, breaking down the cost. He'd even spread it out over the two visits. Maybe she'd have to reevaluate her opinion of him—he wasn't quite as useless as she'd thought.

"Fine," Cat said and scrawled her signature on the work order. "Absolutely do it that way. Thanks. You've got my number. Can you call me when you're done? I'm not sure where on the property I'll be."

She waited for his nod, then headed back to the house to make lunch. Nate would be hungry by now. Though she was pretty sure that taking him lunch was just an excuse to see him. She was almost as bad as the rest of the Nate Stewart Groupies. *Great.*

\* \* \* \*

"Hello!"

Nate jumped at the sound of Cat's voice coming down the hill. She stepped onto the porch and looked around at the new screens. "Wow, what a difference! It's already looking so much better." She toed the wooden bench Nate had found and stuck on the porch.

"You know you don't have to do this? Sleep down here, I mean. I kinda figured you'd given up on this plan." She held up a picnic basket. "I brought lunch."

Cat waltzed inside and pulled a tablecloth, napkins and a bunch of little containers from the basket and in minutes, the table transformed from bare and empty to looking like it was ready for a photo shoot. All it needed was some flowers.

"Thank you," Nate said as he sat down. He wasn't about to get into the discussion of why he needed to get out of the main house. "Septic guy get everything taken care of?"

She shot him a scowl. "He's pumping the thing now. And why do you go and disappear any time there's a workman coming around?"

Nate leaned back and let his gaze travel around the room. Maybe he didn't need to wait to get furniture. He could just lay down a sleeping bag. He'd slept in worse conditions, and it would only be a couple more days before the bed came. He needed to get some space before he did something stupid.

He picked up his sandwich, determined to eat before answering that question. She'd run a business. She should know these things. Hell, she probably did, she just wasn't putting the property in that context yet.

"You don't need me getting underfoot when you're conducting business," he finally replied. "You're the property owner. That's who people need to see. To talk to. Especially locals. That makes it personal."

Cat's scowl deepened. "What are you talking about?"

"I told you—people will talk."

She let out an exasperated sigh and slammed her hands into the table. "And I told you I don't care."

He looked down at the floor and shook his head. "But you should," he whispered. "Pretty soon, there's gonna be more workmen out here. And inspectors. And all sorts of people. Do you want them going to town, sitting down at Dolly's, or at Juan's, and talking about how I'm the one running things here? Because they will, and you know it. People will always assume it's the guy running the show."

He chewed his lip, uncertain if he wanted to dump the entire can of worms on the table, but what the hell. She didn't seem to be thinking about the possibilities. "Add in the fact that you're a pretty woman, and…" He stopped, hesitant to open that topic.

"Look at me!" Her voice was sharp with command, and he looked up to see her leaning forward, elbows on the table. "I don't care one bit what people think. Why do you?"

Nate grabbed her hand, ignored her sudden gasp of air, pulled her to a stand then dragged her into the bedroom before slamming the door shut and turning her to face the full-length mirror on the back of the door.

"What do you see, Cat?"

In their reflections, her eyes shot daggers at him. "You and me. I don't… Oh."

All the fight drained from her expression, replaced with a look of resignation. It was all over her face. She saw it. Finally saw it. She was a tiny woman who he'd lay odds still got carded when she bought alcohol. He towered above her, easily over a foot taller and more than twice her size. A big, burly man in his early thirties.

"I don't care what they think or say. But you should. You need people in town to want you to succeed." He rested his hands on her shoulders, thumbs behind her neck. His hands swallowed her frame and his skin, dark tan, looked weather beaten compared to hers. "That's why I disappeared. Why I'll keep disappearing. People need to talk to you. Not me. I'm just your handyman."

He'd said a version of those words to plenty of other women. "I'm just the handyman." He'd always meant it. Until today. This time, the words stung as he spoke them. He didn't want to be just the handyman. Not for Cat.

"I hope that isn't what you think." Her voice was a whisper. Soft and low. Her eyes pleading in the mirror.

It wasn't what he wanted. Damn it all to hell. The Ice Princess had wrapped him around her little finger. He wasn't sure she was all that cold. It felt more like he was the one who'd been made of ice, and somehow, she was thawing him out.

He swallowed hard and closed his eyes, hoping he was doing the right thing. "Then stop paying me."

She tried to whirl to face him, but he dug his fingers in and held her tight in place. "What? Why? That makes no sense."

He opened his eyes, caught her glare in the mirror. "Stop paying me. I don't need the money."

"But I need your help!" Her voice took on a desperate tone. "I need…"

He tightened his fingers again. "You need someone to help. And I didn't say tell me to leave. I said stop paying me."

Her expression went from angry to confused, then back to angry. "Fine." She spat the word out. "If that's what you want, I'll quit paying you. Now would you please explain…?"

"Good." He cut her off and gently turned her to face him, cupping her cheek in his hand. *Do or die time.* The thing he'd been wanting from the get-go. The desire he'd been fighting, tamping down every time it reared up. "Because if you're paying me, I can't kiss you. And I want to. Tell me what you want, Cat. Tell me if I should stop."

His stomach knotted and he held his breath, waiting for her response. He wanted her so badly he could taste it. The desire for her was so strong he couldn't think straight. He believed she wanted him. Everything in him said it was true, but he had to know. Had to be sure.

"Don't stop." Her whisper was soft, quiet, but clear in the empty space. She turned her face into his hand. He tipped her head further back and brushed his lips against hers, gentle, testing. She reached up, twining her hands behind his neck, pulling him closer. That little move was all the encouragement he needed. He slid his hands down her arms, wrapped them around her waist and pulled her tightly against his body. Soft curves yielded to his touch.

Her lips parted. He ran his tongue along her lower lip, then into her mouth. She tasted of cinnamon and honey. His fingers splayed across her hips. Hers clenched into his shoulders as if she would fall without his support. Except he was the one falling, tumbling down this rabbit hole he'd been trying to avoid.

He broke the kiss before he lost all semblance of control. His hands stayed firmly gripping her hips, holding her close. He dropped his forehead onto hers and breathed a sigh.

"I've wanted to do that forever."

"Then what stopped you?"

"You didn't exactly give me an invite. I told you before, I'm not an asshole."

Cat wrapped her arms around his waist and laid her head on his chest, and every fiber of his being wanted to shout for joy. She felt so good. So right. And he was so screwed.

"Are you still moving into this cabin?" Her words were muffled against his chest.

"Yes," he replied. "Now more than ever."

He stepped back from her, gently, slowly, but still it was like letting go of a part of him. He needed to slow this train down, fast.

"Tomorrow. I kinda thought you might like some privacy back," he said. No matter how wonderful kissing her felt, he wasn't ready to get into her bed. Nate didn't do casual. Sex and love went together for him. Always had. Always would. No matter how many times he'd gotten the painful reminder that not everyone worked that way. No, kissing Cat was one thing. Making love to her was something else entirely. It flat out wasn't gonna happen. He needed to hold on to some shred of sanity.

"Yeah, yeah, I get it," she grumbled. "Finish the cabin."

# Chapter Thirteen

Cat trudged through the fresh snow. A thick layer of the fluffy white stuff covered everything, turning the property into a winter postcard. At least there hadn't been another heavy storm. This wasn't too bad. They kept the drive plowed and the walkways coated with salt and sand and let the rest of it go.

Nate had finished the work on the first cabin and moved his things from the guest room. The first night without him in the house had been quiet. Too quiet. Cat had gotten up in the middle of the night and made herself cocoa. Sitting in the dark, she'd stared out across the expanse of snowy field to the cabins below. She'd considered bundling up and walking down to Nate's cabin. But then what?

There hadn't been any more kisses since the first. Three days since that kiss, and that was it. He'd said he'd wanted to kiss her. He didn't say he wanted to keep kissing her. Maybe he didn't want her. It wasn't like she had a lot of experience in that area. The first brush of his lips on hers had had her trembling with need, then it got better. But then he had stopped, leaving her aching and uncertain. Maybe the kiss wasn't as good for him as it had felt to her.

In the end, she'd stayed where she was that night, staring out into the dark and wondering what to make of Nate Stewart.

Cat climbed the steps of the second cabin and knocked the snow from her boots before going in. Nate was perched on a ladder, running a paintbrush around the edges of the ceiling. Cat leaned back against the door, admiring the view of him in snug jeans. That man had a very fine ass.

"You could grab a brush and start edging the baseboards." He didn't even turn around when he spoke. "Or were you planning on just standing there enjoying the view?"

Cat felt the heat rise in her cheeks. How had he known she was watching? She cleared her throat, struggling, and failing, to find a smartass response.

"You were right about the paint color. This crisp white is a nice touch."

The four front cabins were basically two-room spaces—a broad room with a kitchenette on one end, and a cozy bedroom and bathroom in the back. Each had a deep front porch and the group of four commanded views up the hill to the main house on one side, and down the hill to the river on the other.

Maybe she'd host a picnic for May Day, with lots of activities. That would attract people from miles around. And if they could get the pavilion done in time, show off the amenities, so much the better.

A series of small, connected staff cabins were tucked behind the dining hall, those were in the worst shape and would probably wait until last. The remainder of the guest cabins dotted the hill in small groups—a couple of large, multi-bedroom family cabins sat along the tree line, another series of one-bedroom cabins occupied the far end of the flat meadow, and out beyond those, at the edge of a large field, were four group cabins.

She'd been planning to keep the pale gray with navy trim, but Nate had suggested updating to something fresher. When he'd said bright white, she thought the idea was ridiculous—white could turn dingy in a heartbeat. But the more she let the idea sit, the more she liked it. Bright white, with clear varnish on the wood floors, and gloss-black trim outside, like the house. Simple. Classic. Easy to maintain and repair. Just what this place needed.

"I didn't come down here to join you in painting. I just finished the rec room floor and figured it was time to stop for dinner."

Nate stepped off the ladder and stuck the paintbrush into a plastic baggie. He glanced at his watch, then gave her a look of mock surprise.

"Not bad. I figured you'd be another hour at least."

Cat blew on her nails and pretended to polish them on her shirt. "Once you get into a rhythm, it's quick. I think we have a barn cat." Cat paused a moment over the *we*, then shook her head. "Or rather, a mess hall cat. A calico. They're lucky."

Nate chuckled. "Yeah? Hopefully the cat's a good mouser. Just don't go feeding it."

Cat rolled her eyes at him. "Whatever."

She'd already bought a bag of cat food.

\* \* \* \*

Nate dropped a couple cans of wood varnish into his basket and whipped around as a familiar heavy perfume tickled his nose. Erin stood inches away, her hand raised as if to grab his arm. He took a step back and scowled.

"What are you doing here?" He saw no reason to be polite. She'd left him ten years ago, and their recent interaction hadn't left a positive impression.

She pouted. Typical. She'd always been good at playing those games.

"I'm here working on a project." She stepped closer, put her hand on his cart. "I had no idea you even lived in this part of the country."

"Not buying it. Last time you saw me, the claim was I was a hard man to find. So, which is it? You had no idea I was here? Or you went looking for me? You know what?" He pulled the cart from her grip and pushed it down the aisle. "Never mind. I'm not interested."

Her heels clicked on the floor as she hurried to catch up with him.

"Okay, fine. Yeah, I knew you were here. But it was a surprise." She stopped in front of him, hands on the cart again, forcing him to pause. "I looked for you a while back. I wanted to apologize. I was wrong. I was young and stupid. We both were. But I never found you. Then, I started on this project, and…well…here you were. It's like it's fate."

Nate tugged the cart, but she wouldn't let go. Instead, he reached in, grabbed his things and turned for the checkouts.

"Fate can fuck off, Erin, and so can you."

Mercifully, she didn't follow him this time. Jesus, why did she have to start showing up. They'd started dating in college—against his parents' wishes. They saw Erin as an opportunistic social climber. He'd sworn they were wrong. Then she'd needed money for a broken-down car, then it was that she'd lost her job and couldn't pay rent. One thing after another until he'd gone through his entire savings supporting her.

His parents bailed him out and suggested he should leave Erin. He kept seeing her throughout grad school, and the needs turned to wants, and they'd just kept coming. When his parents finally said no more and cut off their support, she was gone the next week—living with his best friend, a trust fund kid with a helluva lot bigger bank account. She added insult to injury, claiming Nate was abusive and nearly getting him kicked out of school.

Nate spent his last semester mostly drunk. He managed to graduate, barely. After that, he'd crawled into a bottle and planned to never come out, but his parents stepped in—getting him into rehab and threatening Erin with a defamation suit. Faced with a real fight, Erin backed down. Once Nate sobered up and got out of rehab, his parents expected him to clean up his mess and start walking the path they'd laid down for him. Then Erin started turning back up again, claiming the man she'd left him for had been behind everything, that she had just been swept off her feet.

Disgusted and disillusioned, Nate had shoved clothes and passport into a backpack and taken off, with no clue where he'd land. He wound up spending six months volunteering in South America, but every time he came back to the states, every friend he'd ever had would hand him a stack of letters from his parents, urging him to come home. Before too long, Erin would show up again, always needing something. He took a position with an organization coordinating delivery of medical supplies to remote locations, anything that would take him far away from home and keep him there. Nate spent five years traveling the world. And learning he neither needed nor wanted the life he'd been born to.

At one point, he'd have given anything to have Erin back. Then life cured him of that stupidity courtesy of lessons learned in rehab and reinforced by a handful of short, tumultuous relationships that proved he sucked at love.

He mumbled a thank you to the clerk as he paid for his things and hurried to his truck.

He didn't drive straight back to Bristol Park. Cat might worry what was taking him so long, but he needed to think. He drove along Brecken Road until he reached a pullout. He tucked the truck under barren trees then turned off the engine. Too damn cold to go for a hike right now — he wasn't dressed for it. Still, the pullout offered a spectacular view across the valley. The river snaked below, and he could just see the white point of Bristol Park, sitting lonely on the peak.

Nate pounded a fist into the steering wheel. *What the fuck is Erin up to now?*

He grabbed his phone and googled.

Erin Blake, project manager at TravelCorp.

*Shit.*

* * * *

The tiny calico sat under the propane tank, eyes never leaving Cat as she crept along slowly. Ever so slowly so as not to spook the animal. At the edge of the concrete pad, she knelt and poured a small pile of food out, then just as slowly backed away.

142

Nate had warned her not to feed the cat. He'd said putting down food could attract other animals. But she wasn't about to let the poor little thing starve. Besides, if she only put out a tiny amount of food, and swept it up if the cat didn't eat it...

The little calico didn't budge. For an hour. Cat sat there watching until her hands and feet were numb. She couldn't sweep up the food. The cat was still sitting there, staring at her. Maybe she wouldn't come out if Cat was within sight.

Screw it. Cat stood and brushed dirt from her pants. She'd leave the food. And if a squirrel or possum or whatever came along and ate a handful of cat food, well, fine.

Maybe she'd ask Nate what he'd suggest. She'd never fed a stray cat before. Growing up, there was barely enough money to keep food in the pantry, never mind a penny extra to spend on stray cats. Once she'd married Jimmy, well... The guys at the docks fed the wharf cats, just enough to keep them around and friendly, but not enough to keep them from hunting mice and rats.

And what was taking Nate so long? The house was too quiet without him there all the time. He'd help clean up after dinner, then he was gone, leaving Cat alone in the big house. At first, she thought she'd like the quiet and privacy after always having a noisy family around during her marriage—even when Jimmy wasn't there, someone else had been. But this was too quiet. Too lonely.

She turned on music and danced while she cleaned. She listened to podcasts and watched YouTube videos into the wee hours when she couldn't sleep.

It had only been a few days, and they still saw each other every day. All day. But she missed getting up to find coffee already brewed, and Nate coming in from his early morning workout. She missed their late nights, sometimes spent working, sometimes just sitting up, drinking herbal tea or cocoa and staring out at the night sky because neither of them could sleep.

Tires crunched on the gravel road, and Nate's truck came out of the trees. Cat made her way up the hill, trying to sort out what she was feeling. Dominico was right, she thought of Nate as far more than just a handyman. And she didn't want to consider where those thoughts were leading.

Dominico had also warned her to be careful and use her head. Using her head was what had gotten her married to Jimmy. Not an entirely bad thing, to be sure. It could have been worse. But it hadn't led to her being happy.

Nate climbed out of his truck, all long legs and broad shoulders. His hair looked mussed as if hands had tugged at the normally perfect curls. Maybe he'd seen someone in town. A woman. Maybe that was why he'd taken so long. Why he looked disheveled. That familiar knife of fear, of jealousy, stabbed into her gut.

Cat shook herself. No. She didn't need to be thinking that way about Nate. It wasn't any of her business to begin with. She didn't have a claim to him. They weren't even dating or sleeping together. All it had been was some flirtation. And that one kiss. She shouldn't care if he had a string of ladies on a rotating schedule, though despite her first impressions, he didn't seem the type. But…she could be wrong.

He held up a bag from Dolly's Diner. "I brought dinner." The smile on his face didn't reach his eyes. They remained strained and tired looking.

Cat shoved down any misgivings. She didn't have the right to question. She plastered on her best smile and hoped it would cheer him up.

"Good," she replied. "Let's eat!"

Dinner was quiet. Nate barely uttered a word while Cat chattered about what she'd gotten done and about seeing the calico.

"I opened up an entire twenty-five-pound bag of cat food and spread it around the mess hall," she said, watching him for a response.

He poked his fork into the mashed potatoes and mumbled something that sounded like "that's good". Then his head popped up, and his eyes bored into hers.

"You what?"

"Oh good," Cat replied. "You are listening."

Nate looked back down at his half-eaten food. "Sorry, it's been a day. Did you really…?"

"No." Cat didn't make him finish the question. "I put out a small handful. I watched for a while, and the cat seemed interested, but…" She shrugged. "I guess it's too skittish to come out while I'm watching."

Nate rose and carried his plate to the sink. "I'm wiped. I'm gonna call it a night. I'll check on the food. If it's still there, I'll clean it up. No sense attracting critters."

He cleaned up his mess and without another word, was gone. Cat stared at her own barely touched plate. She put the leftovers away, finished the dishes and climbed the stairs feeling more alone than ever. Sleep would be a long time coming tonight.

# Chapter Fourteen

Nate put the last of the dishes in the drainer. He'd barely seen Cat all day. He'd kept busy outside, in the cabins, anywhere she wasn't. Seeing Erin again yesterday had called up too many painful memories. Discovering that she was working with TravelCorp added a whole new layer of stress. He and Cat spent another evening picking at their food and not talking.

He clicked off the kitchen light. Down the hill, the glow of his cabin's porch light shone bright, casting a yellow half circle on the snow. After their virtually silent dinner last night, he'd been outside late, checking on the damn cat, when he'd seen the kitchen light go on at the house. The light had stayed on for a few minutes, then gone out.

She'd been awake, and he'd been tempted to come up. He already knew she was as much of an insomniac as he was, and equally as quiet about it. Maybe she'd enjoy the company, like they'd shared on so many nights—working side by side, or just sitting quietly.

Maybe she'd hate it. Maybe they'd find themselves doing things that could lead to them both sleeping out of sheer exhaustion.

He hung the towel and scrubbed his hands over his face. He needed to stop. This was a dangerous path. He shouldn't have kissed her. He didn't regret it, not one bit. What he regretted was not doing more. Not asking for more. Risking his heart was a mess he didn't need, though he was beginning to think it was too late.

"What are you doing standing here in the dark? Is there something outside?" Cat peered out the window, then drew back. "Oh."

*What the hell. May as well go for it.* "Couldn't sleep last night?"

Even in the dim light spilling in from the dining room, he saw her cheeks flush pink. She closed her eyes and looked down, then took a deep, shaky breath and stared back up at him, almost defiantly.

"No, as a matter of fact. The house was too quiet. I've gotten used to another person being here."

He chuckled. "You've gotten used to me being here."

"Yes." Her voice was a whisper. Her eyes wide. She licked her lips, slowly.

His entire body throbbed with need. The desire to wrap his hands in her hair, to hold her close, breathe in her scent, to sink into her warmth. His fingers twitched, as if to obey those desires, and he clenched his fists, forcing those thoughts aside.

"Nate." Still a whisper. Her hand rested against his chest. When had she stepped so close? She moved again, her body lightly touching his, hand still on his chest, head upturned, looking for all the world like she wanted to be kissed.

His fingers circled her wrist. He meant to step away. Instead, he pulled her closer, his other hand curling around her hip, holding her to him. She felt so tiny in his arms, but not fragile. No. There was nothing fragile about this woman. She was power and strength and steely determination.

She moved, her arm circling his back, her head resting on his chest. Her breath warm through his shirt. The clean scent of her hair, and some soft sweetness. It took every ounce of willpower he had to step away, to place his hands on the island and lean against them. The bereft look on her face almost broke him.

"God, Cat, I want to. I want to kiss you."

"Then why stop?"

He pulled in a deep breath, then another until his body no longer shook with the effort to not touch her. All he wanted in the world was to scoop her up and carry her to bed. Or to hell with a bed, he'd settle for the kitchen island. It was certainly the right height.

"It's been a long time since I've been with a woman." His voice was raspy, husky with desire. He cleared his throat. "And I don't do casual."

She blinked, looking offended. "What in the world does that mean?"

"If I kiss you again, I'm going to want more. Far more than kisses. I don't know whether you're ready for that. Or if you even want that, but I know myself. Sex comes with emotional attachments."

"So, you're saying if we have sex, I'll fall in love with you, and you don't want that?" She turned away from him, her hands on her hips, her shoulders tight and practically vibrating with anger. "Seriously? What kind of garbage is that?"

"That wasn't what I said at all." He bit the words out. Hating that she thought those things of him. "Try it the other way around."

She whirled, her eyes wide, searching his face.

"I don't have a great track record with romantic entanglements." He kept his voice soft. He didn't want her to hear the bitterness underneath. "I've just"—his fingers gripped the island—"just not gone there. It's easier that way. Less painful." The last words came out a whisper, barely audible in the quiet kitchen.

She nodded. "Okay, I'm going to make a pot of coffee, and we're going to sit down and talk. Because that needs explaining."

"Nothing much to explain. I was engaged, we broke up, and I didn't cope with it very well. I...kinda lost myself." That was nowhere near the whole story, but it was enough. Thinking about it still hurt, but not like it once had. "Took me a while to realize she hadn't wanted me. She needed someone, anyone really, and had wanted what I could give her."

"And when was that?"

Nate chuckled. "Ages ago it seems. College. It took some time to get my head straight, and then I moved here."

Cat nodded. "Screw the coffee. How about a bottle of wine?"

Nate shook his head. "I don't drink."

"Let me guess. Bad experience?"

He held his hands up and gave her what he hoped was an apologetic smile.

She poured two glasses of water instead, and then leaned back against the counter facing him.

"I've only ever been with one man." The smile that crossed her face was sad, and a little silly, as if she were mocking herself. "Mother was pretty strict, and virginity was uh...a valuable thing. I wasn't even allowed to date during high school. Not until I met Jimmy." She shuddered, then lifted a shoulder and grinned.

"I loved my husband. Blindly, stupidly loved him as only a kid with no real-world experience can. He was...huh... Well, he was a wonderful provider, encouraging, taught me a lot, put me through school, handed over his business to me. On the surface, he was perfect."

Even in the dim light, he could see the tears as they trickled down her cheeks. If she noticed, she didn't seem to care.

"But...I never got pregnant—no kids meant no legacy. That's not a cool thing in an Italian Catholic family." She wiped the tears with the back of her hand and gave him a smile that was more grimace. "He really didn't see me in the same way after that."

Nate nodded. "Why did you stay?"

A laugh. Short and bitter. "I had everything I'd been taught a marriage was about. Except a baby. And that was my fault."

"You got tested?"

She nodded. The tears fell again. "Aside from some minor hormonal issues that shouldn't be that big of a problem, there was nothing wrong. I was told to just relax. You're too uptight. You want it too much. Maybe you're under too much stress at work." She shrugged. "Whatever. Doesn't matter. It never happened."

She pushed herself up from the counter and crossed to him in two quick steps. She stepped between his knees and pressed her hands against his chest, her forehead against his shoulder. Nate kept his hands on the island behind him. Afraid to touch her. Afraid he'd lose any sense of self control.

"Look, I don't know… I don't know what I want. I liked kissing you. I think I'd like more, but…I don't even know what that means for me. You said you don't do casual. Obviously, neither do I."

She took a deep breath, and Nate was very aware of her breasts rising and falling, the feel of her breath against him.

"Is there anything wrong with taking it slow? Kissing doesn't have to lead straight to sex."

Nate lost his fragile hold on self-control. His hands came up, cupping her ass, pulling her into him. Her arms twined around his neck.

Her lips were soft under his, open, welcoming. Everything about her was intoxicating, and he wanted more. His body throbbed with need at the feel of her against him. Then just as suddenly, she broke the kiss and stepped away. He had to resist the urge to pull her back to him.

"Did you bring a flashlight to get to the cabin?"

Nate took a deep breath. "Yeah." He pushed up to stand, hoping she wouldn't see the raging hard-on straining in his pants. A quiet "oh" and her wide-eyed look put those hopes to rest.

"It's been a while." He shoved his hands in his pockets. "I am a man, Cat."

She shut her mouth, then a wicked looking smile crossed her features. "Yes, I see. That is uh…abundantly clear." She rose on her toes and kissed his cheek. "G'nite, Nate. Lock the door on your way out, would ya?"

She turned and was out the door before he could take a breath and respond. Maybe the walk to the cabin in the cold would calm things down. If not...well... wouldn't be the first time he'd used his hand.

The front door clicked quietly shut. Cat leaned against her bedroom door with her forehead pressed against the cool wood. It had taken everything she had to walk out of the kitchen. If she'd stayed, they'd be naked on the island right now. Though she wasn't sure she could handle that yet. She wanted Nate, but the idea of what that meant—the intimacy, the risk—terrified her. And the size of him—there was no denying, or hiding, the long, hard bulge in his jeans.

She turned for the bathroom—maybe a shower would help. She stripped and reached for the bathroom light, her hand pausing before hitting the switch. The light in Nate's cabin had just flicked on. She shut the bathroom door, cutting off the soft light spilling in from her room, and pressed her nose to the window, but couldn't see him.

*Silly. That's because he went inside. That's why the light went on.*

The cabin door opened, and he stepped out, carrying something. He trudged down the steps and disappeared behind the cabins. Cat waited, watching, looking for a sign of a flashlight. There. By the mess hall. What was he doing? The flashlight bobbled, lowered, then went out for several long minutes, until Cat started feeling silly standing in the dark bathroom, staring out into the night. The flashlight blinked on as Nate headed back up the hill. He stomped up the steps, brushed snow off, and went inside. A minute later, both the porch light and the inside light went out.

Why would he trek down to the mess hall in the dark?

*The cat. He's feeding the cat.*

That mystery at least semi-solved, Cat stepped away from the window and clicked on the light. Under the steamy shower, her skin felt too tight. Her body ached to feel a man's touch—Nate's touch.

Muttering a curse, she grabbed the handheld shower—a luxury Nate had put in for her after the old shower head had sprung a leak, spraying the entire bathroom. She leaned back on the tiled wall and adjusted the spray, a trick she'd learned by accident in the over-large shower Jimmy had installed in their condo. The bathroom had been her one truly private place.

She jumped when the spray first hit, then in moments, her head tossed back, and she hissed in a sharp breath as the tension built. Nate's hands felt so good, so large, pressing into her hips, holding her against him. The scent of him. The stubbly feel of his chin against her skin. Those arms. So huge. He could break her with one hand, but he was so gentle. His kisses, tentative but hinting at something almost primal. Imagine if he allowed himself to lose control. The feel of restrained passion—as if something wild were straining to escape.

What would he feel like, hot, naked, sweaty—holding himself over her, the muscles in his arms bunched and tense? She imagined tracing her fingers along all his ink. How far down did it go?

Her legs trembled and tension coiled in her stomach. The hard bulge in his jeans earlier. The urge to undo his pants had been almost overwhelming. She wanted to taste him, feel him filling her.

She cried out as the tension broke, the orgasm rushing through her, leaving her trembling and shaking against the tiles.

Cat put the handheld back up and ran her hands through her wet hair, conscious of an empty ache inside. No amount of shower massage was gonna scratch that itch. Dammit.

# Chapter Fifteen

Nate came around the staff cabins and was greeted by the sight of Cat's rear end up in the air as she crouched, looking under the mess hall stairs. He stuffed his hands in his jeans pockets, trying to will away the hard-on. Last night's kisses had left him so frustrated that even exercising until he was shaking hadn't allowed him to sleep. Taking things into his own hands hadn't helped either. He still felt like a damn teenager, standing here looking at her ass.

"She won't come out if you're hovering there."

Cat somehow jumped back, whirled and rose to her feet in one fluid movement. A look of chagrin flashed across her features before being replaced with an accusatory frown.

"You're feeding her," she said, tapping her foot. He nodded. She glared at him, hands on her hips. "And you told me not to."

"I said you'd have every critter in the area coming around if you just put food out." He smirked and pointed at the clear signs of animal tracks in the snow. "And you did."

"Why is it different when you do it?"

Nate pushed away from the post and beckoned her to follow. He led her to the path, well away from the buildings.

"I saw where she's coming and going and put a tiny amount of food out at night right after she comes back. If she has a good hunt, she might not touch it, and I'll pick it up after an hour, so it doesn't attract anything else. Last night, I didn't have to—she came out after about ten minutes and ate it all. I'll put a little out every night, same way."

Cat frowned at him, but even the mock scowl on her face couldn't hide the little-girl glee in her eyes. Nate caught the movement from the corner of his eye and made a shush gesture at her. Cat's mouth hung open, and she looked like she was about to give him an earful, then her face softened. The little calico darted around the steps, keeping low and moving fast, a bit of something fluffy caught in her mouth. A flick of her tail and she disappeared under the building.

"Well." Cat breathed the word out slowly. "At least we know she's a mouser."

Nate tried to ignore the thrill that ran through him when she said "we." The last thing he needed to do was get tangled up with Cat and this property and the money-sucking hole it had to be. Especially with Erin around and working with the biggest developer who had their eye on this place. Nope. That was a whole mess he did not need. He swallowed hard and summoned a laugh.

Then somehow his arm went over her shoulders, and she tucked herself against his side as if she'd always been there. Her chin tipped up and those blue eyes bored into his—wide and bright, smiling. His other hand came up, sank into those luscious curls, cupping the back of her head and the need to taste her, to fill his senses with her sent pleasant shivers through his entire body.

A strident quacking sound interrupted those thoughts, and Cat laughed as she reached for the phone in her jacket pocket. That ringtone meant Dominico.

Cat hauled in a deep breath before hitting the answer button. A moment ago, she'd been ready to beg Nate to take her to bed. She wanted him naked and inside her. Right now. This instant. So much for taking things slow. She stabbed the answer button.

"Whatcha got?"

"TravelCorp is not backing down. If you want to reopen, we'll have to address their demands." Dominico's voice held a tinge of restrained anger. Something had pushed his seemingly infinite patience almost to the breaking point. Cat listened as he outlined the next steps and dollar signs swam in front of her.

Nate looked at her, a question clear on his face. She shook her head and waved a hand at him, mouthing "later." She didn't need to burden him with this. As Dominico went on about a nesting habitat for some bird or another, she was mentally totaling up the costs. It wasn't pretty.

"Screw this. We've been playing this the wrong way." She spoke as soon as Dominico paused for breath. "We need to get the town involved. If TravelCorp needs a variance before they can develop this property, they need to be making those plans known. Those require public meetings, opportunities for neighbors and businesses to submit their own impact studies."

The sound of shuffling papers carried through the phone along with the rapid creaking of Dominico's chair. "I've already begun that process. You'll have papers to sign by tomorrow. But until this is settled, you'll have a hard time getting any building permits."

Well, crap. "What about interior renovation? Basic maintenance? Those wouldn't fall under the same restriction, would they?"

"So long as it's not changing the structure," Dominico said.

"Good," Cat replied before he could say anything else. "And I want to know who's behind this. Follow the money."

Dominic cleared his throat. "I can call Tom, I'm sure..."

Cat tuned him out. Tom. Jimmy's younger brother. Physically they were practically twins, but while Jimmy had been a player, never able to be faithful to one woman, Tom was devoted to his wife and kids. Tom was also the more ruthless businessman. What Cat hadn't learned in business school, she'd learned from Tom Corozzo, and that was a can of worms she didn't want to open. Sure, he'd solve her problems here, but the cost would be tying herself back into that family, and the reminders of her failures as a wife.

"No." The word came out flat. Definitive. "Just do what you can. You're good enough on your own, and I don't want Tom involved."

After a few pleasantries, she hung up the phone and looked back at Nate. Whatever magic had woven itself around them before the phone call had disappeared. She could look at him dispassionately, objectively, without the simmering sexual tension that left her breathless and quivering. Or at least that's what she told herself.

The truth was, one look into those gold-flecked eyes, focused on her with so much concern etching tiny lines around them, and she started to melt. Whatever game he was playing—whether seducer, or willing seductee—he was good at it. Could she handle a fling? He'd said he didn't do casual, but that was probably just a line. Something he said because it was what women wanted to hear.

Maybe he was exactly what she needed. But what about when it ended? When he moved on to his next conquest. She'd have to handle that. Learn to enjoy whatever they had in the moment and not worry about tomorrow.

"You wanna share?" Nate's voice cut into her thoughts. His hand captured hers, rough fingers stroking her wrist, and all thinking fled. For once in her life, Cat wanted to feel, to be in the moment without worrying about consequences or what came next.

She shook her head, unable to trust her voice yet. Uncertain that she wouldn't just blurt out something ridiculous, like asking him to take her to bed. Even though that was exactly what she wanted. No, that was what she needed.

She stepped closer to him, wrapped her arms around his waist and went up on her toes, hoping he'd get the hint and kiss her already.

Blood rushed to points south and Nate's pulse pounded in his ears. Last night Cat had suggested they take things slow, and now she was pressed against him looking like she wanted to be kissed. Trouble was, he didn't want to stop with just a kiss. He needed more, but the cost of fulfilling that need was too high.

He slid his hands over her back. One hand cupped her hip while the other traveled to her hair. He loved the feel of her hair in his hand. Her lips parted on an exhale, and he leaned down, pressing his mouth to hers. Gently, oh so gently. Then her lips softened, and her tongue traced his mouth. Her hands fisted into his jacket, pulling him against her.

All thoughts other than Cat left his head.

The tiny gasps she made as his lips explored hers. The way the skin on the back of her neck goose bumped under his hand and the silkiness of her curls sliding through his fingers. The press of her hips, tight against him. He drank it all in.

He traced her ear with the pad of his thumb, and she trembled. A soft cry of protest escaped her when his lips left hers, but soon she was making far more pleasurable sounds when he nibbled gently on her neck.

"Please." She tugged at him, as if trying to get even closer. He stepped in, pressing one leg between hers, wringing a long, shuddering breath from her. Her legs parted, straddling his thigh as she ground against him. Then her hands tugged, pulling his head up. Her lips closed on his in a blistering kiss.

The last time he'd made out like this was in high school, and he knew damn good and well it hadn't been anywhere near this hot. He shifted both hands to her hips, rocking her against his leg.

Cat's fingers clenched on his shoulders and her head fell back, a look of pure ecstasy painted on her features. His dick gave a twitch, as if to remind him of its presence. Not that he needed the reminder. The throbbing was so hard it almost hurt. Worth it to put that look on her face. Her breath came in gasps and pants punctuated with an occasional moan. Nate shifted his hands, pulling her higher up his leg, until her toes were barely touching the ground.

He cradled her body against his as she shook in his arms. His lips closed over hers, swallowing her cries of pleasure. He kept kissing her gently — her eyelids, her cheeks, her neck, her lips — as the trembling subsided and her breathing returned to normal.

Cat opened her eyes, blinking as if trying to focus. Then the blush started. A rosy glow crept up her neck then turned her cheeks into bright apples. She pushed back, awkwardly trying to get her feet firmly on the ground while still straddling his leg.

"Oh my, I-I'm sorry..." Cat stammered, the blush turning even deeper red as she looked down at her shoes, out into the trees, anywhere but at him.

"What are you apologizing for?" Nate cupped her face in his hands, turning her to look at him. "Hm? Talk to me, Cat."

The blue eyes that moments ago had been filled with pleasure now brimmed with tears. "I don't know what got into me," she said. "I never... I've never...come on to a guy like that. I thought— I thought I was ready for...to..." She stopped and looked at him, silently pleading.

"If I recall, you were the one who said kisses didn't have to lead straight to sex," he replied. "There's a whole lotta ground between the two."

A smile crossed her lips, making him want to kiss her all over again. "But what about you? I mean, that was...that was amazing. For me."

Nate smiled and shook his head. Sure, his dick might be screaming for attention, but he'd quickly learned that listening to what that part of his anatomy wanted was a one-way ticket to Hurtsville. Because no matter how hard he tried to convince himself otherwise, love and sex were hand-in-glove for him. And he was already skating too close to the edge of an emotional abyss with Cat. He could give her pleasure all day long and then some if that was what she wanted. Until he could be sure she felt the same, he'd go back to the cabin and take a cold shower. Or use his hand and keep his heart firmly out of the game. Or at least try to.

"I'm a grown man," he replied. "And I'm very patient."

# Chapter Sixteen

Cat sat at the kitchen island, debating what she wanted to say to Nate. She'd been avoiding him for two days and apologizing seemed wrong. As did saying it wouldn't happen again. After all, he was the one who told her to quit paying him — so he could kiss her. She didn't know what she wanted. One minute, all she could think about was dragging him to bed, and the next, the thought of the Nate Stewart Enthusiast Brigade dashed cold water all over that. But then she'd recall how good his hands felt. Or his mouth...

The kitchen door swung open, and Cat pressed her lips together, staring down into her cup. Maybe she could just keep pretending it had never happened. Make believe she hadn't humped his leg like a dog in heat. Her cheeks warmed at the memory as her body pulsed with the need for him.

Cool fingers pressed gently into her shoulder, and she looked up to see Nate, hair squashed flat from his cap, face sweaty from his morning torture hike. She'd avoided him the first night. Barely spoken during dinner, and begged off early, withdrawing to her room as soon as the dishes were done. Ever since that soul-blistering kiss and near-earth shaking and fully dressed orgasm, she'd found excuses to be on the phone, or anywhere he wasn't. And aside from giving her an odd look when she'd walk out of a room as he entered, he hadn't said or done anything. He'd pushed a time or two, but then just gone silent. Maybe he was just as embarrassed and uncertain as she was. Maybe he wanted to avoid the topic as well.

But now he was right here. Unavoidable. Her skin tingled where his hand rested on her shoulder. The warmth radiating off him begged her to touch in return. To slide her hands under his shirt and run her palms over hard muscles. Heat climbed up her neck and she bit her lip, resisting the urge to touch him.

"We're not avoiding this forever," he whispered. "What do you want, Cat? Should I ignore whatever this is between us? Or should I kiss you again?" His hand caressed her shoulder, sending delicious shivers throughout her body. "I won't play guessing games and I won't push beyond what you want, but I need clear signals from you."

His hand dropped, and Cat stifled the cry of complaint that nearly burst from her lips. She wanted him. She wanted his touch. There was something in his tone that made her entire body tingle in anticipation. She wanted that. Lots more of that.

"I uh…" She cleared her throat and tried again. "I'm not exactly good at this. I mean…whatever this is. Between men and women. Us."

Nate leaned against the counter next to her, his arms crossed over his chest and a gentle smile on his face.

"You wanna try that again? Maybe making a little more sense this time?"

Cat glared at him and nearly lost her composure when he raised an eyebrow in response. The man had the sexy-cocky routine down and perfected to panty-melting levels. Cat swallowed hard. Nate was incredibly hot, and she felt like something had shifted between them. Some inexplicable change had occurred, and she needed to figure out what it was.

"Okay." She let out a long sigh. Might as well be honest. "I don't really know what I'm doing when it comes to flirting. Or dating. Or any of the usual relationship stuff men and women do." She shrugged and looked up at him. The smile hadn't changed.

"Oh, I think you know exactly what you're doing when it comes to flirting," he replied. "You might not understand the relationship side, but you know how to use your femininity to get men to listen to you."

Cat opened her mouth, ready to protest, but he was right. She was well practiced at batting her eyelashes when necessary. She'd learned some of that from her mother. Some she'd picked up watching Mama C rule the roost with a flick of her fake lashes. The rest came from practice—years of being a young woman running a business full of men, most of whom believed women were wives and mothers, or simply there for men's pleasure.

"I'm not used to behaving..." She felt the heat rush to her face. "Like...that."

The smile on his face cracked wide, and he laughed. "I gathered. For what it's worth, it's not my norm either."

Cat sat back, stunned. She hadn't exactly expected him to confess to being a ladies' man, but she was stunned at the complete denial. "What? With all the ladies who practically coo at the very mention of your name?"

"Stop it." His voice held a sharp rebuke and she recoiled from it, until she caught his face. The smile had faded, and he looked pained. Stressed. "I wasn't playing games when I said it's been a long time, Cat. Long as in over five years. Before I came here. I don't do casual. Not even kissing."

Something in his tone made her believe. He wasn't just telling her what she wanted to hear. Whatever the ladies in town wanted, or thought, he wasn't the one encouraging it. Still, she had to ask. She had to know. She wanted him like she'd never wanted anyone in her life. And while she didn't really care at this point if she was just another in a long string of lovers, she'd rather know that up front.

"So, all those ladies are indulging in a rich fantasy life?" She tried to keep it light. To not sound like a jealous or possessive shrew. Jimmy used to chide her about that. Time and time again. She buried that memory and focused on the man in front of her.

"I've only had the one serious relationship in my life," he replied. "A few attempts after that, but..."

He stopped, his face set in a mask of distaste. Cat could only think of one way to get him to open up and trust her. To tell her what made him look so hurt. She swallowed her pride and looked him directly in the eye.

"My husband cheated on me," she said. "Repeatedly. Everyone knew. I knew, eventually. And I was just supposed to take it. '*Sit back and be a good little wife and deal with it. This is what guys do*'." She took a deep breath and blew it out. "And the really sad part of it is, that's exactly what I did. Day in, and day out—I dealt with it."

Her admission hit him like a punch to the gut and his fingers clenched on the island at the thought of someone hurting her. That explained so much. About her reactions to the way the ladies in town talked about him. About her own reactions to him. Everything suddenly made so much more sense.

"I told you before, physical and emotional go together with me," he said. "I've been told by the women in my life that I'm demanding, possessive and needy." He grimaced. Not things a man wanted to hear. Especially when one of those women also followed those words with another—abusive. Erin always twisted things, her way of hurting him.

"I don't know that I have any better track record than you do when it comes to relationships," he continued. "What I know is there's something really amazing between us."

Cat's eyes were round and huge as she stared up at him, triggering every protective instinct he had. "I don't know what to say to that. To any of this."

Nate stifled a laugh, certain that would be the wrong response. "I don't think you have to say anything. Unless there's something you specifically want. Or don't want." He looked down at his feet, avoiding those eyes that were so full of questions and promises. "I told you, I'm not an asshole. I'll ask you. Repeatedly. I won't guess. I won't go plunging ahead hoping you're on board."

Her hand snaked out and caught his fingers, pulling his hand toward her. He reached and cupped her cheek as she turned her face into his palm. She was so perfect, so amazing. She didn't even realize how she fit his needs so precisely. Yeah, those were thoughts he did not need to be thinking.

"Is 'I don't know' an acceptable answer?" She spoke against his palm, almost nuzzling his hand. He didn't even think she was aware she was doing it.

"Hell yes," he replied. He slid his hand into her hair and turned her to face him. "There's nothing wrong with 'I don't know'. Hell, I don't know what's going on here either. Or what I want exactly. The only thing I know for sure right now is it involves you, Princess."

The eyes that had closed as his fingers stroked her hair popped wide. "Princess?" She sat up straight and glared at him. "Really?"

Nate gave a chuckle. "You want the truth? I have you nicknamed Ice Princess in my phone."

Cat's mouth went wide in a look of shock and indignation. "Why? Why on earth would you...?"

"Oh, come on," he interrupted. "Think about it for a minute."

She leaned back, her arms over her chest and glared at him. "Fine." She spat the word. "I'll give you that I may have been a touch...brusque to start."

Nate laughed. "A touch? Uh-huh. Don't worry, didn't take me long to figure out the ice part was just a facade."

Indignation took over shock on her face. "Oh really? And what's underneath then?"

Nate curled his fingers into her hair and bent to brush his lips against her ear. Her gasping intake of air rewarded his efforts, and he smiled. "That's what I'm hoping to find out."

He straightened, ignoring the look of protest on her face. "But we have business to deal with. It's the end of the month, and we've made good progress. Time to reassess."

A look of panic crossed her features and she gulped in air. "Shit." The word flew out, and she clapped her hands over her mouth, then smiled as she dropped them and shook her head. "You are not allowed to quit now. Seriously. I…" She shook her head again and her eyes were big and round. If he said no right now, she'd burst into tears. Then hate him for making her reveal that weakness. Good thing he wasn't about to say no.

"Relax." He slid onto the stool next to her and covered her hands with his. "As far as I'm concerned — the project here is on track and I'm happy to see it through to the end."

The tension visibly drained from her. "What about pay?" she asked. "I'm not paying you, and I can't keep asking you to work for free."

He squeezed her hands, trying to reassure her. "I'm getting room and board, right? That's hardly working for free. Anything else? I'm not worried about."

She shook her head. "I'm not comfortable with that. I mean, I know what you said, and…" Her face turned a pretty pink, and she blew out a sharp breath. "I get it. The whole employer/employee thing plus whatever this is between us could be a little, well, awkward at best. Not to mention the ethics involved. But you already pointed out that people talk — you think they won't chatter about you living here and doing all this work?"

Nate held his hands up in mock surrender. "Tell you what," he said. "We've been working on a handshake deal. Draw up a contract that states room and board in exchange for a basic rate. Anything above that, you put in an escrow account or something like that. No ethical dilemma. No fodder for the gossip mill—not that my finances are anyone's business."

"I'll run it by Dominico," she replied. "I'm sure he'll have some suggestions, but he'll take care of it. And give me holy hell for it while he's at it."

Nate laid his hands on her shoulders and leaned in close enough to smell roses and soap. "You planning to tell him you've been making out with the help? Not like he won't figure it out on his own."

Cat reared back and swatted his hands, her face a mix of indignation and laughter. "I hope that was a joke!"

"Of course it was, Princess."

"Do you have to call me that?"

Nate leaned against the counter, propped up on his elbows. He pretended to consider it for a moment. Truth was, it fit her. In so many ways. It just wasn't how she saw herself. She was every bit a princess—if you used a certain character named Leia as your standard for the role. All smiles and feminine charm until it came time to get things done. Then out came the General. He suspected Cat would like that one even less. In fact, he was sure of it.

"Have to? Noooo," he replied, drawing out the word. "You already outlawed Boss Lady." He ignored her scowl and smiled. "So, what's it to be? Are we gonna do this thing?"

She fixed him with a perfectly curled smile that did not reach her eyes. "I outlawed that ridiculous term because I have a name, and you know it." Her expression softened as a blush crept up her cheeks. "And I assume by 'this thing' you mean getting Bristol Park up and running again, and not... Ummm..."

Nate reached and tucked a lock of her hair behind her ear. "I meant both. But sure, Bristol Park."

The look of pure lust Cat gave him had him hard in an instant, then she visibly shook herself, reached for her laptop and pulled up the ever-evolving master spreadsheet. "Of course we're doing this. Why do you think I brought on hired muscle? Though, I'm going to have to bring in more soon. And start the inspection process. And…the list is long."

He resisted the obvious dirty joke and innuendo and covered her hand with his. "And you're good. You've got this." He leaned over and kissed her cheek. "We've got this."

# Chapter Seventeen

Cat was slowly getting used to Nate not being in the house all the time. She set her alarm fifteen minutes earlier so she could get up and make the coffee. They had a daily meeting when he got done with his morning workout, then they'd go their separate ways. All perfectly normal.

Except for the occasional off-color jokes, the more than occasional double entendre and the fact that neither of them seemed to be able to pass the other without touching in some way. Which was equally thrilling and frustrating as far as Cat was concerned.

Nate usually took a lunch with him, and she often didn't see him again until dinner. After spending a day cleaning in the back part of the house or going through the piles upon piles of her grandmother's things, all alone in the big house, his presence at the dinner table was a light in her world. And screw all her reservations. She wanted Nate.

Trouble was, he didn't seem to be in any hurry, and she had no clue how to encourage him. She'd never seduced anyone. She filled a pot with water and set it on the stove. They'd started taking turns cooking. It was her turn to do dinner and she was in the mood for pasta. One thing she could thank Mama C for — her recipe for pasta alla norcina was to die for. And right now, the rich sausage and cream sauce sounded comforting, and oh so good.

She started the sausage browning and instantly the smell of garlic and olive oil transported her to Mama C's kitchen, right after Jimmy had announced their engagement. When her future mother-in-law had discovered the just-turned eighteen-year-old Cat could barely cook, she'd set out to remedy the situation.

"You cannot marry into this family and not know at least some basics," Mama C had said. Then she'd tossed an apron at Cat and told her to grab a notebook and pay attention. They'd started with marinara, and moved on through some basic sauces, meatballs, tender veal and chicken cutlets, and the most amazing eggplant Cat had ever eaten. By the time she'd married Jimmy, Cat was comfortable in the kitchen. After a year of marriage, Mama C had smacked Tom's then-fiancé Lucia when she'd burned a casserole and told her to go take lessons from Cat.

She shook her head as she stirred the fragrant sausage mixture, scraping up all the brown bits before pouring in the wine and letting it reduce for a minute. At least she had something good from her marriage — she could cook. She was lucky if her mother would open a box of Hamburger Helper and be sober enough to get it right. She'd learned to make eggs and ramen out of sheer self-preservation. After Mama C, she'd discovered the kitchen was her meditative space. A place where she could let go of the stress of the day, and know she was doing something good and appreciated. Jimmy had bragged about her cooking skills almost as much as her business skills.

"That smells amazing," Nate called out as he pushed through the kitchen door. He crossed the room in what seemed like an instant. Suddenly his warmth was behind her, his scent surrounding her — clean and spicy, freshly showered. A finger traced down her neck, sending shivers through her entire body. "What is this heavenly stuff?"

Nate reached around her and snagged the spoon, dipping it into the pan. Cat smacked his hand, retrieved the spoon and clapped the lid over the sauce.

"Patience," she replied, then dumped pasta into the boiling water. "Just sausage and garlic so far. Cream and cheese come later. It's really simple."

Nate leaned over her, pressed into her back and inhaled deeply. "Nothing simple or 'just' anything about that."

Then he was gone. He'd turned to the fridge to get a drink, and Cat felt a hollow ache at the loss of his touch. But her mother's voice echoed in her ears — wait for him to pursue you, don't seem too eager, stand off a little so he doesn't think you're too easy. The kind of man Sophia wanted her daughter to marry might have sex with a girl who was easy, but they didn't give them their last names.

Nate was certainly used to being pursued — it would be nothing new or exciting to him. He might even find it distasteful. But he'd said he needed clear signals. That he wouldn't push. He wanted to know what she wanted.

Cat poured cream into the pan and stirred, her emotions roiling more than the food she was cooking. Maybe she should just ask him to kiss her again. She'd never been kissed like that—never with so much passion. A kiss had never sent her into another world and made her want to do unmentionable things. She needed to get her head on straight, and out of the gutter.

"Could you grate some cheese?" She pointed Nate at the block of pecorino on the counter. She tried not to watch as Nate's big, strong hands gently unwrapped the cheese and glided it over the box grater. There was something so sensual about the way he moved. He was like a cat—a big cat. All coiled strength and power hiding behind an easy grace.

Cat focused on the task of finishing the dish—drain the pasta, stir it into the sauce and reduce. She scooped two generous servings into large bowls and dumped a handful of the grated cheese on top, then a few twists of black pepper. She handed a bowl to Nate.

"It's very hot," she warned. "I promise you'll regret it if you just start shoveling, and I know you want to."

He grabbed a fork and moved to the island, sliding onto a stool and pushing one out for her—right next to him.

"Okay." He blew on a forkful of pasta. "So, this is torture. I have to wait to taste this thing I've been smelling from halfway down the hill." He dropped the fork into his bowl and leaned in close to her, his breath brushing against her ear. "How long will I have to wait?"

His fingers traced along her arm, her thigh, her back. It felt like his hands were everywhere—barely touching, gently caressing, teasing. Unsure if he was asking about the food or something else, Cat looked to his face for a clue, but he was all gentle smiles, and something in his eyes that made her think of smoldering embers — just waiting to be stirred to roaring life.

"I...uh..." Cat cleared her throat, trying to find her voice. Or the determination to tell him to forget dinner and take her to bed instead. "I'm sure it's fine. It only needs a minute or two to cool."

Nate blinked, and that fire in his eyes settled a little bit. He nodded and his lips curled into a broad smile before he kissed her temple. "Well then, let's dig in." He stabbed his fork into the pasta.

Cat swallowed, feeling like she'd missed something. Her first forkful of the normally flavorful dish tasted flat. She had. She'd missed something — but it wasn't in the food. She'd done it exactly as Mama C had taught her, and every time she'd made it before, it was good. It took Nate's widened eyes and expression of pure bliss to wake her up.

"My God," he breathed. "That's amazing."

And Cat knew what she had missed. A moment. An opportunity to lean in and savor him, like she would a delicious dish, or a fine wine. She'd caught his double entendre and left it hanging there out of fear and uncertainty. She wanted him to make the first move, but Nate needed to be sure.

This was not going to be easy.

\* \* \* \*

Nate tossed bags of potting soil into his truck just as Cat emerged from Juan's, laughing and chatting with Charlie. For a moment, he forgot to breathe. The sun caught her hair, turning it into a halo of gold and red. When she glanced up at him, caught his eye and smiled, the urge to cross to her and wrap his arms around her was a deep aching need. One that he couldn't fulfill.

Not without knowing that was what she wanted. Not unless he was sure. He didn't want to smother her. Or frighten her. He needed to get control of himself.

"You get everything on the list?" Cat handed him a box filled with who knows what, but it was heavy. "Thanks for splitting the errands with me today. That went so much faster."

Nate grunted a response, unwilling to trust himself to talk at the moment. He'd offered to follow her into town so she could return Juan's truck and then help with the errands. He told himself he was just being helpful, but he wanted the chance to spend time with her. They'd been working apart most days, and since he'd moved to the cabin, he saw her only at their daily meetings and dinner. When they were together, Cat was hot and cold. One minute casually touching his hand or leaning into him while she spoke and the next retreating like a frightened kitten.

Juan came out carrying another box. "That's the last of it," he said as he dropped the box in Nate's truck. "You need anything else, just give me a shout. Hey, Nate."

Cat had insisted on buying as many supplies in town as possible. She preferred supporting the local businesses over the big box stores. The only time she'd break that pattern was if time didn't permit waiting for something the smaller local shops didn't have in stock. No doubt, that habit had gone a long way toward winning over the whole town.

"What'd you think of the flier?" Juan leaned against the porch rail next to Charlie, who suddenly had a broad smile on her face. "Damn graphic artists always gotta stick their noses in and turn something simple into an hours long discussion of what font to use."

Nate didn't miss the elbow Charlie directed into Juan's ribs. Then Cat handed him a bright paper, a flower topped May Pole ran up one side. The rest was information about the May Day Picnic at Bristol Park. *Holy crap. She's serious about that.*

"I love it," Cat replied. "It's perfect! Thank you. There's so much to do still, but we're making good progress."

Nate's head popped up. She'd said "we". He looked down at the flier again. Cat was right, it was perfect. Colorful and attention grabbing, it was just professional enough to not look homemade, but not so slick it looked corporate. The ideal tone for a town picnic.

"Nice work," he said. "Quit giving her shit, Juan. You or I would have hand drawn the thing in Magic Marker, and you know it."

Juan laughed and nodded. "Yeah, and it woulda looked like a kindergartner's art project."

"Hey, Cat!" The greeting came from next door, where Vicky stuck her head out of the coffee shop. "They just pulled those oatmeal cookies you like outta the oven."

A broad smile crossed Cat's lips, making Nate want to kiss her. Then she raised her eyebrows and looked around the group. "Can't pass that invite up. Anyone want anything?"

Nate shook his head, but Charlie jumped up and followed Cat into the coffee shop. Nate set about making sure all the boxes and bags were secured in the truck. Until Juan cleared his throat.

"What's going on with you two?" Juan tipped his head to one side and cast his eyes around. "It's just us, and you know I keep my mouth shut when I need to. So, let's hear it."

Nate sighed and leaned against the truck. "I don't know." Nothing like being honest. Truth was, he didn't know. "Is it that obvious that something's going on?"

That was where he was torn. On the one hand, if everyone saw something, and thought something, maybe that would make Cat less afraid. On the other, if things didn't work out, if Cat tired of him, he didn't want the entire town knowing.

"Well," Juan continued, "let's just put it this way…Gina seems to think so. That group of hens at the coffee shop are all pretty convinced the town's most eligible bachelor is now completely off the market."

*Shit.* Nate glanced down at his watch. Early afternoon. The usual group of ladies would be gathered in the coffee shop by now. And Cat had just walked in there. *Well, hell.*

"You might as well relax." Juan's hand landed on his shoulder and squeezed. "She's likely to be a while. They're just as bad as the old coots who hang out in my shop. Maybe worse."

That last was exactly what Nate was afraid of. He was in the middle of debating whether he should go rescue Cat when the coffee shop door opened and she came out, two coffees and a bag in hand. Nate didn't miss the collection of faces pressed into the shop window, watching Cat's every move. He didn't miss how quickly Juan and Charlie bid their farewells and took off into the store.

He pushed himself off the truck and made the choice. He opened Cat's door and held it while she climbed in, chattering about something Gina had said. He rested a hand on Cat's thigh, and her words dried up. She snapped her eyes up to his, a look of surprise crossed her face, followed by longing, pure and deep. Then she blinked and it was gone, replaced with the plastic smile she adopted when she didn't know what else to do. He didn't move his hand.

"Are you okay with this?" He nodded at the hand on her thigh. She sucked in a breath and the plastic smile dropped, and something far more raw took over. It looked like fear, and he almost removed his hand, until she covered it with her own.

"Yes." It came out quiet and soft. Barely audible even from just inches away. "Thank you."

That was the first clue he had that she needed him to take the initiative. As much as he'd been waiting for her to give him the go-ahead, she couldn't. Just as he needed to know she wanted him, she needed him to see it and act on it.

He squeezed her thigh, gave her the gentlest smile he could muster, then closed her door and went around to the driver's side. All her blowing hot and cold suddenly made sense. He was going to have to figure out how to let her know it was okay. To do that, he'd have to risk himself.

# Chapter Eighteen

Cat stumbled down the stairs and headed straight for the kitchen...and a cold coffee pot. *Dammit.* She'd snoozed her alarm, totally forgetting that Nate was no longer around to make coffee in the mornings. The first week after he'd moved his things down to the cabin had been awkward, but this last week they'd settled into an easy routine. One where the sexual tension between them simmered in the background, occasionally threatening to boil over. She dumped fresh grounds into the machine and poured the water. That routine involved her making coffee for their morning planning meeting.

She'd just flipped the switch to brew the coffee when the kitchen door swung open, and Nate stepped through. He'd peeled off his outer layers and the white tee clung to his chiseled body as if painted there. Cat bit her lip—the only thing she could think to do to keep from begging him to take her right here in the kitchen.

Then, somehow, he was standing in front of her instead of across the room. His hands were in her hair, his forehead pressed into hers, his lips a breath away. Their ragged breathing filled the room and the heat coming off him made her want to strip her own clothes off.

His hands dropped, and Cat stifled the cry of complaint that nearly burst from her lips. She wanted him. And never mind all the reasons not to, and all her fears. She didn't care. She needed his touch.

"I want you." The words were out of her mouth before she could second-guess herself. She traced her finger along his forearm, then up over his hard bicep to those incredibly broad shoulders, and finally, rising up on her toes, around the back of his neck. She dragged her nails along his hairline, still damp from being outside.

"I need a shower." His voice was gravely, rough. "And I don't have condoms, but I'm happy to take care of you."

Cat ran her other hand up his thigh, relishing the way his muscles jumped at her touch. She hooked a finger in his waistband and stepped closer to him.

"I don't think I can get pregnant," she replied. "You said it's been five years for you, I think it's safe. And I got tested regularly because…well…y'know. It's all good."

His eyes squeezed shut, and a flash of panic seized her. He didn't want her like this. He surely had plenty of other women he could turn to.

"Be sure, Cat." The words whispered into her ear. His body practically vibrating against her. "Be sure this is what you want."

She wasn't good at this seduction game. She could play the flirt, but when it came to sex, she'd always backed off. Until she'd married. Because that's what good girls did.

But screw that. She didn't want to be that kind of girl.

She curled her hand behind Nate's head and pulled him down to kiss her. He hissed in a breath as her lips pressed into his, then moaned into her mouth as her other hand moved to cup him through his sweats.

Then his hands were on her hips, holding her tight against him, and the kiss changed as he took control. His tongue slipped between her lips and Cat was lost as her entire body responded, begging for more. He raised his head, eliciting a whimper of protest from her.

"I really do need to shower." It came out almost as a chuckle, and there was a wicked gleam in his eyes. "And I think I have the perfect solution."

His hands curled under her ass and lifted. Cat squealed in surprise, then wrapped her legs around his hips as he headed out the kitchen door and up the stairs. He didn't stop until he set her on her feet in the master bathroom.

Cat cranked the water on and turned her attention to getting him out of his clothes. He kicked off his shoes then started tugging at her sweater as she yanked his damp tee over his head, revealing all the amazing ink that covered his arms and shoulders, and traced down his flat stomach before disappearing into his waistband.

She marveled at the feel of him — all hard muscles and tight bronzed skin. She popped the tie on his sweats and tugged, then caught her breath as he sprang free, already hard. And huge. Cat took a deep breath and kept tugging until sweats and underwear hit the floor. Then she stood and removed the rest of her clothes. She didn't try to cover herself—she wanted Nate to see her.

"Beautiful," he whispered, as his hands caressed her shoulders, down her arms, then to her waist. Her nipples stiffened in anticipation and Cat held her breath. His palms, rough and calloused, slid over her breasts and she trembled. She needed this. Needed him in a way she'd never known before. Her body ached to feel him inside her, and she let out a soft moan. Mustering all her strength and self-control, she guided them to the shower and stepped in, pulling Nate along with her.

She wanted her hands all over him. Wanted to touch this beautifully built man. And he let her. As if sensing her need, or maybe just understanding her unspoken desires, he leaned against the shower wall and let her wash him top to toe.

When she rinsed him, his erection stood out long and hard. Cat wrapped her hand around him, her fingers barely closing. He sucked in a sharp breath, and his stomach tightened. She slid her hand down, then back up, loving the way he reacted to her touch.

Driven partly by some instinct, and partly by things she'd seen in porn, Cat sank to her knees in the shower and let her fingers trail over the ink that traced down his hip to the top of his thigh. Then feasted her eyes on him—her body clenched in anticipation of taking him inside. But first, she wanted to taste him. She wanted to feel him in her hands and her mouth.

She tightened her grip, just a little, then licked the tip. He hissed, and Cat glanced up to see his eyes closed and head thrown back. She opened wide and took him in, as much as she could. His moaning response sent a pulse straight to her groin. She lifted her head to focus on his face, needing reassurance she was doing something right.

"Oh my God." His voice was raspy, harsh. "Don't stop. I want to watch you."

Cat slid a hand down between her legs and stroked slowly in time with her mouth on Nate's hard dick. A long, low groan from Nate pulled her attention back to him. His eyes focused on her, watching. She licked again, took him deeper, and was rewarded with a louder groan.

"I take it back," he said. "Stop, or I'm gonna…"

He didn't finish the sentence. Instead, he cranked the water off and wrapped his arms around her before lifting her out of the shower. He toweled her off, lingering here and there, kissing a nipple, or pressing his fingers into the curve of her ass. As if he already knew every inch of her body, and yet wanted to commit it even further to memory.

"I want to see you laid back on that bed, Princess," he said. "And then I'm going to take my time with my fingers and lips and tongue, until you think you can't take any more."

His words alone sent a rush of wetness between her legs, and Cat would have sprinted for the bed to do his bidding if he hadn't been holding her still.

"Show me this is what you want," he said. "I need to see it, hear it, feel it from you."

Cat planted a kiss on his lips and took his hands in hers as she started backing toward the bed, pulling him with her. When her legs bumped the edge of the bed, she released his hands and eased herself onto the mattress. She slid back until her head rested on the pillows and stretched, hoping it looked as sexy as she felt in that moment. His eyes never left hers, and Cat felt a surge of erotic energy seeing the effect she had on him.

"I thought I made my interest pretty clear," she said. "Do I need to beg?"

That last elicited a growl from Nate as he reached forward and grasped her ankles and began a slow exploration up her calves. True to his word, his lips followed, until he slipped a hand between her legs and parted her thighs. Nate pressed her knees apart and Cat sighed in anticipation of his touch.

Nothing could have prepared her for this moment. Whatever game he was playing, she didn't care. He was being tender, but there was a restrained beast simmering beneath. She wanted to unleash it — to see what Nate would be like completely free to do as he wanted.

She curled her legs over his shoulders, and his breath blew warm and soft against her inner thighs. Then his fingers were on her, stroking gently until she opened for him. He moved with exquisite care, and so slowly. It was maddening.

Then his lips joined in, his tongue found her clit and Cat nearly came at the first touch to that sensitive spot. Nate wrapped an arm around her hips and held her to him as he feasted on her as if he were a man starving, and she was a buffet. She lost count of the number of orgasms. He kept going until she lay back on the bed, breathing hard and shaking top to toe.

She'd never known oral sex could be so good. But, aside from in the shower, she hadn't touched him. And despite all the orgasms, she ached to feel him inside her.

"Nate." She breathed his name out on a sigh, her fingers tugging and plucking at his shoulders, trying to pull him toward her.

He raised his head and the grin he flashed was the most wicked and sexy thing she had ever seen.

"What do you want, Cat?" He rose to his knees between her legs and Cat sucked in a breath at the sheer size and beauty of the man. He was so tall and broad, his shoulders blotted out everything but him. He filled her sight.

He slid a finger inside her, and Cat moaned and ground against him. How could she still want more after all of that? But she hadn't had him yet. And she wanted him. A second finger slid inside, making her clench the sheets and arch her back for more.

"Did you want something?" There was a chuckle in his voice and Cat's eyes flew to his. That wicked sexy grin was still there, along with something else—Cat had no idea what was in store for her, but she had the feeling the beast was about to slip its leash. She arched her back again and ground onto his fingers.

"Tell me." It was a demand, not a question this time, and that tone made Cat quiver.

"Please, I want you," she panted, hoping that would be enough. That he would stop playing whatever game this was and get inside her already.

"I'm right here," he replied. "What more do you want?" He leaned over her, sliding another finger into her until Cat felt stretched and full, but still strangely empty. His lips hovered near her ear. "Yes, Cat, I want you to beg. Tell me you want me to make love to you. Tell me you want my cock in you. Or would you rather plead with me to fuck you? I need to know exactly what you want."

Cat whimpered and writhed against him. She'd never said those kinds of words out loud. But she wanted him. No, she needed him. Right now.

"Please, Nate," she begged. "Please…"

His fingers did something inside her, something delicious, and she moaned. "I want…" She wanted him filling her. But she knew that wasn't what he wanted to hear. No, he wanted the dirty words. The kinds of things good girls didn't say. And wasn't she the one who'd started this game when she asked him if she needed to beg. Cat drew in a deep breath and opened her eyes to find him staring directly at her.

"I want…"

He raised an eyebrow and his fingers twitched, sending Cat into another round of convulsions. She screwed her eyes shut, clenched her hands into the sheets, and sucked in a breath.

"Please, Nate, make love to me." The words came out in a rush, all run together. She held her breath, uncertain what would come next.

His weight shifted and one hand cupped her cheek as he leaned over her. "Look at me," he commanded. Her eyes flew open, focused on him. "Good girl."

Those words from his lips washed over her like a caress and she could breathe again. Then his fingers were gone, and she felt even emptier than before. But he was there, his body over her, his weight on her. And pressing against her.

"Relax," he said. "Take a deep breath and blow it out. I'll go slow at first."

At the first press of his dick into her softest parts, Cat clenched, and her eyes squeezed shut. His fingers smoothed her brow, and his kisses soon had her forgetting the incredible pressure she felt. He went slow — agonizingly, teasingly slow — until she clenched her fingers on his ass and tried to pull him against her.

When he finally sank fully into her, Cat wriggled beneath him, willing him to move, but he shook his head.

"Gimme a minute," he whispered. "It's been a while, and you feel too damn good."

Cat slid her hands over his back, running fingers over tight muscles and reveling in the feel of him. Finally, he moved. Inching from her slowly before plunging back in. The beast had retreated to its cage. She wanted to coax it back out. To set it free.

Nate ground his teeth together and counted backwards from one hundred in his head. Anything to keep from losing it and either blowing his load in ten seconds or less, or flipping her over, pinning her to the mattress, fisting a handful of her hair and fucking her into next week.

He wasn't sure she could handle that. Hell, he wasn't sure he could handle that right now.

Cat's legs slid up around his waist and his eyes about rolled back in his head. Jesus, she felt so good. He forced himself to go easy, to take his time. He wasn't a small guy, in any way, and not all women could handle him even going slowly. Never mind taking what he really wanted to give.

Her hips shifted and the slick warmth around his shaft clenched as Cat reached her arms around his neck and pulled him closer. Sweet Jesus, she was amazing.

"Nate." His name on her lips nearly sent him over the edge. Her eyes were heavy-lidded, and she panted in time with his strokes. "Please…"

*Oh God, that pleading tone.* Nate started that countdown again.

"Please, Nate..." The words in his ear were sweet and soft, begging for more. "Fuck me."

That last was punctuated with her teeth on his ear. Nate roared in response, pinning her knees under his elbows and shifting her hips up. He forced himself to go easy on the first stroke as he watched her face. She didn't flinch.

No, she arched into him, lifting her hips to meet his. "Harder!"

That one word set him free. He sat up and hauled her with him as he drove into the warmth and wetness that surrounded his cock. Her hands clenched into fists and her face buried in his shoulder. Nate's fingers sank into the perfectly round globes of her ass and his teeth found the tender skin at the base of her neck.

She wrapped her legs tightly around him and ground down, taking him deeper. Suddenly her gasps turned into words, begging him for more, harder, deeper. Then she threw her head back and arched against him, her entire body going as tight as a bowstring and trembling. Still, she didn't lose a beat. If anything, she sped up and Nate couldn't take much more of this.

He shifted his hips so she could grind if she wanted. Her eyes popped open wide, and she changed her rhythm, rocking against him until the trembling turned to shaking and her fingers sank into his shoulders. She exploded in a rush as she cried out his name.

Nate followed in about two strokes, the burst of tension and pleasure so intense it almost hurt. He wrapped her in his arms and laid her back on the bed, pounding into her until his body stopped demanding more. He emptied himself into her with a final groan of pleasure and rolled, taking her with him so he cradled her body.

Jesus. He'd never had anyone take everything he gave and ask for more, but Cat had done just that. Unless he missed his guess, she wanted even more. His greedy girl.

That thought made his brain screech to a halt. No, he didn't need to be going down that path. It wasn't that long ago that he'd been thinking how much he didn't need this shit in his life, and here he was thinking 'mine'.

He was beyond screwed.

One thing for sure, he was right that the Ice Princess was definitely all fire underneath.

"Penny for your thoughts." Cat's voice cut through the dangerous rambling in his head.

Nate curled an arm around her shoulders and held her tight against his side, uncertain how much to share with her. He was saved by the rumbling of her stomach. "I think it's time for breakfast." He glanced down at his watch. "Or brunch." They seemed to have skipped breakfast. He shifted and nearly rolled off the side of the small bed. Dammit. The full-size bed had felt plenty big just moments ago. Now he felt like a bull in a china shop.

He stood and went searching for discarded clothing. He found his sweats on the floor of the bathroom, still wet from his hike and the fact they sure as shit weren't thinking about keeping clothes dry when they got out of the shower. No way he could wear those back down to the cabin.

"There's a robe on the back of the linen closet door." Cat stood in the bathroom entry, tugging on an oversized T-shirt and pointing at the small door across from the shower. "You can toss your clothes in the wash. Or at least in the dryer, if you don't want to wait that long."

He opened the linen closet and found the robe — soft and fuzzy and very pink. He'd seen Cat wearing it a time or two. "You really think this is gonna fit me?" He held it up — it looked like it might fit a Muppet. Hell, it looked like it was made out of Muppet.

Cat's face contorted into a twisted grin, and she shook her head. "Maybe just wrap a towel around you, and I'll turn the heat up."

He grabbed a fresh towel from the closet and tucked it around his hips. He waited until Cat was out of the room before holding the robe up again. The shoulders stopped several inches from being wide enough. Nope. That wasn't gonna work. He hung the robe back up, gathered his clothes and nearly ran into Cat as she came back in.

"I ummm..." She cleared her throat and looked away from him as a pink flush brightened her cheeks. It was adorable, but he didn't think she wanted to hear that. "I bumped the heat. You know where the laundry is. I uhh... I need to clean up after...well..."

The pink flush turned almost crimson, and realization hit him. They hadn't used a condom. She'd have a mess to deal with. He tucked a finger under her chin, tipped her head up and dropped a soft kiss on the corner of her mouth.

"No problem, Princess," he replied. "Let me know if you need a hand." He gave her what he hoped was a salacious wink and walked out.

# Chapter Nineteen

Cat leaned in to open the dining room drapes and something wet seeped through her socks. It took all of two seconds to figure out the radiator was leaking. An hour later, and many failed attempts to figure out the problem herself, she called Nate. And an hour after that, he pushed himself up to stand and gave her a look she didn't like.

"You're going to have to call a repairman," he said. "It's not the valve, or the air vent, and as far as I can tell, it's not one of the joints." He let out a heavy sigh. "Which means it's either one or more of the sections themselves, or the connectors."

Cat glared at the radiator. Never her favorite heating option. Jimmy's grandmother — the same one with the ancient toaster with the cloth-covered cord — lived in an old brownstone and refused to get rid of her radiators, despite them being noisy and needing almost constant maintenance.

"Is there a shut-off valve or something, so at least it's not continuing to spew water on the floor?" She peeled her socks off, almost daring Nate to say something. He'd once questioned why she didn't wear shoes, or at least slippers, in the house. She hadn't really had a reason, only that she preferred being barefoot, but it was too cold to go without socks.

"Yeah," Nate replied. "Already took care of that." He pointed down at the valve and Cat caught a glimpse of skinned knuckles. He'd rapped himself more than once trying to get parts to move. She hadn't realized he'd broken skin.

"You're a genius." Cat rose on her toes and kissed his cheek. The smirk on his face sent heat rushing through her. That's how it had been all weekend — one look from him, the slightest touch, and she was dragging him to bed. Or anywhere she could find a flat enough surface. The washing machine had been just about the right height. The memory of that afternoon made her blush.

"I'll text Juan and see who he suggests," she said, anything to get her mind out of the gutter it seemed to have taken up permanent residence in. "And you should go clean up your hand. That looks like it hurts."

Nate caught her around the waist and pulled her against him. "Or we could shower. Together." His lips caressed her ear and then her neck. It was as if he'd been reading her mind, or maybe her body just sent him signals — hey, I want you! "It is about time to call it a day."

She put a hand on his chest, using the last shreds of her self-control to push him away for a moment. "Let me text Juan." The heat in his eyes didn't dissipate, instead, it grew deeper. The look he gave her could have melted polar ice caps—it was definitely turning her into a puddle. "And then I'm all yours."

She skipped out of his reach and snagged her phone from the table, firing off a quick note to Juan, all the while keeping an eye on Nate. His expression was that of a predator watching its next meal, calculating the best moment to strike. And something about that sent pleasant shivers through her.

She still had the sense he was restraining himself with her. Like there was something he kept carefully locked up. She caught teasing glimpses of it every now and then. Sometimes it seemed he'd forget himself and his fingers would clench more tightly on her body, or a growl would form in the back of his throat. Her own responses to those moments only fueled her curiosity—an almost primal, instinctual thing that made her want him even more.

She finished the text and set the phone down, then edged her way to the door. Nate hadn't budged. He stood by the radiator, his eyes glued to her every move. At the door, she spun around and pulled her sweater over her head in one movement.

"Catch me," she called over her shoulder at Nate, then took off running for the stairs. He caught her at the top, his arm closing around her hips and lifting as if she weighed nothing. The buttons on his flannel dug into her bare back. Nate's other hand made quick work of undoing her jeans and pushing them down her hips. She was naked by the time they made it to her bedroom, but he didn't put her down until they were in the bathroom with the door closed and him leaning against it as if she was going to try to run.

"I caught you," he replied, not even winded. "Now what?"

Somehow, he was under control again. The leash drawn tight, the cage door closed and locked. But she knew what he liked. What would tempt him out.

She bent and turned on the water, giving him a view of her backside. His hissing intake of breath was a clear sign he was paying attention. "Why don't you strip and climb in so I can wash you?"

\* \* \* \*

Nate hit the pause button and pulled one earbud out, cocking his head to listen. Yep, there it was. The unmistakable sound of Cat pissed off. She didn't yell, in fact, almost the opposite, but that soft tone somehow carried. Right now, she was giving the radiator repairman an earful. When he heard the man's voice cut her off and say something about the man of the house, Nate understood why Cat was on edge.

He chewed his lip, considering his options. He was in the rec room, painting. There was no way to miss overhearing the conversation down the hall in the dining room. He could go in there and play man of the house—undermining Cat and her authority. He could go in there and stand behind Cat, insist the guy talk to her—which would probably make Cat happy, but the reality would be, the guy would patronize her for it, and piss her off even more. Or he could stay the hell out of it—not entirely a safe option, but he didn't feel like making life easy on the repair guy, and he was reasonably confident in his ability to deal with any potential fallout from Cat.

It had been like that all week. As Cat had to bring in outside contractors, they'd all looked to him, or talked over her head. Even after being corrected by Nate, they'd address him, then turn to her and add, "if that's okay with you, ma'am."

The slamming of the front door reverberated through the entire house, and Cat stormed into the room.

"What an absolute and horrible asshole!" She flopped down onto the floor and dropped her head into her hands. "After bitching for a solid ten minutes that he shouldn't have had to come out here for a valve leak that any competent man could fix, he came right out and said I couldn't understand him, and he needed to talk to the man of the house."

Nate cringed. Yeah, that kind of bullshit was guaranteed to put her in a bad mood. Rightfully. He stuck his brush into a plastic bag, pocketed his earbuds and settled on the floor facing her, his knees brushing hers. She raised her head, lines of frustration etched between her eyebrows.

"I take it he's not fixing the radiator," Nate said. He wasn't sure if humor was the right choice, but it was all he had at the moment. Short of offering to go chase the guy down and pound some sense into him.

"Not only is he not fixing the radiator," Cat replied, giving him a twisted smile. "I'll be calling his company and making a formal complaint. And I'm seriously considering calling Dominico."

What? What the hell had this guy said to push her to those actions. Nate bit his tongue, wanting to give her the chance to open up, and hoping she'd explain that last part. Instead, she leaned back and let her head thud into the wall, tears glittering in the corners of her eyes.

"Hey," Nate whispered. He snagged one of her hands and squeezed. "Talk to me. What happened?"

Cat knuckled the tears away and drew in a shaky breath. "He uh…said he'd be happy to take care of all my pipes — off the clock." She looked away, as if embarrassed. "I asked him to repeat himself. I wasn't sure I heard him correctly. Or maybe I thought I'd misunderstood. But he grabbed himself, y'know." She gestured at her crotch. "And said it again."

Jesus. Had he heard that, he'd have been in the room in an instant, escorting the guy out. Maybe he was doing the wrong thing staying out of her way.

"That's fucked up," Nate said. "And I'm sorry you had to listen to that." He didn't have anything else to offer. She hadn't asked him to fix it for her and stepping in might not be what she wanted.

"I told him to get out of my house," Cat said. "I need to calm down before I call the company. I don't want to sound like a hysterical female."

He hauled in a slow breath and squeezed her hand again. "I'm not sure you want my opinion right now…" He let the words hang in the air. Cat raised her head and looked at him, her expression neutral.

"Let's have it," she said. She looked like she was braced for something terrible.

Nate pressed his lips together and thought for a moment before responding. "You might want to call sooner, rather than later. It's a safe bet this guy is going to be covering his ass and may be ready to spin the tale that you're acting out of spite. Or even that you came on to him."

A moment of pure fury flashed in her eyes before she rolled them, and disgust replaced anger. "Yeah," she said. "Ugh."

She pushed herself up and brushed her pants off. Nate stood with her, caught her hand. "Do you need anything from me?"

Cat looked around the room, at the brush and rollers and paint tray on the floor. The ladder in the corner. She looked back at him, and a tired smile curved her lips. "Make dinner tonight," she said. "And then make me forget that jerk."

He had his arms around her in less than a breath. Those were tasks he would take on with absolute joy and exhausting attention to detail — at least on the second half. "Anything you need." He whispered the words into her hair. "I'm right here."

She leaned into the hug for a moment, then straightened and headed for the door. "If you hear me screaming, just ignore it. Oh, and find me someone else who does radiator repairs. I won't use that company."

Nate almost felt sorry for whoever would be on the other end of that phone call. Almost. He glanced at his watch — time to clean up if he was cooking dinner. He wasn't certain she meant what she said about making her forget the guy, but he was very sure he could meet that need. His dick gave a twitch as if to agree. She might not be in the same mood after the phone call.

Which would be just fine. Now he just had to get past his desire to throttle the guy for making that kind of comment in the first place, and for making his girl feel bad.

Aw, hell. There it was again. His girl. Yeah, he was screwed.

# Chapter Twenty

Snow crunched under her boots as Cat walked the inspector back to his car. He was the last of the lot. The past week and a half had been a parade of tradesmen, inspections and assessments — and it was Monday, a new week, and the circus was set to continue. The result — nothing surprising. The cabin where Nate was staying was the best of the bunch — it had only needed cosmetic fixes. The rest ranged from minor repairs like broken windows or damaged walls, to leaking roofs, faulty wiring and plumbing so bad the water was rusty. The mess hall was also a surprisingly easy prospect — entirely cosmetic. The kitchen would need gutting, though at least the wiring wasn't in terrible shape, and they could get to work without fear of electrical fires.

"If you don't mind me saying, Ms. Bristol, I'm glad it's you taking on this place and not some big corporation." The inspector opened his car door, then turned back to her. "I grew up around here. It's not just that I don't want to see some big company move in and take over, it's that I've seen what happens when they do. It'd spoil this place. This town. You have my info, you need anything, give me a call."

"Actually, now that you mention it." Cat pulled out her phone. "I'm going to email you some information about TravelCorp—a large developer that's been buying up surrounding properties. They've got their eyes on Bristol Park next. I'm pushing for a public meeting to review their development proposals."

The man nodded, a frown creasing his brow. "I'm sorry you're going through that. Send that over and I'll share it around." He opened his car door, then turned back to her. "You've still got a bit of work to do, but this first cabin group is good to go. Though I don't guess you could rent anything out this time of year, and not without a lot of the other work done first."

Cat laughed. "Oh, I don't have any plans to rent anything out for a while. Just determining what needs the most work, and what to do first. We've got a long way to go yet."

She watched him pull down the drive, then went looking for Nate. She found him perched on the pavilion roof, tacking up a huge tarp. Cat shook her head at the giant gray eyesore.

"I suppose that's to prevent further damage?" She stood, hands on hips looking up at him. He was far too nice to look at. Even bundled up against the cold, his broad shoulders belied the powerful build hidden under all those layers. Cat looked forward to peeling them off him later. She shook her head again. As if she hadn't had enough trouble keeping her mind out of the gutter around him. Since they'd wound up in bed last week, her brain had taken up permanent residence there. Not that she was complaining. She was complaining about the fact that he kept disappearing anytime someone came by.

"Yeah," he replied as he swung his leg over the roof and onto the waiting ladder. Cat hastily moved to steady it. "Can't do much about fixing it now, but we can at least preserve what's there. May be salvageable."

His feet hit the ground and one hand crept around her waist. Ever since their first time, it was as if Nate couldn't keep his hands off her. He'd press a kiss to the back of her neck when she was cooking or cup her cheek when he rose from the table at mealtime. And she reveled in his attentions. In feeling special and wanted. Nate's obvious desire for her was a potent thing and only stoked her own fires higher.

Though he'd moved his things to the first cabin, he'd spent every night of the last week in her bed. Whenever they were alone, he was right there—always touching her. Then he'd create distance when others were around. She knew why he did it—so people would see her and talk to her, not him. He'd said as much. But it made it feel like he was just the handyman. Like he wasn't invested. In the property, or her.

"Did the inspector give you bad news?" Nate's eyebrows rose along with the question, and Cat shook her head as she turned to climb the hill, Nate right on her heels. "I'm assuming that's the reason for the scowly face."

Cat shook her head, not wanting to start this conversation outside. She wanted to be indoors, preferably with a cup of coffee in hand. She didn't want to have the conversation at all. Telling him how she felt wasn't likely to get her anywhere. She still wasn't convinced that Nate wasn't just enjoying this for what he could get. He'd be gone the moment he got bored.

That thought sent a jolt of frustration through her as memories of Jimmy came unbidden.

Back at the house, Cat didn't think, she hauled open the door and stepped inside, leaving Nate standing on the porch stripping off his coat. After being outside, the heat was stifling, and she struggled out of the heavy layers. Suddenly she was fighting tears and couldn't even figure out why. She'd known what she was getting into. Maybe she just wasn't cut out for a casual fling.

The door slammed shut, and Cat spun to find Nate staring at her with a frown on his face. "I'm gonna guess you don't want to talk about whatever has you in a snit," he said. He leaned his big frame against the stairwell, ensuring she'd have to pass him to go anywhere but back outside.

Cat heaved a sigh and pushed past him toward the kitchen. "Coffee," she muttered as she shoved through the door, Nate not half a step behind. He took up a spot at the island, watching her with an expectant look on his face. Whatever he was, he wasn't her late husband. Jimmy's response to Cat getting upset was to turn everything around onto her—she was making mountains out of molehills. She was behaving uncharacteristically. Or being irrational. Or jealous. That last was a laugh. She had been jealous. Always. And with good reason.

But Nate just sat there. Quiet. Calm. And waiting.

"You're disappearing again." She didn't like the pouty tone in her voice, but there it was. If she boiled everything down to one point, one thing she could put her finger on, it was that. After spending the night in her bed, Nate had disappeared when the first inspector showed up the next morning. He'd left her to deal with them all by herself. Like he was just some hired help. Who she happened to be having sex with.

"Uhh...yeah." His face creased into a frown. "We had that discussion a while back. What's going on, Cat?" She pushed a cup of coffee to him, but he ignored it and grabbed her hand instead. "Are you okay? Is it that asshole from Friday?"

Cat slid her fingers from his and flopped down to the stool across from him. Screw whatever she'd learned from Jimmy. Screw keeping things quiet and not rocking the boat. She didn't want to live like that — always worried she was creating stress. Being made to feel like she was the one in the wrong.

"No, it's not Friday," she replied. "Not really, anyway. I mean...that, honestly, was my problem to handle. If a guy can't be nice just because there's not a man around, then he's scum. It's..." She looked down at her hands, twisting them together on the countertop, trying to find the words. "Look, I know it's just me and my baggage, but you pulling the disappearing act? It's hurtful."

*There. I said it. I put it out there. No histrionics or tears. No accusations. Just my feelings.*

"I'm sorry." The words came from his lips smooth and easy. "We talked about that. About what people would see. And think."

Cat crossed her arms over her chest. "That was before..."

His eyes went wide for a moment, then softened. He swallowed, hard — his Adam's apple rising and falling. Then he took a deep, slow breath and blew it out. "What do you need?"

Cat scrambled — her brain unable to process that response. She'd expected to be told she was imagining things. To not make a big deal out of it. Instead, he'd asked her the one thing she wasn't prepared to answer. She didn't want this. Didn't want another pretty boy tangling her up into knots, but she needed him. And she needed to know that he wasn't going anywhere. But she couldn't tell him that.

"I need..." She struggled, the right words dancing just out of her reach. How to say what she wanted without actually saying it. "Are we trying to hide? I mean, not that I want to go around announcing we're sleeping together, but..." She toyed with her coffee cup, staring into the barely touched liquid as if it had all the answers in the world.

His big hands landed on her shoulders, and she looked up to discover he'd come around the island and was standing right in front of her. "But what, Cat?" His voice was a whisper, but it echoed in her mind, plucking strings that went straight to her heart.

"What are we doing? I mean..." *Are we just fuck buddies? Are you nothing more than the handyman I happen to be having sex with? I mean, it's great sex, but...* She couldn't ask those things. Couldn't say those words. No matter how much she wanted to.

"I think you know the answer to that one." That smooth drawl, so low and rich, rumbled through her. "I told you before, I don't do casual."

Cat sighed and stared up at him. "What does that even mean?"

Nate hauled in a deep breath. He didn't think she was ready for how he felt. *He* wasn't ready for how he felt. He closed his eyes for a moment, trying not to think about the way they'd spent the morning. He could get used to that. Hell, less than two weeks in and he was already used to it.

Nate squeezed her shoulders, as if somehow his touch would convey what his words could not. He glanced down at her hands—her once perfectly manicured and polished nails were trimmed short. Still buffed to a shine, but right now, there were traces of dirt under the edges here and there. She still looked like she'd stepped from the pages of a catalog.

"I'm not trying to hide anything," he said. "I'm trying to let you call the shots. To give you the space you need."

Cat shifted on her seat, away from his touch, and Nate resisted the urge to pull her back. He wanted nothing more than to gather her into his arms and hold her tight. He wanted to drive all the fears and uncertainty from her head, but he couldn't do that. Only she could. That had to be her choice.

"I don't like you disappearing," she whispered. "It feels..." She paused, her eyes scanning the room as if searching for an answer in the kitchen's rafters. "It makes me feel like we're doing something you're ashamed of. Or like you don't want people to know..." The last word broke off as if she were fighting tears.

*Shit.* Her husband had been a cheater. Nate had been acting to protect her business, her reputation, and yeah, maybe to protect himself from her feeling smothered, or complaining he was clingy or possessive. He'd been sending her an unintentional message. The wrong one, at that.

Nate held his hand out to her and waited. She rested her fingers in his and he urged her up from the stool then into his arms. "Do you remember me touching your leg in the truck when we ran errands the other day?" She nodded, but her face registered confusion. He couldn't blame her, it seemed like an odd thing to bring up.

"I wanted to do more," he said. "I've wanted that for some time. I needed to know you were okay with it." He hauled in a deep breath. Time to lay it out there, or at least as much of it as he could for now. "Have you noticed how touchy-feely I've been the last few days?" He waited for her to nod. He'd tried to restrain himself. Tried to hold back, but it was an ever-present urge — to have her close. To feel her skin against his. To be close enough to smell the soap she used.

"That's the way I am…all the time," he whispered. "Be sure you want that, Cat."

She pushed against his chest, leaning back to look up at him, her eyes full of confusion. "What does that mean? My choice is you disappearing anytime another person is around, or you acting like a possessive caveman?"

That word hit like a punch to the gut, and Nate sucked in a breath, willing himself to count to ten before responding. Cat didn't know, couldn't know, his history.

"No," he replied. "I'm not saying it's all or nothing. Just…" He leaned down, pressed his forehead to hers and closed his eyes. As much as he wanted to, he couldn't express what he really wanted. The sting of rejection was too great. It had taken him a long time to recover from his last relationship. He wasn't ready for that risk again. "Caveman is a bit extreme."

Cat chuckled, her breath washing warm over his cheeks. Her hands slid around his waist. "I was being silly." Her voice whispered around him, filling the air with her, taking over everything. "Why don't you tell me what you mean when you say be sure."

Nate sighed. If only he could. If only he could find a way to put into words the things he'd recognized in himself from a young age. The very powerful sense of 'mine' when it came to someone he cared about. He wanted to possess, just as he was possessed. How could he say that, without scaring her off? He'd known her barely two months. She'd think he was weird if he told her he could sense when she walked into a room. Or feel the changes in her mood before she ever said anything.

"How about we start with what would make you happy," he replied finally and opened his eyes. "You said you don't like me disappearing. What would you like to see happen instead? You want me to stand by your side while you deal with all the business? You got it. Hell, we can go into town and have breakfast together at Dolly's. Hold hands as we walk around downtown, if that's what you'd like."

Her eyes went wide and shocked looking, then she broke into a bright smile. "Yes."

One word and his world soared. One word and he wanted to swing her up in his arms and into bed.

"I want all of those things." She spoke forcefully. "I want to know you're not ashamed of...us. That you don't want to hide it. I want to know that this is more than just a roll in the sheets. That you're not just...fucking the boss lady or something like that."

A blush spread furiously across her face when she said the last, and she looked away as if embarrassed. Her next words were softer, gentler. "You said to be sure, but I'm not sure of anything, really. This house alone is a huge project, and it scares me half to death sometimes. Never mind the rest of the place. I believe I can do this, but I'm not sure."

She pressed her hands into his back, her fingers digging in and holding on. "I don't know what is between us. At first, I thought it was just lust—animal attraction. You are an incredibly good-looking man, you know." She caught her lower lip between her teeth and looked down. "I know I want you. And not just in bed. I don't know what that means. Or where it's going. Or anything else. And I know it scares me a little. No, it scares me a lot. But I don't care."

Her hands unclenched, and she released him, pushing out of his arms and leaving him feeling empty. She stood back, hands on her hips, and shaking her head.

"Am I sure?" She laughed. "Sure of what?"

Nate wanted her pressed close, where he could feel her warmth, smell her scent. He contented himself with cupping her cheek.

"I'm not ashamed of anything," he said. "Nor am I trying to hide anything. I don't ever want to have to guess at things between us. Can I touch you? Can I kiss you? I need to know what you want. Do you want me around? Do you want me next to you, holding your hand? Or behind you, supportive? Or what?"

Her eyebrows knit together in a frown, and she reached a hand up, smoothing her fingers along his jaw and around the back of his neck. "Somebody must have done a number on you." The words were kind and soft, and Nate dared hope that she was different. That she wouldn't feel trapped by his attentions. "Tell you what. I'll try to do a better job of communicating what I'd like—to be clear, I don't ever want you to just automatically disappear. And you will try to do the same. Deal?"

Nate nodded slowly. It was a start. It was a beginning. It gave him more foothold than he'd had just moments ago. He clung to that and tried not to think about the fall that would happen if he was wrong.

# Chapter Twenty-One

Cat pulled the laundry from the dryer and chuckled. Somehow, a few of Nate's things had made it into her laundry. Again—last time it was his underwear. She was certain his things getting mixed in with hers was her fault. It wasn't like he didn't do his own, but she'd been the one yanking clothes off him and tossing them into the corner of her room. This time, it was his gray Henley. Absolutely, her fault. That one came off in the bathroom, and she was pretty sure it had got tangled up in a bunch of towels.

She dropped the basket at the foot of stairs, she'd fold them later. Nate came down the hall, wiping his hands on a rag. His eyes lit up when he saw her, and Cat smiled in response. After the jerk last Friday, and the tense start to this week, things had been amazing between them. The only fly in the ointment was she had to keep reminding herself not to get used to this. But she'd deal with that fallout when the time came. For now, she liked having Nate Stewart as more than the handyman.

"Hey." Nate wrapped his arms around her from behind and nuzzled her neck. "I was thinking maybe we should get dinner in town tonight."

Cat tipped her head back, trying to get a look at him. Was he serious? It was a Friday night. Everyone would be in town. There would be no playing it off as if they were just running errands.

"Are you asking me out on a date?" She wriggled around in his grip until she faced him. A broad smile crossed his lips and those deep amber eyes stared straight into hers.

"Yep," he said. "I am. So, what d'ya think?"

Cat's brain swirled with the possibilities. As things were, if this was just a fling, and he eventually tired of her, she could pretend they were nothing. If they went out, and everyone saw them together, and it ended — she'd have to face the town knowing. But this was exactly what she'd asked him for. To show her that he wasn't ashamed of them. Of their relationship.

"I think dinner sounds great," she replied. "I'm assuming Dolly's?"

Nate gave her a mock scowl. "How long have you been in town and you haven't noticed they close early?"

She hadn't noticed. He'd brought food home a time or two, but it was always an early dinner. She'd never realized they weren't open late. "Okay, you got me. So, where do you suggest?"

He bent his head and pressed a kiss to the side of her neck, sending shivers through her entire body. "It's a surprise."

Cat started to protest. She couldn't dress if she didn't know where they were going. "Fine," she muttered. "But you have to pick out what I'm wearing then." That should get him to produce an answer. No guy wanted to go pawing through a woman's closet choosing an outfit for their date.

"Sure." His easy response startled her. "Shoes, too. In fact, we should go shower now, because I may need you to model things for me so I can decide."

Showering led to other things that led to another shower. She sat on her bed watching as Nate, towel slung low on his hips, opened her closet and sorted through her clothes.

"I was half-kidding," she said, laughing as he made a face at a long charcoal sweater dress. It was soft and cozy, and she loved wearing it over leggings. But it wasn't something she'd ever wear out. Most of her clothes were packed and in storage. She didn't see a need for business attire or eveningwear out here. She'd have to unearth her spring stuff soon.

"This," Nate called out triumphantly as he pulled a deep teal mock-wrap dress from the closet. A baby-soft knit, it had always been one of her favorites. "And..." Nate scanned the top shelf where she'd put a small selection of shoes. "Huh. Somehow I figured you for more of a fashionista."

Cat stifled a laugh. "I didn't bring my entire closet with me, but..." She crossed to the room's other closet where she'd stashed a few pairs of heels. "Trust me, I'm considering some renovations up here. I may sacrifice a guest bedroom to make a proper closet and dressing area."

Nate pointed at a pair of nude heels. "It wouldn't be that tough to do," he said. "The second guest room shares a wall with this one. Open a doorway here, close up the bathroom access in there..." His face scrunched up as he was thinking it through and if she wasn't hungry, she might have grabbed him and suggested they stay in tonight.

"That's a conversation for another time," she said, plopping back onto the bed. "Like, after this place is turning a profit. Now what are you going to wear? I've never seen you in anything but jeans, or sweats. Or...y'know...a towel."

A slow smile crept over his face. "I grabbed a few things from home when I moved into the cabin. Why don't you get ready, I'll see you back here in...?" He glanced at his watch, then back up at her. "Thirty minutes enough? We kinda lost track of time in the shower."

His hand closed over her ankle, sliding her to the edge of the bed. Then his lips were on hers, his hands slipping inside her robe, cupping her breasts and making her gasp in pleasure.

"It won't be enough if you keep that up," she muttered when his lips left hers to trace her neck and collarbone. "Nate, seriously." How could he do that? They'd spent the afternoon wrapped in each other. She'd had more orgasms in a few hours with Nate than she'd ever had in an entire year, and she still wanted to drag him back into bed with her for another round.

He kissed her lightly and stood. "You're right. Time to get moving." He tossed his clothes back on and headed for the door. "See you in thirty."

Cat waited until she heard the front door close, then she bolted from the bed and rushed into the bathroom, digging in the sink cabinet for her blow dryer. No, she didn't have time for diffusing her curls. She'd have to wear her hair up.

She'd just put on lipstick and was headed down the stairs when Nate came back in. And Cat's breath caught. She'd thought him good looking before, but Nate in a pair of trim fitting black slacks and a tailored gray dress shirt, sleeves cuffed up and collar open, was breathtaking. It looked like he'd trimmed his beard as well—though he somehow magically never had more than heavy stubble.

"You look amazing." Nate crossed to her and lifted her off the bottom step, fitting her to his body as if it had been days since they'd seen each other, not just minutes.

"So do you," Cat replied. "As much as I'd like to stand here admiring the scenery, I'm starving. Where are we going?"

Nate released her slowly and led her to the door. "You'll see."

\* \* \* \*

Nate pulled into the lot at Riverfront. He wasn't too surprised that Cat didn't know about it. In winter, they were only open Friday and Saturday nights. Come spring and summer, they'd be open for weekend lunches as well. They wouldn't even have managed that if the place weren't an old family business, long ago paid off.

There were few restaurants in town, and he'd chosen this one for several reasons—it was the nicest of the lot with the most date-like atmosphere, the food was excellent, and, most importantly, coming here with Cat sent a clear signal that they were together. And frankly, he wanted to shout that from the rooftops. Even if the idea scared him more than a little.

Riverfront also had the town's only real bar—which meant most of the town was there on the weekends. If not out for a dinner date, they were there drinking, playing darts or pool, and being social. Everyone would see them. He came around and opened Cat's door, surprised to see her looking a bit apprehensive.

"It's crowded," she said, her eyes scanning the lot.

Nate took her hand in his, leaned in and pressed a soft kiss to her cheek. "Yes. You said you wanted all of those things — to know this isn't just a roll in the sheets." She slid out of the truck, and it was the most natural thing to wrap his arm around her waist, tucking her into his side as they crossed the parking lot.

Inside, the bar opened to the left, and the restaurant to the right. The hum of conversation trickled to silence the moment they walked in, arm in arm. Cat stiffened slightly, and her easy smile took on the polished, plastic look he'd seen whenever she needed to seem pleasant, but it was a sure indication she was struggling with something. He leaned down and placed his lips near her ear.

"It's okay," he whispered. "It's just you and me. That's all that matters."

The plastic look faded a bit as the hum of conversation returned and they followed the hostess to their table. By the time they were seated, Cat looked almost her normal, relaxed self. Something nagged at him — she'd said she wanted this. She wanted to be out in public with him, but she seemed uncomfortable. He reached across the table and took her hand.

"Did I mess up with this plan?" he asked. "Because I thought this would be a good thing, but you seem a little... I don't know, tense."

Her eyes shot up to his, and all his worries came to a screeching halt at the swirl of emotions painted on her face. Joy and fear and happiness and pain all warred for dominance in her eyes.

"You didn't mess up." The words were husky, as if she were fighting back tears. "It was just unexpected. I wasn't prepared for..." She nodded her head back at the bar area. "That. But it's okay. You were right." Her fingers curled around his hand. "Thank you."

With those words, all the tension seemed to drain from her. She relaxed into her seat and when the server came to take their drink orders, the smile she gave was bright and genuine.

"You know the rumors are already flying," she said, leaning across the table and darting her eyes toward another couple across the room—Vicky and her husband. "You're okay with that?"

She was still worried about him being a playboy. Probably always would be. She didn't seem the jealous type, not in any unhealthy way at least, but she had a broad streak of insecurity. Totally understandable considering her past. He couldn't erase it, but he could damn well avoid triggering it.

"More than okay." He caught Vicky staring at them and gave her a short wave. "I told you before, I'm not trying to hide."

Their drinks arrived, and Cat quickly ordered. Nate picked something at random, he almost didn't care about the food. The whole point of the evening out was to spend time with Cat, away from the house and her responsibilities. To relax and enjoy each other's company, and hopefully, put some of Cat's insecurities to rest.

They sat and talked with no agenda, no pressing to-do list. For no reason other than getting to know each other better. He barely noticed the server coming and going, and he couldn't remember what he ate.

She told him about growing up in Vegas and he talked about playing football in Savannah. He still felt like she was leaving out details, lots of them, but then again so was he. She mentioned college—she didn't start until she was almost twenty, and then fast-tracked to complete her business degree in only three years.

"What about you?" she asked. "I know you went to college."

Nate chuckled and stroked her hand. "You have me at a disadvantage. Dominico did a background check on me."

Cat lifted a shoulder and cocked her head. There was nothing guarded in her expression. "Yes," she replied. "I don't think that's a surprise. And he didn't tell me details. Just the basics. Dominico is the soul of discretion at times." She laughed, turned her hand and caught his fingers, holding them tightly. "He can also be a horrific gossip, but in your case, he kept pretty tight-lipped. Which means he likes you, or at least respects you. So, spill."

That did surprise Nate. He'd figured Dominico gave her everything, but either she was lying, and he didn't think that was the case, or he was wrong. He'd been wrong before.

"I uh…" he cleared his throat. He didn't like talking about himself. He really didn't like revealing his background. It gave too many people the wrong impression. "My parents pushed me towards a career in government."

The look of surprise on her face was almost comical. Nate gave a wry smile and shrugged. "But uh, you know how my college days ended. That career path didn't work out so well for me."

That answer seemed to satisfy her. She tucked a loose curl of hair behind her ear and fixed him with a look of childlike innocence. "I want dessert."

Nate tossed his head back and laughed. "I thought you were dessert."

The pink flush that rushed to color her cheeks was at odds with the smirk she flashed at him. She might still be embarrassed to think those thoughts, but she certainly wasn't ashamed of acting on them.

"I'm greedy," she replied, her fingers sliding over his suggestively. "I want both."

Nate sucked in a breath, ready to skip the check and just leave a pile of cash on the table. She'd said she wanted dessert, so he would sit in absolute torture while she indulged.

"What are you thinking?" she asked. "You have a deliciously evil look on your face."

Nate raised an eyebrow and smiled. "Order dessert. And when we get home, I'll have mine." He caressed her hand slowly. "And I plan on taking my time. It's only fair. If I have to wait, then so do you."

Cat's lips parted in a gasp and her eyes glazed over. The server chose that minute to come by with the dessert menu, and Nate had to keep himself from laughing as Cat visibly reined herself in.

If this was what life was like with Cat, he didn't want to imagine things any other way.

# Chapter Twenty-Two

Cat sat in the uncomfortable plastic chair, staring across the scarred desk at the bank manager. In the man's defense, he at least had the presence of mind to muster an apologetic gaze as he pushed the paperwork to her.

"I don't know why none of this turned up during your due diligence." His voice was smarmy and sounded more like a used car salesman than a banker.

Cat opened her mouth to speak, but Dominico raised his hand, silencing her. He leaned forward, bracing his elbows on the banker's desk. "You are telling me this bank holds a five hundred-thousand-dollar loan with Bristol Park as collateral, and this did not turn up on any credit checks, nor in any of Susan Bristol's records?" He crossed himself at the mention of Susan.

"I'm telling you that it has only been a matter of months since she passed. This is not out of the ordinary. The loan was originally for half a million dollars, yes, but Ms. Bristol was making regular payments. It was only when she defaulted on those payments that we tried to contact her."

Cat pulled the papers toward her and scanned the pages. A secured loan for half a million dollars, taken out ten years ago. There was no doubt it was legit. The paperwork was all in order. The question was, why? And where had the money gone? There was nothing to indicate... She glared at the date again. Her birthday. Her eighteenth birthday.

"Huh," Cat muttered and sat up straighter. "Who was the payee on the loan?"

Dominico's eyes went wide. The paperwork they were looking at only specified the terms of repayment—an automatic withdrawal from an interest earning account, at this bank. No wonder Dominico had missed that—it was buried and connected to an account Cat had chosen to close. The bigger question was why the bank hadn't notified her of that when she closed it.

She scanned the paperwork again and handed the stack to Dominico. There was nothing about where the money had gone. Dominico shuffled through papers and shook his head.

The man raised his eyebrows and scanned the papers himself. "That's...uh..." He flipped to the last page and frowned. "Most unusual." He pulled his laptop over and typed for a moment, then sat back. "This was done on the old system. But...ah...here... The entire sum was paid out to Sophia Bristol."

Dominico swore. Cat flopped back in her seat and closed her eyes. "I'm assuming we can resume making payments, rather than pay it all off at once?"

The banker shook his head. "I'd like to say that, but..." He spread his hands over the worn desk. "All of our outstanding loans were recently purchased by another company, and they are not offering terms."

Cat nodded at Dominico, then folded her hands and watched her lawyer turn into a smiling, evil shark.

"I need the name of the loan officer," Dominico began. Cat tuned him out, this was one of many things he was good at — digging into the little details, finding problems, inconsistencies, and making sure they never happened again. By the time they left the bank manager's office, the man was looking pale and shaken. He also seemed genuinely apologetic. Not that Cat was sure she believed that act.

Cat sat back in the plush leather of Dominico's car. "Now what?" She tossed the folder into the backseat and glared at the bank building. "They can't just buy a loan and refuse to take payments."

He shook his head and sighed. "The trouble is this loan is in default and it's the same investor behind TravelCorp's money. We can request terms, and if they refuse, it…"

"Goes to court," Cat finished for him, and thudded her head into the seat. "Can they refuse to accept payment of the total amount due?"

He raised a shoulder. "They can try. They can claim default and move to collect on the collateral."

She sighed. "Giving them the property for a cool two hundred and fifty thousand dollars owed. Not even money out of their pockets. I've got to hand it to them for a slick move." Cat paused, the sting of potential failure digging at her. Everything she'd worked for here could be lost if she didn't play this one right. Not for the first time, Cat considered walking away. She silently cursed her mother, for the umpteenth time in her life. No. She wouldn't give up. *Bristol Park is mine, dammit.* "Can they do that, if we are trying to give them the full amount due?"

He shook his head. "Not really." He cleared his throat. "They can try. They can threaten. They can refuse, and make you take them to court over it — and it will cost. And they have deep pockets. But..." He dropped a wink at her. "You know I'll work for free."

"You don't need to do that," she whispered. Still, it was good to know. "So, my grandmother, who I thought was dead, sent my mother half a million bucks on my eighteenth birthday."

"I gather you didn't see any of it?"

Cat laughed. "Not even the evidence of any of it." No, her mother had threatened to kick her out for her eighteenth birthday. All dreams of state college on a partial scholarship died as Sophia told her only daughter to increase her hours to full-time and start paying half the bills or get out and finally marry that rich boy she'd been dating. There was never enough money to go around, and Cat had taken to hiding her tips, asking one of the casino managers to hold money for her each week so her mother wouldn't get her hands on it. Because the moment Sophia got a dollar in her hands, two dollars were spent.

Cat had tried to hide it from Jimmy. He'd seemed so sweet and charming. So elegant and refined compared to her mother, who on good days managed to stay sober enough to work a full shift at an off-strip casino. And Cat had quickly fallen head over heels for him. But he'd figured it out when she went looking for a cheap place she could afford on her salary.

He promised he'd take care of her. He even promised to take care of her mother. And that's exactly what he'd done. They were married six months later, and he'd moved them out of Vegas to Atlantic City, set

Sophia up in an apartment in the same building as them, and given her a generous monthly allowance. If there had been five hundred thousand dollars around, Cat had no clue where it had gone.

"You took over my mother's finances when I married Jimmy," she said, giving Dominico a side eyed look. "Did you see any trace of that kind of money?"

He shook his head. "No, but I didn't go digging that deep." He spread his hands. "Your mother, God rest her soul, she was a mess. You know that. There were bills overdue. Accounts that were in collections. Who knows? But I'll go back through and see what I can find if you'd like. But you know she was doing more than booze."

Cat held up her hand. Yes, she'd known. She just didn't want to think about it. On top of alcoholism, Sophia Bristol had a taste for a variety of drugs—cocaine to get her through a long shift, heroin to feel good after the shift was over. It was entirely possible she'd owed a dealer. Or several dealers.

"Sometimes I wonder why Jimmy ever took a chance on me," Cat whispered. "She was so much of a risk."

Dominico laughed, not a cruel sound, but not nice either. "Because Jimmy saw you—your brains, your beauty, your determination, everything you are—and he had to have that. I'll say one good thing about that son-of-a-bitch, he could read people. He knew what he was looking at."

"Too bad I couldn't give him what he really wanted, huh?" Cat scoffed. The words stung, not as bad as they used to, but it still hurt.

"Blessing in disguise. Jimmy would have made a lousy father," Dominico replied. "And having a kid would have tied you to Mama Corozzo in ways you don't want. I know it hurts and you see it as a failure. You think I don't know that? But it's not your fault."

Cat hung her head. Dominico's wife had miscarried time and time again, until they'd finally stopped trying. He knew her pain better than any man could be expected to. She squeezed his hand and took a deep breath.

"Enough of the maudlin," she said. "I can cash out retirement and investment accounts, that should get enough. Get me whatever paperwork you need to act on my behalf and deal with this. Pay it. Find out what you can about where the money went, but I'm not sure I want to know. My mother caused enough pain while she was alive. I do not need her coming back from the grave to stir up more trouble."

Dominico crossed himself at her blasphemy before laughing along with her.

* * * *

Nate moved through the dim, early morning kitchen as he started the coffee. His gaze fell on a pile of papers strewn over the counter, and he flipped on a light. It wasn't like Cat to leave paperwork lying around. She'd seemed stressed when she came back from her meeting with Dominico a few days ago. She hadn't been willing to talk about it, and he'd fought the tide of insecurity her silence raised in him.

He wasn't her business partner. She didn't have to talk to him. Hell, despite the fact they slept in the same bed every night, he was barely more than her lover. Because he was too afraid to ask for more.

He picked up the top paper. Delinquent notice. What? She hadn't said anything about a delinquent loan. Or about owing so much money. As far as he knew, she had everything under control. He skimmed to the bottom, looking for the amount due and sucked in a harsh breath.

Even the Ice Princess would have a hard time coming up with a quarter of a million and still have enough money to do what she wanted with this place.

She hadn't been honest with him.

His fingers clenched on the paper. He set it aside and flipped through the small stack. Just the one notice — that was good news at least. She hadn't told him about this. Maybe that was why she left the papers out — something she never did. An ugly voice chimed in his head. She wanted him to find it. To see. Was she waiting for him to offer help?

Nate shook his head. That made no sense. That was his past talking. Cat didn't know his family, his past.

The ugly voice raised up again. *She's got a very high-priced and possibly unscrupulous attorney. Who could have gone digging.*

That thought knocked the breath out of him. He tossed the papers down and rushed from the kitchen to the porch. He tugged on his gear and pushed out the door, needing the cold wind, the physical exertion, to clear his head.

He trudged through the slush and struck out away from the cottages, heading instead for the trail to the river. He skipped the high trail that would take him up the bluff, instead he scrambled down the rocky path to the river's edge where he found a downed tree and sat, listening to the trickle of water and crackles of the last ice breaking up.

Downstream just a few yards, the river churned over rocks in a small set of rapids. From there, it twisted lazily along for miles. A perfect place for tubing. Much of it framed by Bristol Park, or by State Forestry lands.

If Cat wanted to turn this place around and get it operational again, there were plenty of resources to make it an attractive destination.

Abundant hiking, the river — where you could swim, or fish, kayak or canoe, or go tubing. Plus, Bristol Park itself. All within a few hours' drive from New York City.

All just a buttload of expensive work away. Oh, and a quarter million-dollar debt.

Not good. Not good at all.

He wanted to see her succeed. Not just because he was sleeping with her. Abbeydon needed Bristol Park if it was going to survive. A thriving family resort could turn the entire town around for the good. Much better for the locals than a corporate entertainment complex, or casino. Those would just push small business to the side, to wither and die. While what Cat had in mind...that could only benefit the small businesses in town.

Nate shook his head. There was no doubt she was doing something good here.

Cat wasn't his ex.

He shook his head again and pushed himself up.

He didn't want to believe Cat was like Erin. Couldn't believe it. He'd give it time. See how she handled this whole thing, and he'd guard his emotions.

Well, guard them from getting any deeper than they already were. He made his way back up the trail to the house. Cat was in the kitchen, the counter still a cluttered mess, a cup of coffee in her hand.

The tug on Nate's heart was undeniable. Her bright eyes fixed on him, and her lips tipped into a soft smile. Her curls whirled about her face in a riot of coppery red, as if still tousled from the night before. The tug traveled south as his dick woke up with the memories of their middle of the night activities.

Nate leaned down and kissed her quickly, muttering something about showering. He retreated to the bathroom, unable to control the swirl of emotions at war in him.

Either she was the coldest and most calculating person he'd ever met, or she was one hundred percent genuine. The hot water did nothing to wash away thoughts of them tangled in the sheets last night—his hands tangled in those glorious curls as he'd emptied himself into her. Nor did it erase memories of those loan papers this morning.

Nate shut off the water and wrapped a towel around himself. He didn't bother getting dressed. He barely bothered drying off. He needed her wrapped around him now. This instant. To drive those nagging doubts away.

The kitchen counter was clear when he came in, and he entertained the idea of stopping and asking her about the papers. Then she turned from the sink and her eyebrows rose at the sight of him. Her cheeks flushed bright pink and her lips parted in a gasp. She crossed to him in two steps.

Her hands slid up his bare chest, driving all thought from his head except how quickly he could get her naked in front of him. He pressed his lips to hers in a desperate kiss, the ache to be as close to her as possible building.

He tugged at her shirt, pulling it over her head and revealing no bra. He fastened his mouth on a nipple, sucking until she curled her fingers behind his head and pulled him to her other breast. He slid his hands down, pulling the soft pants down her thighs. Hooking his fingers into her panties and tugging them down as well.

She squealed when he cupped her ass and lifted her, balancing her on the edge of the counter before sinking to his knees in front of her.

He looked up. Those beautiful blue eyes drilled into him, full of ache and desire. She wanted him as much as he wanted her. That look told him of her need, as deep and consuming as his own. He pushed her legs apart and relished her gasp as he lowered his head.

Every part of her was intoxicating. Delicious, and demanding to be touched and loved. She shuddered under his tongue, clenched around his fingers.

The sound of his name falling from her lips nearly sent him over the edge. His dick throbbed, demanding to be a part of the fun. Apparently, Cat had the same idea because her fingers clutched at his wrists and tugged, pulling him up to her.

Her legs wrapped around his waist, and he was there, settled into her warmth and wetness. The smooth feel of her drove all other thoughts from his head as she began to rock against him.

She arched and slid, then lay back on the counter, her stunning curves on display—all for him. The sounds coming from her mouth drove him mad. Everywhere he touched, her skin prickled in response. His thumb stroked down her belly, found her clit, and she shuddered into trembling cries.

Her gaze flew to his and held as her body clenched and spasmed. Looking into those blue depths, Nate knew he was lost. An absolute goner. No way to guard a heart that was already all in. He stroked his thumb over her again, eliciting another cascade of shaking and moaning. Then he closed his fingers over her wrists, pulling her hands above her head. He scanned her face for any shred of doubt or uncertainty but found none.

He pinned her hands to the island, bracing his elbows next to her. He nuzzled her neck and she turned, giving him easier access. He let his teeth graze her skin and she moaned. A bit harder and she arched against him. He bit down and she hissed out a "yes", her fingers clenching in his hands. That single word shattered the last shred of his restraint.

Cat cried out as Nate lifted himself up, leaving her feeling cold and bereft, even though he was still buried inside her. The look on his face brought any complaints to an abrupt halt. The beast was at the edge of its leash. Something wild and untamed was in front of her, barely restrained. A tiny shiver coursed down her spine — anticipation, desire. She arched her back, hoping to give him a better view.

Nate uttered a low growl and his fingers tightened against hers. His thrusts, already forceful, came hard and deep. Cat lifted her legs, spread them wide. Again, that low growl as he shifted his body until every thrust rasped against her clit.

He was still holding back. She could feel it — sense how close he was to his edge. She pulled against his hands and felt them tighten. The look on his face — pure pleasure, but something else, a brief moment of uncertainty. His hands loosened. Cat pouted and shook her head.

"Please, Nate." She whispered the words. "Don't stop."

His movements stuttered and his fingers twitched against hers.

"Fuck me." That came out louder. More certain. "Please, Nate. Take me."

Every trace of uncertainty left his face, replaced with a dark passion. His fingers tightened, but he stepped back, slid out of her and Cat wailed in protest. But his strong hands pulled her to stand, turned her so his body pressed into her back. His hands held hers, pinned to the counter in front of her as his teeth found her neck again.

The first rasp of his teeth was gentle. Then harder. He nibbled, sucked, and bit until Cat was grinding her ass back against him, desperate to feel him inside her once more.

He pushed her down to the counter, bending her over so her face rested on the cool marble. Gently, oh so gently, he slid her arms around and clasped her hands together in the small of her back then held them there. His other hand slipped into her hair, fisted and tugged until her head came up and an electric jolt shot straight to her groin.

His body pressed against hers as he leaned down, his cheek rough with stubble as it brushed her skin.

"Cat," his voice rasped in her ear, low and full of desire. "You're mine."

A thrill chased through her at those words. He pushed into her in one stroke, and she lifted her hips to take him, wanting as much as she could get. She'd never had sex like this. Never anything so wild and passionate.

He let go of her hands and cupped her breast, lifting her torso off the counter. The hand in her hair tightened, keeping her arched against him. His teeth grazed her shoulder, and his breath warmed her skin.

"Mine." It was a growl this time. Punctuated with a quick nip from his teeth.

His hand stroked down her body, found her clit, and a rush of pleasure heated her until she was panting, shoving back against him, incoherently begging for more.

Cat cried out as another orgasm tore through her, then shook again as Nate's grip tightened, his pace quickened, and his breath came ragged and harsh against the back of her neck. Her name was a roar on his lips as he crushed her to him and held her there.

She shuddered out a slow breath and Nate's hand stroked, soothing over her body as he whispered into her ear.

"You are so beautiful." Tender words after the animalistic pleasure they'd just shared. "Are you okay?" He trailed kisses along her shoulder, his lips tracing the places where his teeth had been. "I…umm… lost control there a bit."

A dull ache already settled between her legs, and his lips were proving the bites were harder than she'd thought. But…hadn't she been enjoying it, asking for more even? She sighed and melted into him, feeling something tight and brittle inside her let go.

"I'm more than okay." Whatever this had started out as, this was more than a fling. Far more. Cat couldn't imagine letting him go. "Mine," he had said. Well, as far as she was concerned, the reverse was also true. Not that she planned to tell him that just yet. "You can lose control like that anytime. In fact, please do."

# Chapter Twenty-Three

Nate pulled up at Juan's and scowled at the sleek Mercedes in the lot. Not the usual kind of car you saw around here. He pushed into the store and immediately wished he could backpedal out of there, but the bell over the door had caught the attention of the woman standing at the counter.

Erin.

Well, hell.

Except she wasn't alone. Next to her was dark-haired man in a suit that screamed money. The man cast a dismissive glance at Nate, then turned back to Juan, handing him a business card.

"Give me a call if you have any questions." He turned to face the crowd gathered near the wood stove. "That goes for everyone." He raised his voice a bit. "I'm happy to address any concerns you may have."

The man brushed past Nate with barely a glance. Erin, however, stopped in front of him. "You could have told me you were fucking the woman who owns Bristol Park."

She spoke loudly enough that heads turned. Nate didn't think. He grabbed her arm and pulled her into the hall between the Juan's and the coffee shop, away from the gossip crew. Not that a few feet would help. If Erin decided to make a scene, half the town would hear her yelling at the top of her lungs.

"First, my relationships are none of your business." He ground the words out through his teeth. "Haven't been for many years—and that was your choice."

She opened her mouth to say something, but he shook his head. "Don't even start. I don't know what game you're pulling here, but just…don't."

Erin leaned back against the wall and regarded him as if he were an amusement. How had he ever thought they'd be something? "Second, what the hell are you doing here?"

Erin slid a hand into her purse and came out with a business card. She tucked it into his pants pocket, her eyes on his the whole time. The heavy perfume she'd always favored circling him as if it were a snake.

"I'm the project manager on this nightmare," she said, her breath hot against his neck. "And thanks to your girlfriend deciding to keep that damn place, we're facing some struggles that we didn't anticipate."

That didn't make any sense. TravelCorp had bought up adjacent parcels, but aside from the first offer, hadn't done anything about Bristol Park. *Except that damn loan. Shit.* The conversation he'd overheard between Cat and Dominico suddenly made more sense—the company who owned the loan was also TravelCorp's primary investor. And TravelCorp needed the property.

"Don't fight this." Erin's hand trailed from his pocket up his stomach and over his chest. "We've both made mistakes in the past, but we can fix that." She stepped closer to him. Close enough he could feel the warmth coming off her.

Nate reached out and grasped her wrists, pushing her back away from him. He released her and stepped back, creating more distance. The last thing he needed was one of the old coots seeing him here with Erin and then saying something to Cat. She'd brand him a cheater, just like her ex, before he could even blink.

"Sorry, I'm not buying that one." Movement outside the window caught his eye. The suit stood by the Mercedes, flipping his wrist to glance at his watch as he tapped his foot. Obviously impatient. Something clicked in Nate's brain.

Erin was smart, but she'd never been one for doing real work. "What's the matter, hon?" He pitched his voice low and sweet. "He your boss or your boyfriend? Either way, doesn't look like he's too happy with things. Not making the progress you thought you would?"

The flash of worry in her eyes was quick, then covered up with Erin's too brittle smile. The pieces started to line up. The company had been working to get Susan Bristol to sell, and she had refused. Several times. After she died, they'd seen an opportunity. When the executor actually found Cat, and rather than sell on the cheap, she'd decided to stay, that opportunity had got a lot more complicated.

"Nate." Erin sidled close to him again. "This is important to me. And you could really benefit here."

Her eyes flicked to the walkway leading back into the store. She gave a quick smile, closed the distance between them and planted a kiss on his lips. Her fingers trailed down his chest as she pulled away.

"See you around, Nate." Erin waggled her fingers at him and blew a kiss and was gone. Leaving Nate staring into the wide, shocked eyes of Gina.

Nate slumped against the wall with a groan, barely resisting the urge to bang his head into the wall. Repeatedly. Not good. This could not be good.

# Chapter Twenty-Four

Cat picked up her coffee and nearly bumped into Gina as she turned from the counter. The other woman grabbed Cat's elbow and practically dragged her to a table in the corner, far away from anyone else.

"Spill." Gina breathed the word out as she slid into a chair. "Juan said some real estate lawyer was all over him and other businesses, trying to get them on board with some public meeting coming up. And there's rumor you're selling Bristol Park."

Gina leaned her elbows on the table, her eyebrows almost in her hairline. Cat sank onto the opposite chair and sipped her coffee. She'd heard the gossip—and knew what was fact and fiction. Or at least most of it.

Fact. TravelCorp was buying up parcels of property surrounding Abbeydon and had put offers in on a few businesses in town, including the general store. They had also proposed some sort of cooperative, but as far as Cat knew, they hadn't made any foreclosure threats—except indirectly to her. Might as well give Gina some gossip.

"They're trying to get their hands on my place for some sort of big development," Cat replied. "The thing is, that requires zoning changes, and public meetings where business owners have the opportunity to argue for, or against, the zoning change. No public meeting was scheduled. I've tried to get one set, but their legal team keeps getting the date pushed back. I'm not selling."

Gina leaned further in, the smell of Juicy Fruit coming off her in a wave. She grabbed Cat's wrist and caught her eye, her face sympathetic. "Look, I know I have a reputation as a big gossip, and it's true. But I also look out for people." She swallowed hard. Her eye twitched. A weight dropped in Cat's stomach, and she wasn't sure she wanted to hear what Gina had to say next.

"I came into the store yesterday," Gina began. "Some suit from TravelCorp had been hanging around and I was trying to get the dirt. And I saw Nate. With a woman. And they were uh…pretty close."

That weight uncoiled into a snake, twisting and spinning in Cat's insides. "No euphemisms, Gina. No hints. Just tell me what you mean." Her voice sounded dead in her ears, and something must have made Gina think. The other woman released her wrist, and her expression was deep sorrow. And absolutely genuine.

"Some tall blonde has been around. She's part of TravelCorp. And she and Nate were over in the hall — by all the historical pictures and tourist stuff. And they were kissing."

The snake twisted again, hot and then cold as it slithered into her chest. Wrapping around and around her heart. Squeezing. Cold and brittle and strangled. Cat swallowed hard and forced her face to stay calm.

"Define kissing." She had to know. Didn't want to but had to.

"I only saw a moment," Gina admitted. "She was up against him and kissed him. But it was…close. Intimate. Nate saw me down the little hall after she left, and he didn't look pleased."

Cat nodded. No, he wouldn't. He'd been caught. The coils around her heart tightened as a litany of what-ifs ran through her mind. What if it was innocent? Wouldn't he have said something to her when he came home yesterday if it was? What if it wasn't what Gina thought? Well, then what was it? And did it matter?

Cat squeezed Gina's hand, mumbled a thank you and stood. She managed to get out of the coffee shop and halfway to her car before the tears hit. She ignored them and kept walking, trying to remind herself that Nate wasn't Jimmy, but Gina's story robbed that of its power.

*Turns out, Nate is just like Jimmy.* Content to have Cat at home but playing around with someone else on the side. And someone from the development company trying to steal her property no less.

Cat fumbled her car key. Pushed the wrong button. Tried again, yanked the door open and slid into the seat. She had to get out of town. Away from anywhere people could see her. And not home. Nate was there. She couldn't face him right now.

She drove out of town, blindly turning down whatever looked like the least traveled road. Twenty minutes later, she pulled into a narrow gravel strip alongside the blacktop. A break in the trees offered a spectacular view of the valley below. And Bristol Park—the white house just visible through the early spring trees. She sucked in a shaky breath and let her head drop onto the steering wheel.

This wasn't supposed to happen. She wasn't going to get caught up with another playboy. But Nate had seemed different. He'd said he was. He'd shown her time and time again that he was. And she'd believed him. She'd fallen for him, hook, line and sinker. There was no other reason for her to feel this way. No other reason for the empty pit that was her stomach. Or the cold bands now firmly wrapped around her heart and squeezing tighter every breath she took.

She loved him.

Goddammit. She'd gone and fallen in love with Nate Stewart.

And look where that had got her. She fumbled her phone from her purse and punched out a text to Dominico.

*TravelCorp – who's the suit in town right now? And there's a woman on their team. Who is she?*

She hit send and tossed the phone into the passenger seat. She took a deep breath and blew it out on a measured count, then pulled down the visor and checked her reflection in the mirror. Haunted eyes stared back. Cat scrubbed a hand over her face and snapped the visor shut.

It was time for her to treat this like the business that it was. And business? That, she understood. TravelCorp wanted to fight dirty? Well, okay then. Caitlin Bristol-Corozzo was not the type to back down.

Her phone quacked with a text. Dominico.

*The man is Gerald Spade and he's an attorney for TravelCorp. The company is close-mouthed about whatever they're doing up there, but Erin Blake is listed as contact for some surveys they've applied for. She's also listed as a project manager on their site. I'll do some digging on both.*

Cat tucked her phone into her purse and smiled. Dominico was on the job. And he would not let her down. He never had. Maybe the only person in her life she could say that about.

* * * *

The afternoon sun slanted through the trees as Nate tossed yet another roll of ugly carpet into the rolloff. Why anyone had thought it was a good idea to cover the beautiful heart pine floors in the big house's guest rooms, he had no idea. Cat had been right—the carpet had to go.

Tires crunched on the gravel. Cat had been gone longer than expected. She had just run to town to mail a bunch of paperwork to Dominico. Knowing her, she couldn't resist stopping for coffee. *And…oh shit. If she bumped into Gina…*

Nate looked up as the car door slammed, and his heart sank. The Ice Princess was back, and not in a good way. Cat was dressed the same as when she'd left, but something had changed. Her hair was still a riot of curls—partly his fault, as he couldn't keep his hands out of the glorious mass while they were tangled in her sheets, her body wrapped around his in ways that made the world fade away. Something in the way she carried herself was different. Cold and distant.

He brushed carpet fuzz from his pants, suddenly feeling sweaty and sloppy in her presence. *What the hell?* When had he become that kind of puppy dog? Who was he kidding? He'd given up trying to control his feelings for her before they'd ever gotten naked together. Now, he was too far gone. Seeing her return to Ice Princess mode shook him hard.

"I want you to pack your things and move to the cabin tonight." Cat's words rang cold in the spring air. "You can stay at the cabin for one week if you need to, but that's it."

She hadn't looked at him. She had addressed the tree behind him. Her chin tilted, that stubborn look on her face, and pain. A flash of something deep and hurting in her eyes before she blinked and it was gone, and her eyes were as cold as everything else about her.

"I'm guessing Gina had some juicy gossip." He tried to keep the bitterness from his voice. He'd known how Cat would react if she heard. Well, no…he hadn't known. Nothing could have prepared him for this degree of cold. As if every level of hell had frozen over, and she was the new queen of the underworld about to crush his soul.

"Does it matter?" Cat shook her head. "It's bad enough to hear from someone in town that you were kissing another woman. But for that woman to also be a project manager at the company trying to take this property from me is even worse."

"It isn't what you think…" Shit. The words were barely out of his mouth, and he knew they were wrong. So wrong. The flash of anger on her face confirmed it.

"I don't care what it was or is." Her voice was tight. Controlled. Her expression dead. "I care that you didn't have the courtesy to tell me — if you are seeing someone else, you should have told me. If you two met and sparks flew and one thing led to another, you should have told me. If it was her coming on to you, you should have told me. Do you see the pattern here?"

Nate nodded. Every fiber of his being screaming at it all. The hell of it was, she was right, but he'd been a coward. Too afraid of her response. Too afraid of hurting her, and now it was too late. Nothing he could say or do would fix that mistake.

"I'll get my things. I'll stay in the cabin tonight, then be out of your hair in the morning." He turned for the house, every step feeling like another crack in an already broken vessel. He stopped at the door and turned back to her. "Business is business, Cat. If you want me to continue working for you, I will."

Those blue eyes flashed again, something he couldn't name, and wasn't sure he wanted to. "I'll pay you back wages, if that's what you're worried about."

The words were a slap in the face. "Hell no." Harsher than he intended. "Jesus. I asked you to quit paying me…"

"And I should never have agreed," she cut him off. "Just…let's end this like responsible grown-ups. It was a mistake. You and I were a mistake."

Nate winced. She might as well have stuck a knife in his heart. "Don't say that," he whispered. He came down the steps, intent on telling her they weren't a mistake. The look on her face stopped him cold. "I'll get packed and go tonight. I'll give you the names of some guys who can help with the work around here."

Nate turned and made his way upstairs, into her bedroom, where even now, the scent of them lingered. Her soft rose soap. His beard oil. And them. The unmistakable smell of sex coming from the unmade bed.

His eyes stung and he swallowed hard, forcing back emotions he didn't want to admit. Never mind give in to. He did debate giving in to the desire to pull the sheets back up, fluff the pillows, and make the bed neat and pretty so she would have to deal with that reminder when she crawled in to sleep tonight.

Instead, he stripped the sheets and blankets and tossed them into the hamper so Cat wouldn't have to do that, then gathered his clothes and scoured upstairs, leaving not even a sock behind. He made his way downstairs to gather his tools — every item a reminder of how intertwined their lives had become. How at home he'd been here, in her house. In her space.

She sat outside on the porch, eying him as he tossed load after load into his truck. He kept expecting her to stop him. Or maybe it was hope. She didn't. Not even when he trudged down to the cabin and out to the shed to pick up the rest of his tools. Things that normally lived in his truck when he was on a job, but this hadn't been just a job.

Nate pressed his lips together on the final run to his truck. He wanted to drop to his knees in front of her, apologize for being a coward, for not talking to her, for not trusting her. Now was not the time. He wanted to beg for a chance — do whatever it took to convince her he wasn't what she believed. That would only make things worse.

Whatever was going on with her, whatever fears had been triggered, she wasn't in a place to hear his pleas as anything more than the things she likely heard time and again from her late husband. He'd just be pounding more nails into his coffin.

Better to walk away softly. Give her some space and hope they could find a way to get through this later. He'd wait. He had to. She had him, heart and soul, and he had to believe they could try again.

He cleared his throat and stood at the foot of the porch steps. "I'm sorry, Cat, and I know that probably doesn't mean shit to you right now, but it's true. I'm sorry. I'll text you the names of some good…"

"Don't bother," she said. "I can get names from Juan. If you're done just leave your keys on the porch bench."

With that, she turned her back on him and went inside. Leaving Nate standing there feeling empty and so lost he didn't know which way was up.

"I love you." The words came without him planning, or even thinking them. Whispered into the early evening wind and carried away to be lost in the trees. The truth of them chipping away at his resolve until he shook with the effort to rein it all in. The cracked bits of his heart shattered like glass, slicing into old hurts and reopening old wounds. This was why he'd denied himself for so many years. He knew this pain. Only this time, it was far worse.

He loved Cat. As completely as he'd ever loved anyone. Bone deep and steeped into his soul. He couldn't imagine a life without her by his side. Didn't want to. He forced his hand to let go of the banister. To dig the keys from his pocket and leave them. Forced his feet to turn toward his truck. When all he wanted to do was stay rooted to that spot until she relented and listened. Until she forgave him.

Now was not the time for that. For now, he'd go home and wait.

# Chapter Twenty-Five

The empty towel hook mocked her. The space in the shower where Nate's shampoo usually sat seemed to glare in anger. And when she finally crawled into bed, exhausted from crying all night, all she could smell was Nate.

She'd made the bed with fresh sheets, but his spicy scent was everywhere. On the pillow. The comforter. Every time she moved, reminders of him washed over her, bringing on a fresh spate of tears and she wondered if she'd been too harsh.

Then she'd remember Dominico's call later that night. Erin Blake. Project manager for TravelCorp and Nate's ex-fiancée. The woman he claimed used him for money and left him for his best friend when Nate's money ran out. The woman he claimed had hurt him.

And the woman Gina had seen kissing him in the general store.

His ex-fiancée.

There was no reason he should have kept that a secret. He'd told her how hurt he'd been. She'd seen that truth in his eyes. Felt it in him, the same truth she recognized in herself when she'd first found out about Jimmy's extracurricular activities.

There was no reason he shouldn't have trusted her with that.

And the only reasons she could imagine were not good. The first that occurred to her, he was still in love with Erin — which would go a long way to explaining why he didn't dally with the women in town, despite them fawning all over him. At least she knew he'd been honest about that. Gina and crew had made that clear. No matter how much they all might have wanted, Nate was always the gentleman.

But then what was she? What were they? If he still loved Erin, was Cat an attempt to get over his ex, once and for all?

No, that didn't make sense.

Then maybe it was a plan. Maybe he was trying to seduce her. To convince her to sell. Or create some scandal that would drive her out of the town. But that didn't make sense either. Nate had been nothing but helpful. Supportive. And he'd acted time and again to protect her.

No matter what excuses or causes she came up with, she could shoot them all down based on her experiences with Nate. All except one.

He was just like Jimmy.

And there, all reason fled. Even Dominico couldn't get through that wall, despite the logical arguments he threw at her.

Cat tossed the covers back and stripped her clothes off. She grabbed a fresh towel and pajamas and trudged into the room Dominico had used when he visited. The sheets had been washed and the bed made. More importantly, Nate had never slept in this room. After showering, she climbed into a bed mercifully free of the smell of Nate, and the reminder of what they had shared just that morning.

She pushed those thoughts aside. She needed to sleep. In the morning, she had a lot of work to do — starting with finding a new handyman.

\* \* \* \*

The smell of sawdust tickled his nose even through the face mask. A flash of movement at the back door distracted him and he powered down the Skilsaw. Charlie stood at the door, waving to get his attention. Nate pushed the earmuffs back and waited for her to speak.

"Lunch is on," she said. "I hollered twice." She huffed back into the house, ripping a rare laugh from him. He'd never met her mother, the woman had passed shortly before Nate came to town, but he imagined Charlie was a carbon copy.

He dusted off his hands and took off the goggles and mask before heading inside to wash up. Juan had been meaning to tear down his old shed and build something bigger, but he'd never get around to it — he was always busy at the store. After sitting at home a few days, with nothing but time to think about Cat, Nate had gone to Juan's one morning, tools in hand and gotten to work. To his credit, Juan hadn't asked questions, but he sent a sandwich out at lunch time. That was a week ago. Nate was almost done with the shed now and had no clue what he'd do to occupy his time next.

Charlie tossed a plate of sandwiches on the table just before she ran out the door, hollering something about meeting her boyfriend for a movie. Juan heaved a sigh and sat down, shaking his head. Nate grabbed a plate and joined his friend.

"She does know I can make my own lunch, right?" Nate asked, bringing a chuckle and a wistful smile from Juan.

"Yeah," he replied. "She knows I can make my own, too. She's still got a wide streak of take-care-of-dad going on. I figured dating might change that, but so far..." He trailed off. "She'll grow out of it eventually."

Nate wasn't so sure. Charlie hovered over her dad, as if she could ensure she wouldn't lose another parent by sheer force of her will and presence.

"Besides," Juan continued, "you're one to talk. I remember when you moved here. Kept quiet and just threw yourself into working. Helping anybody who needed help. Like fixing people's things could fix all your problems." He nodded out the window at the nearly finished shed. "Not that I'm complaining, but..."

Nate chuckled. Then, like now, figuring out a solution to a tangible problem kept his mind from dwelling on thoughts he didn't want to entertain. He worked himself hard enough that he'd just fall into bed at night—too exhausted to do anything but succumb to sleep.

"Things make sense," he replied. "Something's broken or not working, you figure it out. People..." he blew out a breath. "People have history."

Nate drew in another slow breath, counting to ten before letting it out. Talking about his feelings was not his strong suit. The week without Cat had twisted him up in ways he could never have imagined. He'd considered going to the liquor store and getting a six pack. Or hell, a bottle of something stronger. Had even gotten in his truck and was halfway down his drive before good sense took over. He'd started on Juan's shed the very next morning.

"I messed up with Cat." Just saying the words out loud hurt. Juan paused mid-bite, arched an eyebrow at him, then nodded and continued chewing. "And I don't know how to fix it."

The story came out between bites of sandwich. Juan listened, nodding occasionally, laughing a time or two, and when it was done, he leaned back in his seat and shook his head.

"TravelCorp has been on me about a shopping complex they're planning," Juan said, the change of subject making Nate's head spin for a moment. "They had some fancy looking renderings of a big mall. It doesn't take a genius to figure out they can't do that with the little parcels they've bought up. And the big parcel, smack dab in the midst of it all, between the highway and the forestry land, is Bristol Park."

*Shit.* Nate hadn't been paying much attention to the business side of things. He always gave Cat her space, never asked questions. He knew the developer was purchasing plots of land, but not that those purchases all virtually surrounded her property.

"The song they're singing is how they want to make a big Main Street type experience a central part of this thing," Juan said. "All the local businesses, in shiny new digs made to look quaint and cute and have a hometown kinda feel. Trying to get us all to sing their praises at some public meeting."

Something nagged at the back of Nate's mind. "If the local businesses all move to the new shopping center, what happens to the town?"

Juan made a face and shook his head. "No idea. They tend to pull out a lot of talk of creating a walkable living space, which sounds great on the surface. But...I dunno. It feels...hollow."

Nate nodded. If the goal was a large shopping center, there would need to be affordable housing for the retail employees. What would be better than a nearby small town, properties recently vacated by merchants who moved to the shopping center? Juan was right, the idea of a walkable residential area downtown sounded charming, but the reality would likely be anything but. Housing around shopping centers tended to be very high end — and out of the price range of the typical retail employee, or borderline slums filled with cheap apartments where people never lived for long. It would change the entire character of the town.

On top of everything else, Cat thought he was somehow a part of all that. Just great.

# Chapter Twenty-Six

Cat stared down at her computer and nearly pitched it off the kitchen island. It had taken almost every penny she had to get the loan paid off and hire men to replace Nate. She pushed the thought of him aside. Dominico had suggested she talk to her brother-in-law, Tom, and she'd refused. Instead, she'd found local and semi-local help and the place was almost finished. The only things left were the pavilion, which needed a new roof, and some landscaping. And all the supplies for the picnic. And the catering.

With two weeks to go before the picnic, she wasn't worried. Or hadn't been.

She practically sighed in relief when tires crunched on the gravel outside. She automatically poured a coffee, Dominico would let himself in.

"Wow, Cat! This doesn't even look like the same place." Tom Corozzo stood in the kitchen doorway, with his hands shoved in his pockets. He nodded at the older man next to him. "I had to twist his arm to get him to bring me back out here."

Cat glared at Dominico. The last thing she wanted was the Corozzo family getting their fingers into this place. But right now, she might not have much choice. She heaved a sigh and spun the computer to face the two men while she poured another coffee.

"We were doing okay so long as we were getting local supplies, or things readily available." She dropped two coffees on the island and grabbed her own. "I had an order for supplies for the pavilion and got all the permit applications done. And they've postponed the public meeting, again." She pointed a finger at the screen.

Tom whistled and Dominico glared, then leaned back. "The delays to the permits are ridiculous, and I can put an end to that with one phone call. It's just politics and stalling tactics. Getting the public meeting set? That's beyond me."

Tom leaned back in and scrolled through the emails she had called up. "That part may be easy, but you've got a massive order for lumber that the supplier just said they can't ship before June. What the fuck?"

Cat threw her hands in the air, frustration finally getting the better of her. "The big box stores nearby are all sold out, can't seem to get any new supplies in before June. Juan at the general store tried to order from his usual supplier — same story." She sat her coffee cup down and shoved her hands through her curls, fighting back tears of frustration.

"I've got two weeks before the picnic and I can't get anything done." She leaned forward and tapped the computer, pulling up her list. "The lumber is just one part. The landscaping list is huge. I can't get the propane tank filled—which means I've got enough to get through into June, if it's just me on the property, but nothing extra. I'm just..."

She blew out a breath and flopped back against the counter. She'd planned. She'd organized. She'd pushed every bit of her emotional pain over losing Nate into a dark corner to be dealt with later and instead channeled everything into making Bristol Park work. She'd busted her ass harder than ever for the past two weeks, and the end was in sight. And now this.

Tom cleared his throat. "So...uh...you know I can help." He laid a gentle hand over Cat's.

She shook her head vigorously. "I don't want the family..."

"Hey," he interrupted. "I said I. Not we. Are you forgetting what company you sold me? Huh? C'mon, this corporation has deep pockets. You aren't gonna win this in court. You're gonna win this by out-thinking and out-stubborning them. And frankly, you're the most stubborn human being I've ever met. Not to mention one of the smartest. So, seriously, let's figure this out, huh?"

The resistance bubbled up and Cat clenched her fists, turning away from the men. "I don't have the money." She whispered the words into the window. She could throw it all in. Quit and walk away. Sign the agreement to sell the property and be done with it. She heaved a sigh. *No. Hell no.* She would not be pushed out and bullied like that.

Bristol Park had worked its way into her heart and soul. The idea of seeing the place thriving and open again made her spirit sing. It was the first thing in her life she'd felt was truly her endeavor. And completely free of her mother or the Corozzo family. But to do it, to keep it, she'd need help.

"You two talk over shipping and supplies." Dominico laid a hand on her back. "I need to make some phone calls about those permits, and I think I can get you a small business loan. But whatever, don't worry about the money. We'll take care of that."

Cat's ears perked up at that. The bank had not been too thrilled with the idea, as she had recently liquidated all her non-real estate assets and already gone through every cent. It was a big risk, and not one most lenders would be willing to take on. Dominico headed to the dining room, leaving her in the kitchen with Jimmy's little brother.

And for the first time, she felt nothing when thinking of Jimmy. Seething anger, abject humiliation and shame, hurt and most of all betrayal. All those she was used to. The absence of any negative emotions was new and welcome. It gave her hope that the gaping hole Nate had left in her heart might eventually heal as well. She shook herself and turned back to the computer.

"Let's see what you need," Tom said and pulled a notepad out of his bag. "Corozzo Shipping at your service."

Twenty minutes later, he tossed his cell phone onto the island and smiled. "You got a delivery coming with everything for the pavilion. I'll front the cash for the goods and delivery, you can take it outta what I still owe you on the business."

Cat chuckled. She'd been thinking of that as her emergency money. If this all fell apart, and she had nothing left, Tom still owed for the purchase of the shipping business. That would get her out of here and into a small rental somewhere nice. From there she could get a job. She'd survive.

Dominico came back into the room, his smile positively shark-like. "The permits for the picnic are handled. You should already have everything in your email."

Cat leaned back against the counter. Dominico, she trusted with her life. Tom, well, Tom wasn't Jimmy. And he at least understood her reluctance to involve the Corozzo clan. He'd made that clear when she sold him the shipping company. Maybe, just maybe, they could do this.

At dinner, Dominico cracked open a bottle of wine he'd brought, and they sat at the dining room table, the room glowing in candlelight and filled with their happy voices. This was what the place needed—life, laughter, love. Cat choked on that last thought and fought back tears. She should be content, no, ecstatic. But all she felt was emptiness. As if something were missing. No, not something. It was someone. *Nate*.

She'd seen him around town a few times. He looked as haggard as she felt. At the time, a small part of her had rejoiced in his discomfort. Once again, she shoved thoughts of him aside. Nope. He was just like Jimmy. He'd proven that.

"What happened between you two?" Dominico eyed her across the table while Tom gave a confused look.

"Drop it," Cat growled at him. She'd told him Nate was no longer in her employ and that was enough. Should have been enough.

"You know, I found no signs of him being involved with TravelCorp," Dominico pressed on. "Whatever did happen, it wasn't him using…"

"I said drop it." Cat hissed the words through gritted teeth. Dominico looked down at his plate, but Tom's eyes narrowed as he contemplated her over his wine glass.

"What'd this slug do? And do I need to do anything about it?" He leaned forward in his seat, his gaze soft and out of place in the hard expression on his face. "I should have slapped my brother for being the asshole he was. I shoulda done a lot of things. If some man did to my little girls what Jimmy did to you...well..." He shook his head, the cold look on his normally open and happy face telling the rest of the story.

"I'm not sure anymore," Cat whispered. "But he kept a secret. One he knew would be a big deal to me."

Dominico sighed and shook his head, his expression gentle. "Cat, he is not Jimmy. You don't know..."

She glared at him, and he shut his mouth with a snap. Tom grabbed the wine bottle and topped them all off, then sat cradling his glass.

"So, he did something that would break your trust, and didn't say anything about it?"

Cat nodded, swallowing hard at the memory of Gina telling her what she saw at Juan's.

"Look, I know you've been through some shit at the hands of my asshole brother," Tom said, and Dominico hastily crossed himself. "But at some point, you have to lay the blame where it belongs—squarely at Jimmy's feet." He reached across the table and took her hands in his. "I know you loved him. You were just a kid when you two met. Hell, you both were. You were starstruck, and Jimmy gave you everything you'd ever wanted. Or believed you wanted, anyway."

Tom shook his head and let go of her hands. "Mama C might be overbearing, and obnoxious, but even she saw Jimmy for what he was. A class-A slug. So, she made sure you were taken care of."

"That was for the family," Cat spat out. Tom laughed, his mouth wide and his flat stomach shaking with it.

"Yeah," he managed. "It was. And it was also for you. If she didn't think you'd be an asset, she woulda let you fall apart the first time you found out Jimmy was sleeping around."

Cat opened her mouth, but no words came out. She glared at Tom. He'd made excuses, just like everyone else. The message loud and clear — just deal with it.

"But…" she sputtered, trying to get something out past numb lips.

"But nothing," Tom replied. "He was a prick, and sure, telling you to deal may not have been the best thing, but it was the only thing. You really think Jimmy would ever change?"

Cat shook her head. No. Jimmy Corozzo was his own man. A player through and through. And when she looked back on their relationship with the gift of hindsight, she could see how he'd played her. Perfectly. To get what he wanted. Only he didn't get everything he'd wanted. She never gave him a child.

"So…maybe the thing to do is have a conversation," Tom continued. "Because I'm betting I know just what you did. You shut that shit down in about two breaths, because nobody is ever gonna hurt you again the way Jimmy did."

Cat fought back the tears. He was right. She hadn't thought of anything beyond that. Tom's hand closed over hers again.

"Maybe at least consider it, anyway," he said. "You look like you did whenever you'd see pictures of Jimmy out on the town. So, something hit you hard, and you can say you don't care, but that's bullshit, and we both know it. Think about it. And on that note, I'm hittin' the sheets. Got a long-ass day tomorrow. We're gonna get this place up and ready by May Day, just you wait."

Cat and Dominico cleared the dishes in silence. She could almost feel the waves coming off him. Something was weighing on him. She hung up the towel and kissed his cheek.

"I'm heading up too. How about you?"

Dominico shook his head. "No, and if you'll stay a minute, there's something you need to know. Pour a couple brandies, you're going to want one."

Cat poured the drinks then joined him in the living room, where he'd settled into a well-stuffed chair. Dominico sipped his drink and pondered for a moment, then heaved a heavy sigh.

"I should have had this talk with you when Jimmy died. Before he died," he said. "And I sure as shit should have had it with you since then. God knows I've tried, but..." He hung his head, looking so forlorn that Cat wanted to grab his hands and tell him it would be okay. "I'm sorry, this is going to be painful for you."

Cat smirked and shook her head. "If it's about Jimmy and his mistresses, I don't care anymore."

Dominico ran a finger over the edge of his glass and spoke without looking at her. "One of his mistresses turned up pregnant once. Only a couple years after you two got married. Started pushing for money. She wanted Jimmy to ensure their child would be taken care of. He paid her off. Or tried to, anyway." He took a large gulp of brandy.

Cat braced herself for whatever she was about to hear. The idea that Jimmy had fathered a child with some other woman wasn't a new one to her. She'd always hoped he was at least careful, but knew the risk was there that any day, some woman could pop up claiming her child belonged to him. And she wouldn't put it past him to find a way to divorce her or annul their marriage to marry that child's mother. Anything in the name of keeping up the family.

"She had the kid, and asked for more," Dominico continued. "That's when I stepped in. Mama C woulda had a fit if she'd caught wind of this. We demanded a paternity test—long story short? It was inconclusive. Knowing you and Jimmy had been trying to have kids, and that you'd been tested, and everything was good, I talked Jimmy into getting tested."

He looked up at Cat, sorrow written across his features. "I'm sorry, Cat. I can only imagine what you had to be going through. I knew he'd never tell his mother, but I never imagined he wouldn't tell you. Jimmy had really low...uhh..." Dominico looked uncomfortable for a moment, then hauled in a breath and visibly steeled himself. "It wasn't like he was shooting blanks, but he might as well have been. Highly unlikely that kid was his. The woman backed off, and Jimmy figured he had carte blanche to sleep with whomever he pleased with no risks."

Cat swallowed, her throat clicking painfully. Her tongue was dry and stuck to the roof of her mouth. Jimmy was sterile, or virtually sterile. Which meant it wasn't her fault they never had kids. The doctors had been right—there was nothing wrong with her.

*Oh no. Crap. Oh, hell.*

Images of her and Nate together in her bed flashed in her mind. No condom. Not once. "I don't think I can get pregnant," she'd said.

She choked on the mouthful of brandy. She needed space. Needed to be alone. One look at Dominico's worried face told her she needed to do something else first. Whatever he was, he'd been her good friend through everything. He'd kept one little secret from her — one that he thought Jimmy had told her. One that he knew would just add to her pain and misery. The irony was not lost on her.

"Y'know what?" she said, finally. "I don't even care anymore. I'm glad you told me. At least that burden is off my shoulders. So, thank you." She leaned down and kissed Dominico's cheek. "Now I'm going to bed. Seriously, thank you, and I understand."

Cat forced herself to walk up the stairs. Forced herself to not slam her bedroom door. To calmly pull up the tracker app on her phone and look.

Cat sank back against the bedroom door, a low moan escaping her lips.

Her last period had been the first of March. About a week before they'd first had sex. Cat hitched in a shaky breath, willing herself not to cry. She was nearly three weeks late. *How in the hell have I missed that?*

The answer was obvious when she thought about it. She'd been due to start just a few days before everything blew up with Nate. *Shit.* She couldn't tell anyone. Not Dominico. Not Tom. And certainly not Nate.

※ ※ ※ ※

Nate pulled into his drive and came to an abrupt stop. A large black car sat parked to one side, Dominico leaning casually against the driver's door, and some guy pacing next to him. *Great. Just great.* He'd long ago figured out who Cat's late husband was — it didn't take a genius — and had a brief moment of worry that he was about to have a very unpleasant experience. Then he shook himself. The Corozzo family wasn't that kind of family. At least not anymore. He hoped.

He got out of his truck and shook Dominico's hand, then looked pointedly at the pacing man. Only an inch or two shorter than Nate, with thick black hair and olive skin, the guy could have seemed intimidating. He looked the part of a hit man. Until you got to his eyes. Every hint of danger was wiped away and all Nate could think was puppy dog.

"Good to see you again," Dominico greeted. "This is Tom Corozzo." He nodded at the other man, who stopped pacing long enough to take Nate's offered hand. "Cat's brother-in-law."

That last part wasn't necessary. Nate could have figured that much out on his own. The question was, why were they here?

"I have a couple of questions for you," Dominico continued. "And depending on their answers, a business proposition."

In the short time Nate had known him, Dominico had proven himself to be a straight shooter who didn't mince words. More importantly, he absolutely had Cat's back one hundred percent and then some. In Nate's book, that was a good thing.

He nodded, gestured for them to follow and led them into his house. It had been tough moving back in after being with Cat. He'd built the one-bedroom cottage for himself — a place meant for just him. An open downstairs with kitchen, dining, and living room all overlooking a tree-covered slope that led down to a small tributary of the East Branch Delaware River, and upstairs, a loft office and his bedroom. Simple. Easy. With no space for overnight guests. Or any guests really. Just the way Nate had liked it.

He put on coffee and pointed his company to the sofa, then pulled up the single dining chair. That took up all his available seating.

"Okay," Nate said. "Let's hear the questions."

"What happened with you and Cat?" Tom Corozzo spoke up. Those puppy dog eyes looked less friendly, and Nate realized it would be a mistake to underestimate the man.

Nate gave it a moment before answering. "Stupidity on my part, and a big misunderstanding."

The two other men stared at him blankly, so he sighed and leaned back in his seat. "Look, I'm sure Cat told you…"

Dominico waggled a hand back and forth—a little. Tom shook his head. Interesting. So, Cat had kept her hurt to herself. Made sense. She'd been very publicly humiliated by her late husband. She wouldn't want to go and tell the world it had happened again. He hauled in a deep breath. What the hell. Nothing to lose.

"Turns out my ex is the project manager for TravelCorp, only I didn't know that at the time," he began. Before he knew it, he'd spilled the whole story, right down to catching Gina's eye after Erin kissed him at Juan's.

Dominico sat, hands folded over his belly, nodding. Tom started chuckling.

"I hardly find it funny," Nate growled.

Tom got control of himself, barely by the looks of it. "Oh, it's hysterical from my point of view. You're basically innocent in that whole mess, but you said nothing to her because… I'm gonna guess, you figured she'd misinterpret everything. Trouble is, she found out, and then your silence served to convict you. Cat finally grew a backbone and takes it out on someone who doesn't deserve it. Sorry, it's funny."

"Not to me," Nate mumbled. Though if he were being honest, he'd probably have the same reaction if he were in the other man's shoes. "You said questions. That was one."

Dominico nodded and leaned forward, elbows on his knees. "You're in love with her."

The words hit the air and exploded. They shouldn't have surprised Nate. After all, Dominico had nailed his growing feelings for Cat before he'd really admitted them to himself.

"That wasn't a question," he replied. "But yes." There was no sense in denying it. Cat was his world. He'd been in love before, but it was nothing compared to this.

"And you are not quite what you pretend to be," Dominico stated.

"Again, not a question," Nate said. What was the man getting at and where was this going?

Dominico smiled and nodded at Tom, who shifted to the edge of his seat as he faced Nate. "Why wasn't Cat paying you?"

Was this what they were on about? She'd offered to pay him his back wages and he'd refused. She'd sent a check and he'd returned it. He might as well be honest. Brutally honest.

"I didn't think it was appropriate to start a relationship with my employer." He glared at Tom.

Dominico piped up, "I have a business proposition for you. But first, full disclosure, Cat would never agree to this."

"Then why are you here?" Nate replied. "I think I've made enough mistakes keeping things from Cat. Don't you?"

Tom leaned forward. "Even if it's something that could keep her from losing Bristol Park?"

*Shit.* Now they had his attention. He'd do anything for her. At any cost. Whatever it had started as, Bristol Park had become her dream. He'd watched as it took root in her mind and grew until it held her as much as she held it. Just like the two of them. Only he'd screwed that up royally. He nodded for them to go on.

"She won't accept help from the Corozzo family," Dominico stated. "And a traditional business loan is iffy, considering the history and circumstances, plus TravelCorp pushing on so many fronts. I'm organizing private funding—a small group of willing investors. It will look like venture capital to Cat. She won't know who is behind it. A straight up investment, meant to be paid back over time."

Jesus, the man was cagey, and smart. Cat would have his head on a platter if she ever found out. Still, Nate had nothing to lose. He'd already lost her. He could at least help her keep her dream.

"I'm in."

# Chapter Twenty-Seven

Cat looked away from the thin white stick on her bathroom counter. She'd driven two towns over to be certain she wouldn't run into anyone she knew when she bought the home pregnancy test. She'd debated going to her doctor, not sure she wanted to be alone when she saw the results. But she hadn't gotten around to getting a new doctor yet, and the idea of driving all the way back to New York to see the doctor who'd told her for years to just relax, everything would be fine when he had to know about Jimmy, turned her stomach.

Her watch beeped. Time was up.

She hauled in a deep breath and looked back at the stick.

*Pregnant.* The word vibrated in her brain. After years of trying with Jimmy — taking her temperature every day, planning sex for during her most fertile times. Things that Jimmy had said made him feel like a piece of meat. Her tears every month when she'd feel that familiar heaviness and reach for a panty liner before the bleeding even started.

And all that time, Jimmy knew. She should be angry. Furious at him. At Dominico for keeping it from her. But none of that mattered now.

She, Caitlin Bristol-Corozzo, was pregnant. And all her money was tied up in this place. The temptation to cut and run hit strong, but Cat threw that idea out the window. No. Now more than ever, she needed to put down roots. And she couldn't go back to the Corozzo family. This baby wasn't a Corozzo, he or she was a Stewart.

No. That wasn't right. This baby was a Bristol. Same as Cat. And her mother and grandmother. She laid her hand over her belly. She was pregnant. She'd have to find a local doctor. Everyone would know. Everyone would know the baby was Nate's. He would know.

Maybe she should sell the place. Just give up. Walk away. She could get a job anywhere. She had the skills and experience.

No. She belonged here. She felt that in her bones. And she would raise her baby here. She could tell Nate... What? Maybe she could say it was artificial insemination—Jimmy's from when they were trying. Or some anonymous donor. But she'd told him she couldn't get pregnant. He'd think she'd lied to him. And then when the baby came, if it looked like Nate...

No. She'd have to be honest. She'd have Dominico draw up papers releasing Nate from any responsibility. That was the only thing to do. People would talk, people always talked, but it would die down if neither of them made a big deal about it.

She had time before she started to show. She'd figure things out. Meanwhile, she had a never-ending to-do list that wasn't going to finish itself.

The crunch of gravel outside startled her and she pulled the curtain aside. She wasn't expecting anyone. She certainly wasn't expecting a big delivery van. She rushed downstairs to find Tom directing a small army of men.

"What are you doing?" Cat wrapped her arms over her chest, uncertain what to do with her hands. A larger truck parked near the pavilion and Tom turned to her, hands on his hips.

"Exactly what I said I would," he replied. "And nothin' that ain't on that big planning sheet you've got. I know who's Boss Lady around here."

A pang of regret washed through her at his words. Not for the work, but Boss Lady. She'd bristled when Nate called her that, now she was wishing she could hear it again—from his lips, not Tom's.

"I do remember our conversation," she replied, "but that was about the pavilion. What is all this?" She waved her hands at the truck in front of them.

Tom shrugged and slipped his phone from his pocket, in seconds, her project spreadsheet filled the screen. He pointed at the list.

"Paper and plastic goods for the picnic—even found the eco-friendly compostable type you had listed." His fingers slid down the screen. "Bedding and a few sundries—I'm guessing to dress up a cabin or two and a guestroom, so they look pretty and inviting. I sent you an email with the whole list."

Cat shook her head. She hadn't looked at her phone all day. She'd been too busy worrying about the fact that she was somehow pregnant. She stifled a laugh.

Somehow. As if she didn't know exactly how she got in this state.

"There's even a construction crew for the pavilion," Tom continued. "They'll be here tomorrow morning bright and early. You said you had caterers for the picnic handled. And I called in a favor, propane truck will be here later today. And they're delivering a second tank."

Cat's head swam and she blinked rapidly. "I had the second tank on the list, yes, but it doesn't need to be done before May Day." That tank would cost a fortune. And was only worth it if she managed to save the place. And a million other things.

"I got a deal," Tom replied. "Besides, easier to have them come out once. It's a helluva haul."

Cat had a sinking feeling he'd run into the same problems she had. TravelCorp had either booked up or bought out anyone local. And while no one would say it, she was willing to bet there was some strong-arming and threats going on as well.

"Paper goods and stuff for the picnic can go on the screen porch." She shook her head. She'd wanted to do this without calling in the Corozzo family, but here was Tom, without the rest of the clan, and maybe, well, maybe she didn't have to do this all by herself. "I wasn't sure if the pavilion would be ready, so I figured I'd put the food on the porch and patio behind the house."

Tom smiled and dug an elbow into her side. "The pavilion will be ready. I've been assured this is a crack team who'll knock it out in no time."

\* \* \* \*

Nate set the power saw down and surveyed the pavilion roof. With all the damaged parts removed, it didn't look so bad. In fact, it was a hell of a lot better than he'd thought.

"You gonna stand up there all day?" Juan yelled up. "We're burning daylight, man!"

Nate climbed down and helped finish cleaning up the demolition debris. If all went well, they'd have the repair framed out and completed by the end of the day. Nothing like calling in every favor he'd ever been owed.

Juan tossed big chunks of the old roof into the rolloff Tom had somehow arranged. Randall Drake and Grant Bishop pushed brooms, sweeping up the smaller stuff. Lyle Redman, a former construction foreman, was helping Rachel measure and cut the new pieces. They were an odd team—assembled in a hurry after he'd agreed to Dominico's proposal and heard Tom fretting about the pavilion. Nate had picked up the phone and started making calls—and everyone he'd talked to said yes. Hell, Gina and Vicky even offered to babysit for anyone who needed it.

All he had to do was say Cat needed help saving Bristol Park.

She might hate it. She'd hate him for it, but that wasn't anything new. She hated him already. He might as well make something good come of it.

A shock of red hair moving down the hill caught his attention. *Aw, shit. Time to get outta sight.* He tapped Juan on the shoulder and nodded in her direction.

"Yeah," Juan said. "Haul your ass up to the roof. Probably safer up there."

Nate didn't argue. He'd rather she didn't know he was even here. Everyone on the crew knew that. Nate scrambled up the ladder and watched as Cat unloaded the cart she'd been pushing.

"Coffee and pastries!" she called out. "I'll get them set up. And I can't...oh my goodness, I just can't thank you all..." Her voice broke, and she fished a handkerchief from her pocket and wiped her eyes.

Since when was the Ice Princess emotional? She hugged Juan, and a handful of the others. Shook hands or patted shoulders all around, and even poured the first round of coffee—all traces of the prissy city girl who'd first come to Abbeydon wiped away. She looked like she belonged here as she laughed and chatted with each person. Nate pressed his lips together and sat back on his heels.

He should be there, by her side. She smiled up at Juan and something seemed off. Her eyes were red rimmed. Her face puffy, like she'd been crying. He wanted to reach out and smooth the hair off her face, cradle her chin in his hands and promise she'd never have reason to cry again.

He wanted to fix whatever was wrong in her world, but she'd pushed him out. He couldn't help that, but he could make damn sure Bristol Park was ready to open for the May Day picnic.

He watched her every move, drinking her in—the flash of sunlight on her curls, the way her cheeks dimpled when she laughed. That sound carried on the breeze, making him feel all was right with the world, but also digging a knife even deeper into his heart.

His breath caught in his chest when she turned and looked up the ladder. He slid back on the roof, away from her view, but her voice carried.

"Wow." The single word came out on a breath and was filled with so much joy it almost hurt to hear. "It looks a lot better with all the damage gone. How long do you think it'll take to fix?"

"Best-case scenario?" Juan's voice was clear and confident. "Have it done by this evening. Tomorrow morning at the latest."

They chatted for a moment, Nate not listening to the words, but basking in the sound of her voice. Then she was gone. He watched her trek back up the hill before sliding down the ladder to find Juan holding a coffee and a donut out to him.

"You could just tell her you're doing this," Juan said shaking his head.

"Oh, hell no," Nate replied. "You want me on this project? She doesn't know I'm here. Simple as that."

Juan's shoulders shook with his chuckle. "Suit yourself, but she'll figure it out at some point."


"It's like an Amish barn raising down there." Cat waved her hand out the window at the sea of people crawling all over the pavilion. After they'd cleaned up from the demolition, the construction had begun, and it was an impressive thing. Occasional shouts and the sound of power tools carried up the hill, bringing unwelcome thoughts of Nate. She sighed and turned back to Dominico.

"So, you're telling me no matter what I do, those assholes might be able to force a sale?"

He'd come saying he had good news and bad news. Of course, she'd chosen the bad news first.

"Yes, and no," he replied. "They've bought out any loans they could, and they're foreclosing on any that are in arrears." Dominico cleared his throat. "If they can demonstrate that the remaining businesses are poorly maintained, or that the buildings are dilapidated, and can show cause, and a whole list of other ifs, and buts, and ands, they can attempt to force sale through eminent domain. But" — he waggled a finger at her — "that's mostly just a threat."

"Because they can't really do it?" Cat was confused. She knew a lot of legal wrangling could go into land and property grabs. Not all of it above board. But this seemed extreme.

"Yes, and no," he said again. "The likelihood of it being granted is minimal."

"And how does that impact me?" she asked. "I'm not in town. We've paid off the loan, and there is no possible...wait... There is, isn't there?"

Dominico sighed. "It's a long shot, but yes. If they're somehow able to get all the surrounding property, they can take it to court. One common approach is roadways and traffic control, like when a highway is built. You can argue it, and you might win — if you could afford the battle."

Cat nodded as understanding dawned. This fight was not just hers, but the entire town's. "So, we need to make sure they can't get everything they want. Or anywhere near that. How are we doing on getting a public meeting set?"

The shark-like look was back on Dominico's face. A look Cat had learned to love, because it always meant Dominico was being exceptionally smart, more than a little devious, and yet somehow managing to stay on the right side of the law.

"That was the bad news," he said. "The good news is, them delaying the public meeting is working in our favor. I spoke with a...colleague, and we were able to create the Main Street Historic District and the

Abbeydon Preservation Association." He waggled his eyebrows and smiled.

Cat snagged the folder he held out and waved her hand at him to continue.

"Most of Abbeydon's Main Street is made up of historic buildings," Dominico explained as he motioned for her to open the folder. "Many are over two hundred years old. A couple are three hundred years."

He pointed at the map and showed her the highlighted properties. Abbeydon General Store and most of the places she shopped on Main Street were all in buildings dating to the early 1800s.

"Not that it means anything on its own, but Abbeydon is not too far from the Hudson River Historic District," Dominico continued. "New York State has the highest number of national historic sites in the US. We're taking a cue from that, and several small towns similar to Abbeydon."

He pushed another stack of paper across the counter to her. "This house was built in the late 1800s, but the well house, and that old stone building along the northern edge, they date to the mid-1700s."

Cat whistled as she flipped through the paperwork. "You applied for historic designation for Bristol Park."

Dominico nodded. "The pavilion is over one hundred years old. There is documented history of this property being used for community events going back at least that long. The application has been filed. That will buy you some time. TravelCorp can't force anything with Bristol Park, or any of the shops downtown, until a decision is made on their historic designation."

Cat launched herself at Dominico and hugged him. "That's amazing!"

He laughed and sat back as she let him go. "It's not a guarantee of success. If it's granted, they would have to completely change their development plans. That might cause them to give up, or it might not. But at least it keeps them at bay until we can figure out more options."

"As you said, it buys us time," Cat replied. "And right now, that's a win." She leaned into the kitchen window, seeing the pavilion with a new hope. A loud whistle carried up the hill, pulling her attention to the crew working on the damaged roof. A group of men huddled near a pallet on the ground. Juan, it looked like Juan, gathered a rope in his hands and looked up. A single man stood on the roof—legs braced wide. He easily caught the rope and threaded it through a pulley. Cat could imagine the muscles straining as he pulled the rope tight. Then Juan was on the roof as well, the other man towering over him. Cat groaned. There was only one man she knew around here who was that tall.

Cat reached for her binoculars, but Dominico's hand landed on hers. "Don't."

Cat glared at him. "You knew? You knew he was on the property?"

Dominico nodded. "How do you think this is getting done? That man, who you are so angry at, is the reason all of these people are here to help you. He made this happen. Not me. Not Tom. Not Juan."

"But how did he know?" Cat poked Dominico in the chest. "How?"

Dominico's eyebrows knit together, and the corner of his mouth drew down. "I do what I have to do to get things done. And sometimes those things are distasteful to the people I do them for."

His hands gripped her shoulders and steered her back to the window. "Look out there, Cat. Look at the town, working to help save this place. Bristol Park is part of their history. In many ways, this is as much theirs as it is yours. You don't have to see him. You don't have to talk to him."

She wanted to be angry. But he was right. Whatever Nate's reasons, he wasn't trying to talk to her. When she'd been at the pavilion this morning he was nowhere to be seen.

"Fine." She spat the word out. "If he wants to spend his time doing this, that's on him."

# Chapter Twenty-Eight

Cat stuck the flier up at Juan's and smiled at Charlie behind the counter. Less than a week to go and everything at Bristol Park was complete. Now TravelCorp was pushing for the town meeting and threatening legal action, but the Abbeydon Preservation Association seemed to be doing the job of keeping things at bay.

She waved at Juan as she stepped out of the store and into the bright spring sunshine. A tall blonde woman stood on the sidewalk, blocking her path.

"So, you're the pain in my ass," the woman said. "Erin Blake. Project manager at TravelCorp." She held out a business card. Cat looked down at it, then back up at the woman.

*Wow, this is Nate's ex.* Everything he had worried about with Cat came into sharp focus. While physically they looked nothing alike—Cat was a petite and curvy redhead, while this woman was tall and lanky and tan and blonde—Erin had the same facade Cat recognized in herself. A plastic veneer designed to create a particular impression.

Cat shook her head. "No thank you. I'm sure my attorney already has your contact information." She moved to go past the woman, but a hand closed on her arm. A cloyingly sweet perfume smell hit her senses as Erin leaned in close.

"You think you've won," she whispered. "But you are almost tapped out of funds, and we can keep this going for a very long time. The legal battles have only just begun."

Her nails dug in briefly, then she released Cat with a little push before walking away with a laugh. Cat rubbed her arm and texted Dominico. Who did that woman think she was? She typed up the details to her attorney, not paying attention to where she was walking until she ran into a wall.

Cat looked up as she stuffed her phone back into her bag. Not a wall. Nate—with a cautious-looking smile on his face. *Goodness, he is a fine-looking man.* That thought sprang into life before she could react and no matter how hard she tried to stomp it down, desire for him kept popping to the surface. She opened her mouth, trying to form the words to demand he get out of her way.

Pain like she had never experienced lanced through her stomach, making her gasp for breath. The smile on Nate's face faded, replaced with abject concern. Cat felt something inside her give with a horrible tearing sensation and she clutched a hand out, catching Nate's shirt.

"Cat!" His voice sounded a million miles away and his mouth kept moving, but she couldn't make out the words. She followed his eyes down and saw red. Her pale-yellow shorts were stained red and that made no sense. She was pregnant. She shouldn't be getting her period.

Without warning, her legs refused to support her, and Cat felt herself sliding down. But Nate was there. His strong arms scooped her up. Cat caught sight of his worried expression as he pushed his way back into the store.

"It's okay, Princess, I've got you." Nate's voice washed over her. She closed her eyes and rested her head on his shoulder.

\* \* \* \*

Everything smelled wrong. Everything felt wrong.

Cat opened her eyes, expecting to see the inside of Juan's, or maybe the coffee shop, but this looked like a hospital room. She turned her head to find Nate sitting there, a haggard look on his face. His fingers curled around one of her hands. Cat was about to ask what happened when a woman in a white coat came in.

"You're awake," the woman greeted. "I'm Dr. Sands, and umm…" She glanced at Nate. "Are you the husband?"

Cat tried to push herself up in bed. Nate squeezed her hand and tried to push her back all at the same time. Then the door opened and Dominico barreled in. And everyone started talking at once.

"We're not married." Cat managed to squeak the words out.

"You need to sit back and rest." Nate, trying to calm her down.

"What in the hell happened?" Dominico, in full lawyer voice.

And the chatter continued, each overlapping the other until the doctor cleared her throat.

"I need both of you gentlemen to leave the room," she said into the sudden silence. "Immediately."

Dominico looked stunned for a moment, then turned and walked out. Nate pressed his lips together and sniffed, as if trying to hold back tears. He squeezed Cat's hand again and followed Dominico out the door.

Suddenly Cat felt very alone. And she had a feeling she knew what the doctor was about to tell her. She wanted to call Nate back. To hold his hand as she got the news. She needed his strength, his warmth, to face it. But she couldn't do that to him. She was the one who had turned him away. Who wouldn't listen to him. But here he was. He'd carried her into the store, and he must have sat with her the whole time. Had anyone said anything? Did he know?

"How are you feeling?" Dr. Sands stood next to the bed, a look of concern on her features.

"Shaky," Cat replied. "Hurting. And... I lost the baby, didn't I?"

The doctor looked down and nodded. "I'll want to order a complete scan, to be sure, but yes. You suffered a miscarriage."

The doctor continued, something about her hCG levels not being right, but the words washed over Cat. She'd lost the baby. An ache settled into her chest and tears leaked from her eyes.

"Is the gentleman who was here with you the father?"

Cat nodded, everything miserable and numb at the same time.

"Do you want me to have him come back in?"

Cat didn't have an answer for that. "He doesn't know…"

The doctor's eyebrows raised. "Well, he may not have before, but I'm sure he figured it out."

Cat looked at her, confused. Dr. Sands smiled gently. "You were semi-coherent when he brought you into the ER and you were saying you didn't want to lose the baby. And, well, not to be too graphic, but that amount of blood doesn't happen for too many reasons."

*Well, crap.* She'd hoped to keep that information to herself. At least for a little while longer. All she wanted right now were Nate's arms around her, his voice in her ear telling her she'd be okay. And what kind of selfish bitch was she for that? And a hypocrite. She'd gotten angry at him for not being honest with her about his ex. But she'd withheld something far bigger.

She couldn't ask for his emotional support right now — she didn't deserve it. But she could apologize. Had to. She owed him at least honesty.

"Yes, please," she said. "Send him in."

Dr. Sands nodded then left the room. Cat stared out the window, trying to decide how to tell Nate. Before she could formulate any thoughts, he was there, his big hands cradling hers, his lips on her forehead, his eyes anguished.

Cat took a shaky breath. "I guess I can get pregnant." She tried to laugh, but the chuckle turned into a sob. Nate's arms were around her in an instant, holding her against him as she cried and cried until she felt like she'd emptied an entire ocean of tears into his shirt.

"I'm sorry." She muttered the words into his soggy shoulder. "I'm sorry for the way things ended between us. For not listening to you. For not trusting you." Cat pushed back and looked into his eyes, as gorgeous as ever. "I was not nice to you, and you didn't deserve it."

"Cat, I…"

Cat held up a hand. "Please. I need to say this." She straightened up in the bed, as much as she could anyway. "I was a complete and total bitch to you about Erin. And I'm sorry. But I'm even more sorry for not telling you about this. About being pregnant. I found out after…well…after the Erin thing, and I didn't want you to think I was trapping you or something like that."

Cat hitched a breath and forced down the tears that threatened to overwhelm her. "I don't blame you if you're pissed at me. Or if you never want to speak to me again. Or if you hate me. I get it. I…"

His hand cupped her cheek, his thumb settling over her lips, gently shushing her. "I don't hate you." His voice was raspy with emotion. "And I think I'd go crazy if I had to go through life never speaking to you again."

He hauled in a deep breath, his chest shaking. The pain in his eyes made her want to weep even more. "You mean the world to me. You're right." He blew out a sharp breath. "I should have said something to you the day I ran into Erin. I shouldn't have let you find out the way you did. When you got mad, you had the right, and I figured you just needed time."

Cat shook her head. The man was too good to be true.

"So, you're not mad at me?" Cat asked.

Nate slid his arms around her, cradling her against his chest. "About that? Nah. Not even a little. About not telling me you're pregnant? A little, yeah. But under the circumstances, I understand. What were you planning to do when you started showing? Tell everyone you had in vitro or something? I mean, that would've been interesting when the time came."

Cat laughed. "I considered that. No." She snuggled into his arms. "I was planning to have Dominico draw up papers releasing you from responsibility."

Nate drew in a sharp breath. "I think you and I have some serious talking to do."

Cat opened her mouth to respond, but a large bouquet of flowers came in the door with Dominico's voice echoing from somewhere behind the mass.

"Oh good," Dominico said as he put the giant vase on the bedside table. "You two are back together."

Cat arched an eyebrow at him, then looked at Nate, who smiled down at her.

"Were we ever really not?" His eyes never left hers.

\* \* \* \*

Pregnant. Nate tried to wrap his head around the idea as he drove to Bristol Park. What had started as just an overnight observation turned into two nights in the hospital as the doctor and Cat decided on a D and C as a just-in-case measure, but then Cat had had trouble coming out of the anesthesia. Adding to the fun, she'd spiked a fever and the bleeding had got heavy enough that the doctor worried Cat would need a transfusion. She hadn't, but it was a scary thing to watch—Cat looked tiny and pale in the hospital bed. He knew they weren't fixed, not by a long shot, but at least it was a start.

His eyes darted to the list on the passenger seat. Cat would need a change of clothes to go home in. She had written down options and where he might find them. She'd been horribly apologetic for asking him to do that. He'd made light of it, but it made him feel good—a level of intimacy that didn't exist between just lovers. He'd gotten a little choked up when she handed him a set of keys—the same ones he'd left on the porch at her request. She must have had Dominico get them from the house.

He pulled into the drive and marveled at how far the place had come in a few months. The house had a fresh coat of paint, now gleaming white. The black shutters hung straight and glossy. The landscaping crew had just finished with the plantings and the large expanse of lawn was a vivid spring green. Even the pavilion sported new paint—the once sagging and collapsing structure restored to its original glory. He felt a stab of pride at having been a part of that, and a twist of hope that she would allow him to continue to be. It wasn't like they'd really talked about it yet.

Nate made his way to her bedroom and rummaged until he found a selection of items on her list. Yoga pants, T-shirts, a loose dress. Everything went into a small tote. He paused at her underwear drawer. He pushed aside the scraps of lace and floral fabric until he found what she'd told him to look for. In the back corner. Plain cotton. Dark colors. A little faded and worn. "Period panties" she'd called them. He'd never known that women had period panties.

He stuffed a handful of them into the bag then moved on to the bra drawer. How was he supposed to navigate that pile of straps when it wasn't on a human body. Sports bra, she'd said. Or a bralette. What the hell was a bralette? Something with no wires, she'd instructed. He found a silky thing, soft and light, with no wires and added it to the bag. Then came across something heavily structured with Velcro that looked like it might be related to a bulletproof vest. That had to be the sports bra. It went into the bag as well.

He tossed the bag on her bed and looked around for the slip-on shoes she said would be up there. His eyes fell on the nightstand. A scribbled note about an appointment with an OB/GYN—next week. Nate sagged onto the bed, head in his hands.

He hadn't even known about the baby and the loss hit him. He hurt for Cat—for what she had to be going through. That she'd gone through it all alone up to this point. Yeah, that had been her choice, but it was his stupidity that had pushed her that way. His fear.

Never again.

He wasn't Jimmy, and she wasn't Erin. While he couldn't change the way Cat thought about things, he could sure as hell do something about the way he did, and spend every moment of every day proving to her that he wasn't like that cheating shit.

He traced a finger over the scribbled note. Maybe, one day, when she was ready, they could try again. If she wanted. Bristol Park would be an ideal place to raise a family. Those were thoughts for later. Much later.

Right now, he just had to be here for her. They could figure out the rest as they went. He didn't need all the answers. So long as he had Cat in his life, that was all that mattered.

He stopped in the kitchen to grab her notebook. She was firmly in the digital world, but still made all her early notes on paper. He'd been baffled by it at first, but it was just the way she thought about things.

The book was open to the master checklist for Bristol Park. Everything checked off—except one thing. There had been some follow up questions about the permits for the picnic.

He shot a text to Dominico. Thirty seconds later, the reply came in.

"On it. Don't sweat it."

Why wasn't that done? Cat had everything else figured out down to the last millisecond. Something must have gone wrong. Which would explain the highlight, the asterisk, and the question mark next to that item.

Dominico was on it. He didn't need to worry. He did need to get his ass back to the hospital for Cat, however. He grabbed the bag and headed out the door.

\* \* \* \*

Cat winced as Nate's truck bounced onto the gravel drive. She tried to hide the response from him, but he was watching her like a hawk. He slowed the truck to a crawl, and she wanted to tell him never mind the wincing, just hurry up. She wanted to get home. There was so much to do. She'd lost time in the hospital and while she could stand and move around, there was no denying she was moving slowly.

And the picnic was tomorrow.

They inched around the drive and Cat sat up and gasped as the pavilion came into view. Flowers adorned every corner and topped the giant May Pole. Picnic tables dotted the lawn, and more flowers decorated the back porch.

"What...?" Cat leaned forward, trying to take it all in. "What in the world? How? Who?"

Nate smiled and squeezed her leg. "I called Gina. And she called everyone, I think."

As they pulled up to the house, Gina and the other ladies from the coffee club were gathered on the porch. Cat spied Dominico and Tom as well, and Juan and Charlie, plus several others from town. And suddenly she felt self-conscious of her yoga pants and long T-shirt. She smoothed her hair back, glad she'd taken time to make herself look semi-presentable before leaving the hospital.

"This explains the cryptic text from Dominico," she muttered.

Nate chuckled. "Yeah, he said you'd be livid if half the town showed up and you weren't looking at least semi put together."

A moment of panic seized her—she had on no makeup. She'd just come out of the hospital. Then Nate smiled at her again as he parked in the drive. His fingers gripped her chin and turned her gently to face him.

"You've made a home for yourself here, Cat," he said. "And you fought for this town, not just for your piece of it. Bristol Park was always something special here, and you've made it that way again. That's why everyone is here. Neighbors take care of each other."

He'd said that to her ages ago when he'd stayed during a snowstorm, stranding himself to make sure she was okay. Even then, even before they really knew each other, Nate had been there for her. He had never failed to be there for her. Never failed to be looking out for her best interests.

Even when his ex had cornered him in the store. Something clicked for her and it all made sense. She had cornered him in her own way, same as Erin had. He would have been afraid to tell her anything—no matter how innocent he was. He took the risk of saying nothing to protect her. To avoid hurting her. Dammit. She owed him one monstrously huge apology.

And then maybe, maybe they could try this relationship thing again. Because life without Nate kinda sucked. And the last couple of days at the hospital—having him by her side had made all the difference in the world.

Oh God. Everyone knew what had happened. She'd been on Main Street, right in front of the store. She couldn't handle the questions right now. Didn't want people asking if she was okay. And she definitely didn't want to talk about being pregnant. Her fingers clenched in her lap, and she pulled away from the door, turning into Nate.

He leaned closer, and for a moment, Cat thought he was going to kiss her. With everyone watching. She tipped her head up. He pressed his forehead against hers, cupping her face in his hands. "You've got this," he whispered. "These are your friends. Your family. And I'm right here. I always will be, so long as you let me."

Cat sucked in a breath and let it out on something between a sob and a laugh. She nodded. She'd be fine. She could do this. One thing her mother had taught her well was how to put on a smile and make people feel good, no matter how you felt. And she'd honed those skills to a fine edge in the Corozzo family.

Cat plastered a smile on her face and nodded at Nate. His lips pressed into a thin line before he pulled her into a tight hug and whispered in her ear.

"None of that plastic crap, Princess." His breath was warm and soft against her skin. "No one expects perfection from you. Just be yourself. Trust me."

He pulled back and she gave a shaky smile, too rattled that he'd seen through the facade to do anything more. She nodded again. "Okay. Let's do this."

Nate sprang from the truck and came around, opening the door and helping her out. No pain. That was good. Or at least, no increase in pain. The doctor had said the pain would fade over time, and it could be a few weeks before she was back to normal. Right now, she seemed okay. A little weak feeling, but not terrible.

Dominico hugged her. Then Gina. And then it was a blur. Just as she was starting to feel panic, uncertain she could continue to stand on her own, Nate's hands closed over hers, and he pulled her into the living room. He settled her into the big chaise and pulled a chair up next to her.

For the next half hour, Cat listened as Gina and Tom regaled her with how everything had gotten finished. The flowers that had come from the local florists, and gardens all over town. The calico making an appearance when the yard clean-up disturbed some gophers — the little cat caught at least two of them, and Cat vowed to give her extra treats somehow. She caught Dominico's eye — there was more. Much more. But she was tired. She glanced over at Nate. In seconds, he helped her up and she made her excuses then let him help her upstairs.

Dominico waited in her room. Nate got her settled into bed, and Cat looked at the attorney.

"We finally got everything cleared for the picnic today," he announced. "The caterers are still waiting for the results of a surprise health inspection, but if it doesn't come through, we've got a back-up plan."

Cat hauled in a slow breath. "At this point, I don't care if we tell people to bring their own hotdogs and we just light a bunch of bonfires. This town, these people, deserve to have some fun, and fuck TravelCorp for making this such a pain."

Nate's mouth dropped open, but Dominico laughed. "Say the word, whatever you want."

Cat gave it a moment. She'd been playing nice. Taking the high road. Then Erin had threatened her — face to face, telling her they'd drag this out and make it so expensive she had to give up. Well screw that.

"Rip them apart," Cat replied. "I'm sorry, Nate, I know that's your ex, but..."

"Don't apologize on my account," he said. "There's no love lost."

"Good." Cat looked back at Dominico. "Find some dirt. Shady dealings. Anything. Make it public. Go after them in the press. We get the jump on them and file every injunction we can. See if there's any history of TravelCorp or its subsidiaries, investors, or anyone having ever run up against the Corozzo family — safe bet if they've got entertainment complexes and hotels, they have, and since I know they're not partners, they lost that fight."

It was Dominico's turn to raise his eyebrows. "You do that, you're going to involve the family. And everyone is going to know you're Jimmy Corozzo's widow."

Cat nodded. One more thing she'd have to apologize to Nate for. "Yep, they will. And maybe they'll think twice about fucking with the former CEO of Corozzo Shipping."

She glanced over at Nate, expecting to see concern on his face. Instead, she found him looking at her with eyes filled with admiration.

"I don't want the family here, as part of Bristol Park. This is mine. And Abbeydon's." She leaned back on the pillows. She was tired, but she had one more thing she had to know.

"Who were the investors, Dominico?" She stared him right in the eyes, daring him to lie. She knew he wouldn't, not when she pressed. "I know this took money I didn't have. More money than Tom owed me for the business. Which leaves Mama C. Or someone else in the family. Who were the investors?"

Dominico's eyes darted from her to Nate. He opened his mouth, shut it again, and made a sound like a cough. He was stalling.

"Me," Nate spoke up. "Tom offset what he owed for Corozzo Shipping. The rest came from me."

Cat glared at Dominico. "I think that is my cue to leave," he said. "I'll take care of everything and keep you posted."

Cat waited for a count of ten after Dominico closed the bedroom door. She should be mad at Nate. At Dominico. But she trusted them both. And she knew Dominico would have set up a straight-forward investment—nothing risky. But where had Nate come up with the funds?

"You?" She shook her head. "Nate, we're talking a lot of money. I can't..."

He took her hands in his and sat on the edge of the bed. "Since we seem to be in the let's be completely honest with each other phase, and I just got confirmation that you're related, by marriage anyway, to a former crime family..."

Cat wasn't sure she liked the look on his face. Half laughter, half trepidation.

"I don't tell people about my past, either, for different reasons," he continued. "My parents bailed me out after my engagement fell apart. Made sure I had funds, got me into rehab." His mouth twisted into a cold smile. "I was young and stupid, didn't want anything to do with them, or their money. I walked away. I haven't seen or spoken to them since I left rehab. I send cards on the holidays. Gifts to my brother's kids."

Nate swallowed hard. "I was able to ask you to stop paying me because my grandparents set up trust funds for me and my brother. My folks had control of it until I turned twenty-five—but by that time, I was long gone. When I finally quit wandering and settled here, I started taking small monthly distributions, but otherwise, it's been sitting there untouched for ten years."

His fingers squeezed hers. "When Dominico asked, I knew it was the right thing to do. The investment in Bristol Park is just that, an investment. No strings. No expectations other than getting my money back eventually. Dominico set it up because he knew you'd never agree to me fronting the funds."

Cat gave those thoughts a moment to sink in. She wasn't thrilled to admit it, but he was right. At this point, she didn't care. She'd wanted to do this on her own, without any help. But that had proven impossible. And maybe she didn't need to do it without help. Maybe what she needed to do was learn how and when to stand on her own two feet, and when to lean on friends and family for support. Without feeling bad about it.

"I'm tired," she said. "Do you want to go back down there? I can hear a party going on."

She hoped he didn't. She wanted him to stay right here with her. She wanted his arms around her. Needed his warmth, his strength. Most of all, she needed him.

"It's a big day tomorrow," Nate replied. "I'll see everybody at the picnic." He pushed off his shoes and slid down in the bed, tucking her into his side. "I'm right where I want to be."

Cat curled into his warmth, Nate reached over and turned out the light. With the drapes mostly closed, the room turned dim, Cat felt ready to drift off.

"Nate," she whispered into the darkness. "I'm sorry I didn't tell you about the baby."

His muscles tensed under her fingers and his breath hitched once, then twice. His throat clicked as he swallowed.

"Shhh," he whispered above her head. "I told you before, you and I have some serious talking to do. But not right now."

Before, Cat would have worried about what he meant. Those words could be taken so many ways. Before, she would have stayed up and fretted. Or pestered him to know the answers to her many, many questions. That was before. Before she knew, beyond any doubt, that she was hopelessly and completely in love with Nate Stewart. And it was before she knew, without any reservation, that he loved her, too. She didn't have to hear him say it to know. She felt it, in everything he did.

# Chapter Twenty-Nine

Nate surveyed the crowd and shook his head. Somehow, Cat had pulled this off — despite everything getting in the way. She'd mustered the help, and inspired the entire town, and this was the result. Even the last-minute scrambles to finish were made easy by the fact that everyone wanted to pitch in.

The morning had started off on shaky ground with Dominico having to call in a few favors to get the health inspection report released so the caterers could do their damn job. Sheriff Duane had set a patrol car up at the drive after Nate had smelled gas coming from a car in the lower field — he'd found a couple of kids making Molotov cocktails in their trunk. Five minutes of questioning and it turned out they'd been planning to torch the mess hall — a relatively safe target, considering it wasn't yet renovated. Still... Nate was pretty sure they'd been offered money for the shenanigans, though proving it would be next to impossible.

Cat was taking it easy — mostly sitting and enjoying the crowd. She had grabbed his hand and dragged him to the May Pole for the first dance. He'd practically had to carry her back to her chair after that, but she insisted it was worth the effort.

The weather was perfect, the entire place looked amazing, and Cat was beautiful. A little pale still, but she'd left her hair in wild curls and woven flowers and ribbon through it. She wore a bright yellow dress, flowing and light, that made her look like a walking flower. Or a fairy. Something ethereal and otherworldly, and far more amazing than he ever thought he deserved. He'd seen this Cat — in his imagination when they were first struggling to figure out what they were to each other.

"Hey." Cat slid up next to him on the porch. "Wanna walk me down to the pavilion? The DJ is setting up. There's gonna be dancing. Who knew?"

Nate laughed and took her hand. She'd known. Of course she'd known. She'd put all of this together, while overseeing the renovations, and torn up thinking he'd cheated on her, and knowing she was pregnant. Without him there for the last month of it all.

They made their way down the hill, and he took a place over to the side as she climbed the steps to the small stage. Dominico smiled at Nate, making him wonder what was up. Then he spotted Tom, who had a beautiful, and visibly pregnant, woman next to him, a toddler in his arms and a slightly older child hanging on to his pants leg.

Cat had said Tom was the spitting image of Jimmy — that could have been her. Should have been. Except from what she'd told him, she and Jimmy were never the happy couple that Tom and his wife seemed to be.

He understood why being around Tom would be so difficult for her—it was a constant reminder of what she didn't have.

"Is this thing on?" Cat's voice came through the speakers and the crowd came to a hush. All eyes turned to Cat. "First off, I have to thank everyone for coming out. You've made this a very special day."

Cat blinked as if she were fighting tears and flashed a big smile. "Welcome back to Bristol Park."

The crowd cheered and clapped. She let it die down before continuing. "Some of you are old enough to remember when this place was an important part of this community. And thanks to the help of so many here—Juan and Charlie, Gina, Lyle, Grant, Randall, Harry, Rachel, Duane, Vicky—it can be again."

Nate shook his head. She was a natural at this. She had the crowd eating out of the palm of her hand, with just a few words. Everyone she named was beaming with pride for having been a part of it.

"I had some outside help as well." She waved a hand at Tom and Dominico. "People I know and trust, and who came through above and beyond to help me, and this town. Guys, I appreciate you more than you can ever know."

Now everyone in town would look at those two as the good guys. The crowd whooped and cheered some more, until Cat held up her hands.

"I came here looking for something—for myself. For a home. For a family. And I found it all. This is my home, and you are my family."

More applause and cheers and foot stomping. Cat smiled and laughed, and then her eyes were on him. Everyone followed her gaze. Suddenly, everyone was looking at him. Nate only had eyes for Cat, and she was staring at him as if he were the only man in the world. The crowd went silent.

"The local handyman," Cat started, and someone, probably Gina, wolf whistled. "An all-around good, no, great guy. Whom I underestimated from the start."

Nate's stomach clenched. He had no idea where she was going with this. While she'd been very vocal about not wanting to hide their relationship, she hadn't exactly gone around telling the world either. Putting her emotions on her sleeve where everyone could see them wasn't her style. She feared rejection and humiliation too much to risk that.

"I have to tell everyone, that if it wasn't for Nate, I could not have done this." She paused for a moment, giving a little shrug. "It's true. I'd have quit. Or failed. But he was always there when I needed him. Always. And I did something stupid."

Her shaky breath echoed into the silence as everyone hung on, waiting to hear. "I let past hurts color what I saw in Nate. And I didn't trust him. And that was a mistake. Because if there's one thing I've learned about this guy? It's that he's absolutely, one hundred percent, a man of his word."

Several people burst into applause, and a few hoots and whistles. Then Cat lifted the microphone again. "Nate, I owe you an apology. And not a little one. I acted in fear, and I hurt you, and I'm sorry. You deserve so much more than that."

Her fingers clenched around the microphone. She wasn't done. Cat was doing something she never would have done when she first came here — dropping the perfectly polished façade and baring her soul, trusting her friends and neighbors. Most important of all, showing Nate just how much he meant to her. She was giving him everything he'd ever needed from her.

"I guess everyone here knows why I was in the hospital." She turned back to the crowd with a chuckle, and a collective aww went through the group. "I uh…" Tears streamed down Cat's face, and she sniffed, shook her head and gave a tiny smile. "I didn't mean for this to turn sad, or sappy."

A chuckle rippled through the crowd and Cat's smile broadened. "Enough of the unpleasant stuff. I wanted today to be positive. There's one more thing I have to say before we all get back to celebrating."

She wiped her eyes and turned to face him with the biggest, brightest smile he'd ever seen glowing on her face.

"I love you, Nate Stewart."

Her words hit Nate in a rush, tearing down his last remaining fears. He was on the stage with her in less than a breath, crushing her in his arms, her lips warm against his. He was dimly aware of the hoots and wolf whistles echoing through the crowd. The DJ had the good sense to take over and start the music. Nate scooped Cat up and carried her from the stage, down the steps of the pavilion and across the lawn to the first set of cabins. He needed quiet. He needed a moment alone with her.

"I love you." He breathed the words into her hair as he set her on her feet, then again against her lips, and again holding her face in his hands so he could stare into her eyes. "With all my heart and soul, with every breath I have."

Cat settled her head against his chest. "So…you keep saying we need to have a talk."

Nate chuckled. "I think you covered most of it."

"Most of it?" Cat tipped her head back and looked at him.

"For now," he whispered and kissed her again. "I'm not going anywhere. I think you know that. And I don't believe you're going anywhere. There's more, but it can wait. Don't you think we should be getting back?"

Cat shook her head. "In a minute. I'm enjoying kissing you."

Nate lowered his head and traced his tongue over her lips. "I will never stop wanting to kiss you."

# Epilogue

Nate left the wagon at the drive, stepped onto the broad porch and ran a finger over the sign next to the door. Once dull and tinged with a heavy patina of age and neglect, the brass Bristol Park sign now gleamed. It hung over a second sign declaring the property was on the National Register of Historic Places. He shook his head. He never would have imagined this six months ago, when Juan Neeman first handed him the keys to this place along with the request to get it ready for Susan's granddaughter.

He double checked the small tote bag had everything in it before he headed inside to find Cat. She was in the kitchen, tossing an ice pack into a cooler and gesturing at the folded picnic blanket on the island. "Can you grab that? We need to get going or we won't get a good spot for the fireworks."

Nate kissed the top of her head. "Relax. Juan promised he'd save a spot. Besides, it's your property, can't you kinda do whatever you want?"

She rolled her eyes at him. The way she looked, she should be glad he wasn't throwing her over his shoulder and carting her up the stairs. Tight denim shorts and a bright orange tank top that matched her sandals and set off her curves in ways that had him thinking very impure thoughts. Something he'd been doing an awful lot of lately.

Even after the doctor had cleared her for sex, and she'd started taking birth control, Cat hadn't been interested. Or rather, she had, but even touching her hurt. He was content to wait — give her whatever time she needed. She'd insisted she could take care of him, but he felt so damn guilty over it being one sided, even that had stopped. Until this morning.

Cat had woken him up with her mouth around his dick. He'd made love to her slowly, so slowly — first with his tongue, then fingers, and finally, deliciously, he'd eased himself into her warmth and wetness, where he'd lasted about ten seconds. Fortunately, he recovered quickly, and she was up for round two. Unfortunately, that meant they'd missed lunch with Juan and Charlie.

Now they had to get out to the dock for fireworks over the river. They could see them from the house, but the whole point of opening up Bristol Park for the community was to be a part of it. Not keep themselves locked up in the big house alone.

Besides, he had plans for tonight.

They made their way down the hill with five minutes to spare. True to his word, Juan had saved them a spot — front and center. Perfect for Nate's plans.

Cat chatted with a few people, patted Lucia's growing belly, and finally came back to their blanket, knelt down, wrapped her arms around him and kissed him before settling down between his knees, her back resting against his chest.

As the fireworks started, Nate figured it couldn't get much better than this, but if everything went right, it would.

Cat oooh'd and ahh'd over the fireworks along with everyone else. Nate's arms cradled her, his warmth welcome even in the heat of a July evening. This morning had been magical—she'd been afraid, so afraid, but she needed his touch, to feel him inside her, and he'd been so patient. He was so gentle. Almost too gentle. She wanted what they'd had before. The wild abandon and passionate sex that left them both tired and aching. It would come, in time. She was sure of that. Still, this morning had been sweet and slow, and exactly what she'd needed.

In the two months since the picnic, Dominico had found evidence TravelCorp had suppressed environmental studies that would have made a negative impact on their development plans, plus he'd managed to instigate an investigation into Erin Blake and the attorney Gerald Spade. They had acted well outside the bounds of not just ethics, but the law. More than likely, nothing would come of it, and everything would be swept under the rug. But Cat couldn't resist a moment of joy at the news.

Tom and Lucia had bought a second home nearby — a place to vacation with their growing family, away from the city.

The cabins were almost done, and they had tubing set up for August, and two weddings in September, plus several more in October, and two in December. And next year's camp schedule was already filling up.

She had done it. They had done it. Bristol Park was up and running again.

Nate tapped her shoulder and she shifted so he could move. He stood and pulled her up with him, turning her to face the river. The fireworks lit up the water, giving a show above and below, and Cat knew contentment. This was where she belonged. Right here, in this place, with this man.

"I love you." Nate's voice whispered in her ear. "I think it's time we have that serious talk."

Cat pulled away and looked at him. "Here? Now? Why?"

Nate's smile grew, something in his eyes telling her to trust. "Yes. Don't worry, it's pretty simple. I told you from the beginning that I don't do casual."

Cat chuckled. He had. "And I told you I don't even know what that means."

Nate's arms tightened around her waist. "It means I'm yours, Princess. Every fiber of my being. It means I'm here for you through thick and thin."

He stepped back and took her hands in his, raising them to kiss her knuckles. "When you said you were going to have Dominico draw up papers to release me from parental responsibility? That's not the way I work."

Cat shuffled her feet. "I worried you would feel trapped. Or tricked. Or something like that."

"I think you know better now," he whispered.

She did. Oh, how she did. Nate would be here for her, no matter what. It was just the way he was.

"I'm yours, Cat," he repeated as he sank down to one knee. Fireworks exploded over his head as he looked up at her, his love written all over his face.

"I love you," he said, his words carrying even over the booming fireworks. "I want to spend the rest of my life loving you. You've shown me that broken hearts can heal. Will you be mine? Will you marry me?"

Cat tugged at his hands, trying to get him to stand, but he shook his head.

"Not until you answer my questions." There wasn't a shred of doubt on his face.

Instead of answering, she sat on his upraised knee, wrapped her arms around his neck and kissed him like her life depended on it. His hands cupped her ass, pulling her closer to him, and by the time she finally came up for air, her body hummed with desire.

"I'm not sure how to interpret that as an answer." Nate's brow furrowed as if he were troubled by some deep thought. Cat grabbed his face in her hands and kissed him again, quick and hard.

"Yes," she said between kisses. "Oh my God yes!"

Nate's smile was a mile wide, and his kiss deep and sweet, a promise of more to come later. Seemingly from nowhere, he produced a small velvet box and pulled out a two-tone band set with a large solitaire. Happy tears sprang to her eyes as he slipped the ring on her finger.

Applause burst out behind them, and Cat turned her head to see the entire crowd of people on their feet, watching the two of them instead of the fireworks. She tucked her face into Nate's shoulder, relishing the feel of his arms cradling her.

She'd started the year uncertain about where she would go or what she would do, but knowing she needed to find a place where she belonged.

And here it was. Nothing like what she would have imagined for herself, but oh so perfect anyway. A place she felt at home. Surrounded by friends and chosen family. And a man she loved more than anything, and who loved her in return.

"Hey Nate," she whispered against his neck. "Was that the serious talk?"

The chuckle rumbled through his chest. "Yep. Told you it was simple."

# Want to see more from this author? Here's a taster for you to enjoy!

## Bristol Park: Abbeydon Academy
### Roxanne Blackhall

## Coming September 2023

### *Excerpt*

The big round wall clock clicked as Gina Tellis slid past the empty front office. She picked up her pace, despite being five minutes early. She was a fully grown adult on her way to see her boss, not some troubled teen who'd been sent to the principal's office. Still, in the otherwise silent room, the low hum of the clock caused her stomach to knot. It was about time they replaced that thing with something digital. Or at least from this century.

"Gina! Come on back." Principal Kerr's broad face wore an overly bright smile that told Gina she was not going to be thrilled with whatever he had to say. The knot twisted tighter, and she tried to will it away. She had no reason to be nervous. She was a good teacher coming into her sixth year at Abbeydon Academy. Her students consistently performed well, and her parent reviews were always top notch.

Principal Kerr waved her to a seat in front of his desk, and for a moment, she saw herself sitting there as a high school senior—overly bleached hair and too much eye makeup, trying to hide her uncertainty behind a tough look and even tougher attitude. Gabriel Kerr wasn't the principal back then. A woman had just taken over the job, and she had looked at the rebellious teen in front of her with a kindness and warmth Gina wasn't used to.

The laugh Principal Kerr gave as he sat yanked her back to the present. "Thank you for coming in. Teacher days don't officially start for another week, so I appreciate you giving up some of your free time."

Gina plastered a smile on her face to match his. "It's not a problem. I just got back from vacation yesterday and your message seemed a bit urgent. What's this about?"

She'd asked for a new set of microscopes for her classroom last year and been put off. Maybe that was it. Though she couldn't imagine Kerr calling her in for that. No, he'd save that for unveiling when the parents were here in a big 'look what we got' gesture.

"We finally hired a new coach," Principal Kerr said, as if this were not only great news, but something that she should be excited about. His eyebrows raised and he leaned forward, clearly expecting some response from her.

"That's terrific," she replied. She wasn't sure she understood the 'finally' part. Coach Doyle had broken his hip in late July and had decided to retire a year early. No surprise. The man was nearly seventy. "A month feels like a short time to me."

The words were out before she could think twice. Fortunately, Principal Kerr chose for once to ignore her smart-ass remarks.

"Coach Waters will be taking on boys' sports, as well as four physical education classes and a study hall," the principal said. Well, that was new. Franklin Doyle had taught only two PE classes—both filled with students in the athletics program, and two health classes, also usually filled with athletes.

"No academics?" Gina replied.

The principal shook his head. "He feels it's important to focus on his strength—physical education. And I agree." He leaned back and sighed, running a hand through thinning dark brown curls. "Between the two of us, Coach Doyle should have given up teaching those health classes ages ago."

Gina managed to stifle her laughter. Barely. The state mandated health education and that usually fell to science teachers or PE teachers. She'd been offering to take it on for years, but...

"Wait, is that why you called me in today?" Two weeks before school started was nowhere near enough time to prepare a decent curriculum.

"In part," Kerr said with a nod. The overly bright smile was back, and the twisting feeling in her gut returned. "We've had to make some schedule changes since we can't have science and health classes overlapping now."

She braced herself. Whatever he was about to say couldn't be too bad. On the bright side, she was getting the health classes she'd been asking for. Maybe the new coach would be less of an old-school locker room jock than Doyle. Maybe, just maybe, he'd rein in Gerald.

Gina suppressed a shudder. She'd come very close to quitting when he'd come on as an athletic assistant during her second year of teaching. She wasn't sure what drove her more nuts, the damn toothpick he always had in his mouth or that he acted like the sports programs were all that mattered.

Yeah, and maybe pigs would fly. Gerald hadn't changed since high school. He sure as shit wouldn't change now.

Principal Kerr slid a piece of paper across the desk. Her schedule. She already had it programmed into her phone. She taught five classes and her first started at nine in the morning. She took the second lunch period and had lucked into having no class scheduled during the last period. As far as she was concerned, it was perfect.

The schedule sitting on Kerr's desk was not perfect. "I have classes periods one and eight?"

"But no students during period four," he replied.

True. She had office hours during period four. Which would have been annoying but fine if he'd also moved her to the first lunch slot during period five, but no. She was still set for the second lunch during period six.

"You realize this is a choppy schedule that really messes up the organizational plan I'd already made?" Gina didn't see any reason to be nice about it. She wasn't a new teacher. She'd been here long enough to have paid her dues. "And now I have six classes to teach. Six!"

"Well, we needed to give you both of Coach Doyle's health classes," Kerr replied, his voice rising in defense. "You've been asking for those."

"Yes, I have," she said. "I've also been asking for environmental science as an elective. I have two biology classes. What is up with that? What happened to Stephen?"

She glared across the desk at the principal. If he wanted to hire a new coach who refused to take on academic classes, fine. She was happy to take over the health classes, but she wasn't the only science teacher at the school. Stephen Schubert taught the same classes she did. His wife, Christie taught math, and only math—four periods of it every semester. A prospect that made Gina cringe.

"He's picking up the earth science and advanced physical science classes," the principal responded. "And Micha Lewis only teaches chemistry. Look, I know this isn't ideal, but no one expected Franklin to get injured and retire."

"Seriously?" The word burst out before Gina could think twice about it. *Oh well, may as well go for it.* "It's terrible that he was injured but come on. Really?"

Kerr spread his hands in a what can you do gesture. "We thought we'd have this academic year to find a replacement and plan." He shook his head and looked down at his desk. "We had to cobble this together in a hurry. Stephen isn't comfortable teaching health classes to…ah…well…"

A lightbulb went off in Gina's head. "More like Christie isn't comfortable with him teaching health classes to girls."

Principal Kerr had the decency to blush. Stephen had never done anything inappropriate, but he was young and good looking, and a devout Christian. Come to think of it, Gina couldn't blame the principal for not asking him to teach a health class. Susan Becker, the head of the girls' athletics department, was already teaching two health classes, so she couldn't take on more.

"Fine." Gina allowed a sigh to escape. "You know me. I'll always do what needs doing."

The principal visibly relaxed and sat back with the first genuine smile she'd seen in this meeting. "Thank you."

The note of sheer relief in his tone almost made Gina feel guilty about getting pissy. Almost.

"Have you sent out the updates to parents and students yet?" Safe bet he hadn't. The office staff were slowly trickling in, but they wouldn't be up to a complete full-time staff until next week. Cutting things a bit tight.

Kerr shook his head. "That'll go out right before the meet and greet."

*Oh boy.* She didn't envy the office staff when that news went out to parents.

After she left, she had the realization she hadn't asked about Coach Waters. Who was he? What was his background? Where did he come from? Since he was replacing Franklin Doyle, it was a safe bet he coached football and lacrosse—two sports that were practically a religion in the area. There's no way the school would be without them.

She checked her watch—before lunchtime. No one would be at the coffee shop yet. She could still stop by. Grab a cuppa and maybe see if anyone at Juan's had heard anything.

A group of older men sat gathered on the porch in front of the general store as Gina pulled up. Two were hunched over a checkerboard, while Grant Bishop and Lyle Redmond sat in rocking chairs. She crossed her fingers Grant was in a talkative mood.

"Gorgeous day," she greeted as she climbed the steps.

Grunts from the men at the checkerboard. She hadn't expected much from them.

"Ayuh." That was Lyle. He was tamping tobacco into his pipe. Not that he'd ever light it up. He'd given up smoking years ago. He just liked the familiarity of the process.

"I'm guessing you just heard 'bout your new colleague." Grant folded his hands across his chest and leaned back in the rocker. His dark eyes staring out from under steely brows. Ever the grump.

"I was kind of on vacation," Gina said, as if she needed to explain her lack of knowledge. Asking Grant direct questions was an uncertain prospect. He'd either talk your ear off or clam up. He nodded at an empty chair and waited for Gina to sit.

"Cat was in getting supplies for Nate's old place," Grant said once she'd settled. "Said she hasn't met him yet. They worked with some rental agent. All she knew is he's moving from San Antonio. Couldn't even recall his name."

Hell, Gina didn't even know his first name. "It's Waters," Gina said. "That's all I know."

"The hockey player?" One of the men at the checkerboard turned around. "Betting it's him. Took a bad injury a while back. Right at the height of his career."

"Yeah, but which one?"

"The one that got hit on the ice. Some fight."

"It's hockey. There's always some fight."

Gina tuned the bickering out. *Sports. Whatever.* She went inside to get a coffee and sent fresh cups out to the men. It paid to be nice.

Maybe she should call Cat. She might've heard something new.

* * * *

Brandon Waters turned down the gravel lane and parked behind the large pickup truck. The place was a little further out than he'd like, but it wasn't too bad, and the price was right. Perfect to see how he settled in at the new job, and the small town.

He stepped out into air that was surprisingly cool for how sunny it was. When he'd left San Antonio, it was already pushing ninety degrees before ten am, and the humidity was stifling. A year of living there and he'd never gotten used to the oppressive heat.

The house sat at the top of a tree-covered slope and the sound of rustling leaves filled the air. Well, the rental agent had said it was semi-rural. The whole point of the job here was to get away from the pressure and noise of big cities. To be someplace that felt quiet and safe.

The crunch of gravel behind him had his heart hammering as he whirled around to see a huge man with a big smile on his face and his hand outstretched. Brandon clamped his teeth firmly into his tongue before he let out a string of obscenities at the guy who was probably the owner of this place.

"Sorry to startle you," the man said, his hand still hanging in the air. "I'm Nate Stewart."

*Pull it together!*

Brandon shook the man's hand. "Brandon Waters. Pleased to meet you. And it's no big deal. My head was in the clouds, I guess."

Stewart gave him a long look, then nodded toward the house. "It's open. Go on ahead and check it out. The agent didn't say whether you wanted it furnished or not. Everything's still in there, but that's an easy fix."

Brandon stepped through the front door into what felt like a fishbowl. Dark stone floors stretched through the wide-open space and huge windows lined every wall. No curtains, or blinds, or shutters. Nothing to cover the giant panes of glass.

"Not big on privacy, I guess." He glanced over his shoulder, hoping Stewart hadn't followed him in. At a couple inches over six feet, there weren't too many men who made him feel short. Nate Stewart towered over him.

Brandon made his way upstairs and found the bedroom and a big loft space outfitted like an office. Both with lots of windows. The bedroom commanded a view down the slope to a stream tumbling over rocks.

He took a deep breath, closed his eyes and tried to imagine himself in this space. It was only twenty minutes from the school, so not as rural as it might seem. The furniture was sleekly modern and good quality. Aside from feeling like he was on display with all the windows, and the fact that he wasn't used to not being able to see his neighbors, it was pleasant.

He was comfortable, and that was a feeling he'd forgotten. He scanned the room—he'd bring in his own bed, and his desk set up. There was room in the loft for his weights and treadmill. The rest of the furniture could stay.

The tension in his chest eased as he took another slow breath before heading down the stairs. He found Stewart outside, pulling weeds from the flower beds.

"Looks great," Brandon said. The other man straightened, wiped his hands on his worn jeans and smiled. "Do I need to fill out an application?"

Stewart shook his head. "I figure you're working at the high school. They've already done background checks on you. The rental agency sent over a straightforward lease agreement. Did you need the furniture?"

It took all of fifteen minutes to complete the paperwork and hand Stewart a check for the first month's rent—no deposit.

His new landlord fished in his jeans pocket, pulled out a set of keys and handed them over. "It's all yours." Another handshake and he was out the door.

Brandon leaned in the doorway as the other man cleaned up the gardening he'd been doing then headed for his truck.

"Oh, hey." Stewart paused and leaned on his door. "When's your furniture arriving? You want me to wait on taking out the bedroom and office stuff, so you've got a place to sleep?"

*When is the furniture getting here?*

By now, the truck that had pulled out of his driveway late yesterday afternoon with Brandon's Jeep and the few things he'd decided to keep was somewhere between San Antonio and Abbeydon.

"Good idea," he replied. "I'll check with the movers and get a date. Thanks!"

He meant it. That would have been a horrible oversight.

"One other thing..." Stewart had to be the smiliest man Brandon had ever seen. The hell of it was, it seemed entirely genuine. "Cat would kill me if I didn't invite you over for dinner sometime. Whenever you're ready, of course. May be easier after you've settled. Or heck, before, if you haven't had a chance to go shopping and all. Just shoot me a text, and we'll figure out a time."

Another reminder of things he'd have to do—stock the kitchen. A morning without coffee would be hell.

"Will do." Brandon waved as Stewart climbed into his truck and pulled out of the drive. After a lifetime living in cities like Boston, Portland and San Antonio, the quiet was both unsettling and strangely calming. He'd be willing to bet the entire county here had barely more people than his college town of Ithaca.

*What the hell did I sign myself up for?*

The answer was simple. A chance at something that passed for a normal life. More important, the opportunity to make a difference. Neither of which he'd accomplish standing on his new front step listening to the wind in the trees. Time to make a list and see if the store in town was as well stocked as the rental agent had implied.

"You gotta be kidding," Brandon said as he parked the rental car and stared at Abbeydon General Store. The place looked like something time had forgotten. He gave a polite wave at the group of old men gathered at one end of the broad porch and stepped into a store that seemed at odds with its old-fashioned exterior.

Sure, there was a wood stove off in one corner, but the rest of the place was bright and modern. It took him only a few minutes to get the basics and carry them up to the checkout where he was greeted by a man with a shock of thick salt and pepper hair and deep brown eyes.

"You must be Cat and Nate's renter," the man said, offering his hand. Brandon shook reflexively. He still had some people skills. "Juan Neeman. If you need anything we don't have here, just let me know."

Brandon cleared his throat and willed away the tension wrapping his chest in tight coils. "Brandon Waters. And thanks."

He left it at that, hoping it would end there. But no such luck.

"I knew it." The voice came from by the door. An older man, holding a coffee mug in one hand, his other still on the doorknob. "I'm sorry for what happened to you. Terrible thing, that."

The man nodded at Brandon then turned sharply and headed down a hallway.

"You get used to them," Neeman said with a shake of his head. "That whole group is here most days. They're good people, despite being some of the biggest busybodies anybody's ever seen. Gina said you're coaching up at the high school."

Something about Neeman's tone knocked the rising tension out of Brandon. He'd been prepared for the awkward conversations that happened when he was recognized, but these folks treated it like it was no big deal.

"Yeah," Brandon replied, trying to be normal. Sociable. "Coaching and phys ed."

The shop owner's eyebrows rose. "You're not taking on Coach Doyle's health classes?"

There was something about the way he asked, the laughter that seemed to be bubbling just under the surface that hit Brandon weird.

"Noooo," he said. "Why?"

Neeman shook his head. "I'm sorry, I'm forgetting you're new. The man taught all of his health classes using sports terms. For everything. It was kind of a running joke."

That partially explained the laughter.

"I guess that explains why Gina was in here all in a tizzy the other day," Neeman went on. "You'd think she'd be thrilled. She's been pushing to teach those for years."

Brandon should ask about Gina. Whoever she was. He thanked the owner, grabbed his bags of groceries, and headed out the door, giving nods to the gathering of old men as he passed. He couldn't bring himself to jump onto some gossip train. He'd had more than enough of that in his life already.

*Welcome to small town living.*

* * * *

Gina checked the email again, sure she'd misread it, but nope. The meet and greet had been moved to the gym. Tonya Pinks stood outside the double doors, clipboard in hand.

"Well don't you just look tan and rested. How was the beach?" Tonya handed Gina a name tag, then leaned in with a sly smile. "Have you met the new coach?"

Gina shook her head. "Thanks. It was Key Largo. Hot, but gorgeous and totally worth it." She cast a quick glance into the building but couldn't make out anyone. "And no, I haven't. Any clue why we're in the gym this year?"

Tonya's wide-eyed expression didn't change. "No clue, but I'm betting all the single moms are going to be signing their boys up for sports." She made a show of fanning herself.

Gina chuckled. Tonya often caught the attention of single dads with her Bettie Page bangs and pin-up looks, but she made no secret of the fact that not only was she happily taken, but she also preferred women.

Just inside the double doors, the office staff sat behind a long table covered with file boxes of manilla envelopes. Tape marks on the floor matched the signs overhead — directing parents to the correct line to pick up their incoming freshman's class list. Beyond that, long tables dotted the room. Each table had a sign with a teacher's name, room number and subjects. She quickly spotted Micha Davis with Stephen and Christie Schubert and made her way over to them.

"I've got to admit, this is kind of a brilliant idea," Stephen said.

"It is," Gina replied. "I just wish we'd had notice so we could prepare."

She was used to parents trickling into her room over a two-hour window. Her class was filled with colorful charts, specimen jars and all the trappings that proclaimed science is fun! Now, all she had was a table with a copy of each of her textbooks.

"You're telling me," Micha replied. "I usually set off a series of smoke bombs to keep people moving along."

"Have you met...?" Christie waved her hand toward the opposite side of the gym where a small group of teachers gathered.

Gina glanced at the crowd, but all she could see past the bulky frame of Gerald was the top of a ginger-blond head. She shrugged and turned back to Christie.

"Nope. Guess I'll wait for the official intro," she said. "Wonder if he's the reason for the change of venue."

A loud squeal of feedback brought the bubble of conversations to a halt.

"Folks, can I have your attention, please?" Principal Kerr stood under a basketball hoop, microphone in hand. "If you will all find your tables. We have a few important announcements."

Gina shrugged and made her way to the table with her name on it, right between Stephen and Micha. Christie headed to the math tables on Stephen's other side.

"First let me address the elephant in the room." Kerr gave a short chuckle. "In response to parent feedback over the past few years, we're trying something new for tonight. Our hope is this set up allows more time to talk as opposed to parents rushing from class to class."

"Hey, I liked the mock bell schedule," Stephen muttered, just loud enough for Gina to hear.

"We've had some last-minute changes to staff workdays. Those updates will be in your emails by the end of this week." Kerr flipped a page on his notes, and Gina wondered when he'd get to the real elephant in the room — the new staff member.

"There are four temporary classrooms set up on the east side of the staff parking lot," Kerr continued. "Over summer, a hive of bees formed in classrooms ten and eleven. Beekeepers are working to remove them and out of an abundance of caution, we have closed that entire block of classrooms. Affected teachers are, Mrs. Kirch, Ms. Davis, Mr. Johnston and Mr. Ritt."

A totally inappropriate giggle tickled the back of Gina's throat. She must not have been the only one as the room erupted in nervous chuckles and hushed whispers. The idea of bees in her classroom was horrifying, of course, but...

"And on to our final announcement before we let the parents in." The entire room went silent. "We were sad to say farewell to Coach Franklin Doyle after nearly forty years with us. But we are thrilled to welcome a new staff member to Abbeydon Academy."

Kerr waved his free hand in a come here gesture, and all heads whipped toward the sports and physical education section to see who stepped forward. Gina stared right along with everyone else as a tall strawberry blond man rose to his feet and strode toward the principal as if he owned the place and had all the time in the world.

Even a well-groomed beard couldn't hide the boyish features. Dimples creased his cheeks when he flashed a quick, devastating smile. Track pants and a fitted polo clung to a long, lean physique.

A sharp pain in her shin brought Gina's attention back to Stephen at the table next to her. "Did you just kick me?" she whispered. He nodded.

"You were drooling," he whispered back.

The redhead...strawberry...ginger...whatever he was stood next to Principal Kerr.

"Some of you have already met the new addition to our athletic staff," Kerr said. "Coach Brandon Waters..." He paused as a few hoots and hollers echoed in the gym. "Whose reputation precedes him, will be taking on the boys' athletic department—coaching football and lacrosse..."

"Are we getting a hockey team?"

Coach Waters' eyes narrowed, and those impossibly full lips pressed into a grim line. He shoved his hands in his pockets and tucked his head down. Principal Kerr gave a settle down gesture.

"Coach Waters is not taking on academic classes but is instead focusing on PE and athletics. He will also be taking the period five study hall, so those of you who hate that duty can thank him for that." Kerr's gaze swung to the science tables.

"We tweaked the life sciences schedules a bit to allow Gina Tellis to take on two health classes, which means minimal impact to the rest of the teaching staff." He cleared his throat and continued, "Please join me in welcoming Coach Brandon Waters to the Abbeydon Academy team!"

The room erupted in thunderous applause, and Gina made a note to google the man. Clearly she was missing something.

"And no, we are not getting a hockey team," Kerr shouted over the noise. When things settled down, he picked up the microphone and launched into his usual start of year welcome speech. Coach Waters was gone.

Gina looked around, but he wasn't at the sports tables either. It was like the man had disappeared.

The staff whirled into action, clearing away the microphone and putting up a big sign with arrows pointing to the different departments. Gina grabbed her phone and typed in the new coach's name. Then she sucked in her breath.

Brandon Waters—former pro-hockey player and two-time Stanley Cup team captain, and a bunch of other stuff that meant nothing to Gina. He retired after a post-game attack left him with a career-ending head injury.

Oh great. So hot dude was not only a jock, but a pro-jock who likely had a monster ego and was probably a jerk after losing his career at his peak.

*Yeah, no drooling over this guy.*

# About the Author

Roxanne Blackhall is a former magazine and newspaper editor from San Diego, California, now living in the heart of Baltimore, Maryland. When not at her desk coming up with new ways to torment her characters, she can often be found in the kitchen, glass of wine in hand, cooking a meal for friends.

Roxanne loves to hear from readers. You can find her contact information, website details and author profile page at https://www.totallybound.com

Home of Erotic Romance

Sign up for our newsletter and find out about all our romance book releases, eBook sales and promotions, sneak peeks and FREE romance books!